The Kill Code

J.L. Hays

The Kill Code/ J.L. Hays. -- 1st ed.
ISBN 978-0-9908759-6-3

To my husband, David

Your support, enthusiasm, and love are invaluable.

Part One

The Teacher

1.

COLLIN DRAKE PUSHED ASIDE THE CURTAIN and peered out the front window of his first story apartment. Only a couple of cars were parked along the darkened street, which was unusual for this late in the evening. None of them looked out of place, but something was definitely off. It was too still; too quiet. Not a person in sight. Not a light on in any of his neighbors' windows. Not even the cats were out slinking around the dumpsters. He let the curtain fall back into place and turned away from the window.

The boy stood on the other side of the room, staring at him with hollow eyes. He'd lost his spunk days ago, and his cheeks had sunken quite a bit in the last week. He'd stopped eating. One or two more days and he wouldn't be worth much to the buyer he'd lined up.

"Get in the closet," Collin commanded. The boy stared at him, unmoving. Collin sighed and pointed at the closet behind the boy. "I said, 'Get in the closet!'"

The boy flinched. Then he stepped back toward the closet door. He didn't look away from Collin, just stood there like a freaking moron. This was why he hated dealing with kids. That zone, where their fear and hope were in perfect balance to keep them in line, was too fragile to maintain for any length of time. Too much fear and they'd freeze up. Like this little brat. If he hadn't been worth a solid fifty grand, Collin would've passed up on the job.

Taking a deep breath, he plastered on a smile. "Listen, everything's fine. I have some work to do. Remember those pictures we took? I have to send them to your parents. They'll be very proud of you for being such a good boy. You go lie down for a bit on your bed. Tomorrow's the big day. Mum and Dad are coming to pick you up. So you need your rest." The boy finally took hold of the door and went inside the closet.

Collin took a long drag on his cigarette. He peered out the window again. Something moved in the corner of his vision, but when his eyes shifted, he could see nothing. Then it hit him why everything was darker than normal. The streetlights were off. All of them. He stepped across the window and looked down the other direction of the street. All the lights, as far as he could see, were shut off. It couldn't be a power outage. His bedroom light was still on. He looked the other way again, and this time he saw a tiny glint of light, a reflection of...what?

Crossing the room in three strides, Collin downed the last of his vodka that was sitting on the bar separating the tiny living room from the even tinier kitchen. Then he headed into the bedroom to figure this whole thing out. Maybe the cops were on to him? He glanced around the room, wondering where to start. Should he destroy the camera equipment? Maybe the lighting and props?

Taking a deep breath, he gathered his wits. The computer would need to go first.

He rounded the bed and sat down at his desk, gazing over the hardware. How much could he save? He connected to the dark net, logged in, and sent a brief message:

Believe I am being watched. Instructions?

His skin tingled as he waited for a reply, and the hairs rose on his arms. The air around him felt like it might pop with electricity at any moment. The cursor on the screen blinked. It kept blinking and blinking. Nothing came. He was on his own.

The living room exploded, and shockwaves sent him flying to the ground. Smoke poured into the bedroom. His ears ached with loud ringing. He climbed back onto the stool and raced his fingers across the keyboard. Men in black SWAT gear began streaming through the bedroom door shouting orders.

"Police! Get on the ground! Get on the ground!"

Collin raised his hands high into the air and sat as still as he could while coughing. The screen in front of him raced through lines of commands. He began to turn slowly, keeping his hands high.

"What is this all ab—"

Suddenly he was hurtling toward the ground, his face planting into the carpet. His cheek burned like it had been set on fire, but before he could scream, something hard pressed into the back of his neck, nearly suffocating him. A cop yanked his arms behind his back, securing them in cuffs.

"Where's the boy?" reverberated in his ear. Then louder. "Where's the boy?"

"Closet," he croaked.

Feet shuffled around him. His mouth filled with the metallic taste of blood. One of the cops yelled from the living room. "Got him! We've got the boy!"

The cop with his knee in Collin's neck shifted his weight, nearly cracking Collin's spine. Another set of boots went by his face, and stopped in front of his computer.

"What is this? Clarke, get over here!"

More boots went by. "It's a kill code."

"Can you reverse it?"

"No. It's done. Probably wiped everything."

The one on his neck got up and yanked Collin up with him. Pain shot from his shoulder down his arm and into his hand. The cop pushed him onto the bed and shoved a blurry finger in his face.

"Listen, pervert. You've got one chance to help yourself out. Either you rot in a cell for a long time, or you rot in a cell for the rest of your life. We've got the boy and evidence connecting you to at least two more missing kids. The only thing that's going to help you now is to talk. So spill it!"

2.

ALEX WALKER SAT UP AND DROPPED HIS FEET
over the side of his bed. Right into a pile of
toilet paper. He let out a long sigh and
stood. The trail of shreds led into his bathroom. He
scooped it all up and dumped it into the trashcan
beside the toilet, muttering curses. Grabbing his
toothbrush, he turned on the water. A moment later, a shaggy head peeked over the counter next to
his reflection.

"Had some fun last night, huh?" Alex said,
through a mouthful of toothpaste.

The dog's ears shifted forward. He sat back on
his haunches and barked.

Alex rinsed his mouth and put away his toothbrush. Then he knelt down and patted the dog on
the head, enduring a few licks. He had to be the ug-
liest dog ever, but he'd shown up nearly a year ago,

starving and shivering, and Alex hadn't had the heart to turn him away.

"Hey, Mutt. You stink," he said.

He made his way to the tiny kitchen, throwing away last night's takeout box as he passed by the counter. Sunlight streamed in through the sliding glass door and sent a ripple of pain through his eyes until they adjusted. He poured a cup of coffee then slid the door open, and Mutt bounded into the overgrown yard. Alex stepped out onto the wooden deck and sucked in a big breath of morning air. The weekend was coming up. He'd hoped he was done mowing the grass for the season, but a couple of rainy days combined with unusually warm temperatures in the past week had given the grass enough courage for one last push.

Across the yard, Mutt sent a wave of squirrels over the fence. He leapt at them, posted his paws halfway up the fence, and began his incessant barking. Right on cue he heard the scraping of Mrs. Anderson's sliding glass door. He turned a big smile to her over the top of his mug.

"Morning, Mrs. Anderson."

"Mr. Walker, I don't suppose you could tell that good-for-nothing dog of yours to pipe down?" She pinched her already wrinkled face into a frown and pointed at Mutt, as if Alex needed reminding to which dog she was referring. Her paper-thin nightgown danced around her knees, revealing more than Alex cared to know.

He took a sip of coffee before replying. "Yes ma'am. He's just excited to be alive on such a beautiful day." She pursed her lips, and Alex smiled again. "You look radiant, as always."

She touched her hand to her mop of white hair, frowned again, and went back inside. Alex chuckled to himself and called Mutt away from the squirrels. He went back inside to the bedroom, intending to find his shoes and go for a run before work. But his phone vibrated on the bedside table, drawing his attention. He glanced at the screen. *Steve Albright.*

Steve was Alex's partner from his days as a local cop in Brunswick. Technically, he was also Alex's brother-in-law, but since his sister Chloe might as well be a perfect stranger to him, he preferred to think of Steve as the best friend who married a chick he couldn't stand. He let it ring through to voicemail. Then he listened to the message.

"Hey there!" Steve's voice drawled. "Just checking in. Haven't heard from ya in a couple of months. Give me a call, okay, brother?"

He knew why Steve was calling, and he appreciated his friend's concern, but he preferred to at least attempt to let the day pass on by without commemorating it in any way. He wasn't one to remember anniversaries of good events, much less the worst day of his entire life.

3.

CARRIE REYNOLDS TOOK A DEEP BREATH outside her parents' front door before breezing in like she didn't have a care in the world. "Good morning," she called, placing her jacket over the back of the couch. She rounded the corner into the large kitchen and straight into her dad's arms.

"Good morning, sweet pea." He kissed the top of her head before letting her go.

Her mom swept around the counter that separated the kitchen from the breakfast nook. She stopped and looked Carrie over from head to toe.

"Oh honey, you look wonderful! So professional."

Carrie tried to take the praise as it was intended: genuine encouragement. But she couldn't help but wonder if she hadn't looked professional every other day she'd gone to work. It was a new suit, and she had tried to make sure the skirt and blouse communicated how seriously she was taking this new job, but still, her mother's adoring gaze gave her pause.

"Mom, let's not make a big deal out of it."

Her mother dismissed her with a wave of her hand and gave her a quick squeeze. "Grab a plate and whatever you want. It's all on the table."

She followed her parents to the breakfast nook and filled her plate with scrambled eggs, bacon, toast, and orange slices. When she took her seat across from her mother, their gazes met. Carrie caught the disapproving look in her mother's eyes and looked her plate over again. She dropped the bacon back onto its serving dish in the center of the table.

"So," her dad said. "You nervous about your first day?"

Carrie shrugged and did her best to sound relaxed. "Not much. I mean, it's a little scary to start something new, but most of the cases I'll be working on are similar to cases I tried at the State's Attorney's office."

She caught the look her parents exchanged. Her dad's worry lines deepened. Her mother's lips formed the thin pink line that said, "You're making a huge mistake, young lady."

"So, tell me again what you'll be working on," her dad said.

She took a mouthful of her eggs and tapped her fork against her plate. There was no good answer. The truth would just have to do. "Child exploitation and human trafficking cases."

Her mother dropped her fork and leaned onto the table. "Carrie, dear, do you really think that's wise for a young woman in your position?"

"I think it's exactly the kind of job a young woman in my position should be doing." Carrie steeled herself for an argument. "I don't see how it's any different from what you and Daddy are doing."

"Your mother and I prayed for many years before moving forward, and we knew exactly what we were getting ourselves into."

Carrie stopped herself from rolling her eyes. She'd gotten used to her parents' use of prayer as license to do whatever they wanted while passing judgment on her own decisions. She'd long since come to the realization they would never be able to stop trying to protect her from monsters. Some small part of her couldn't blame them.

"Listen, I know what I'm getting into," Carrie said. "I tried several child abuse cases with the state—"

"And nearly had a relapse," her mother interrupted.

"Mom, that was the first case. It was very difficult, but I got through it. And I tried other cases with no trouble." As long as you didn't call nightmares and weight gain trouble.

"Sweetheart, we know your heart is in the right place." Her dad covered her hand with his. "We just want to make sure you're all right. If the cases bother you, you can always come to us or talk to Pastor Daniels."

"I know," Carrie said. "I know you both love me and want to protect me. But I need to do this. I can do a good job, and I can make a difference in the lives of kids who are suffering. Can't you see that? I just want a chance to make the same difference you have. Just in my own way."

Her dad smiled, and her mom's tense face relaxed. Carrie wondered if maybe this was the beginning of a new life for her. A new job. A new mission.

And finally getting her parents to see her as a healthy, independent young woman.

4.

"WALKER, BLAKE, GET IN HERE!"

Alex dropped his feet off his desk and set his coffee down. Time for his morning scolding. He weaved through the cubicles of the Child Exploitation and Human Trafficking division of Homeland Security Investigations until he reached the office of his group supervisor, Nicole Masters. He deflected a grin from Tony Blake, who joined him. Together they rounded the last cubicle on the left, knocking on Nicole's door.

"What's up?"

She pointed at the chairs against the wall, her large eyes narrowed with the intensity of an impending lecture. "Sit."

He plopped down and thought through the various scenarios he could be in trouble for this morning, one in particular that was most likely. He suppressed a chuckle as Tony took the chair beside him. Wednesday mornings seemed to be his regularly scheduled lecture about proper office behavior. Like he cared.

"Agent Walker, Agent Blake," she started. "First of all, I'd like to ask that you make sure all evidence is secure before leaving the evidence room."

So that was it. He'd been right. "Look it was late, and Williams wasn't around to unlock the back of the evidence room. We planned on moving them into our section when we got in this morning. They were secure when we left." Forcing his face to remain serious, he avoided looking at Tony at all costs. "We had no idea the drug team would be in there so early."

Nicole narrowed her eyes into that hard expression he'd seen her use with her kids a time or two. He hated it when she went all parental on him. "That may be the case, but we can't have people tampering with the evidence."

"I can assure you, I did not tamper with the evidence." He stifled his laughter with a cough.

Tony too cleared his throat. "I can also confirm that none of our guys tampered with the evidence. We brought it in, saw Williams wasn't around, set the mannequins in the corner, and left. When we went back to secure them this morning, we noticed they'd been moved."

Alex couldn't help himself. He caught Tony's eye, and the two of them flew into a fit of coughing. Alex stood and tried to walk it off. Pausing, he leaned onto the back of the chair. "Come on, Nicole. Lighten up. It's kind of funny."

Her mouth tipped just slightly, and her forehead relaxed. "Maybe you should've left a note explaining that the mannequins were evidence."

"But then we would've missed out on seeing their faces when they found out the mannequins were sex toys!" Alex said. Tony finally let out the laugh he'd been holding back, and Alex couldn't help himself any longer. He doubled over.

"Look, you two," Nicole said. "If that business compromises the case, it's on your heads."

Regaining control of himself, Tony rested his elbow on her desk, flashing the crooked smile that chicks swooned over. "We're sorry if it got you in the hot seat this morning. Maybe the drug group just needs a refresher course on evidence handling."

She sighed and ignored the smile, turning her attention to Alex. "On a more serious note, we got a lead early this morning from Australia. Some guy arrested on kidnapping charges claims he's part of an exclusive international child pornography group with some pretty serious requirements to join."

"Like what?" Alex said.

"Video proof of actual contact with a child."

Alex's humor evaporated. "Why's the tip coming here?"

"Because the suspect claims he traveled to Atlanta last spring to meet up with some guys in the group. He claims to have made a deal with someone they call El Maestro for producing child pornography as well as selling these kids through auctions on the dark net. He says he went to a house here in Atlanta, where he believes this El Maestro lives."

"Any information on the website?" Tony asked.

Nicole shook her head. "The Australians haven't been able to gain access. But from what the suspect is saying, it sounds like a massive international case. They believe the main server is housed either in the Netherlands or here in Atlanta. Your job is to find the house, locate the server if it's here, and take down this El Maestro."

"Can we take over the suspect's account?" Tony asked.

"He deleted everything from his computer as soon as the police busted into the house. Apparently it took some persuading to get him to cooperate."

"Good," Alex muttered.

She rolled her eyes and stood. "It's not much to go on, but I'll forward you all the details we have. Walker, you'll be the case agent on record. You and Tony see if you can confirm any part of this guy's story. If he's telling the truth, we can take down a major highway of CP traffic."

Alex nodded. "We'll get right on it."

Alex went to his desk and made himself comfortable. He opened the email forwarded by Nicole, and read through the report of the arrest in Australia. As he put together all the details and images, his stomach did its usual churn. Working child exploitation cases was such a mixed bag of emotions. It sickened him what people were capable of doing, but the drive in him to save these kids would kick in and override his disgust.

He twisted in his seat away from the computer screen. He'd need help with this. More than just Tony. Glancing around the opening of Craig's cubicle across from him, he ascertained it was empty, and he'd left his computer on. Alex snuck over and opened his email. Then he went in and changed his signature line.

Craig Warner
The Most Specialest Special Agent, if ever there was...

Alex chuckled to himself, closed the window, and slid back over to his cubicle. Craig was in need of a good laugh these days. He took a sip of coffee and printed the info he needed from the email. Then he went to work identifying all the cab companies that had serviced the airport the day Collin Drake had arrived, as well as their destinations within a two hour window. The list was long.

This was going to take forever.

5.

THE SUN WAS HANGING LOW IN THE SKY BY
the time Alex and Tony approached the
twelfth house on their list. This one was in a
nice neighborhood in Marietta.

"I'm starting to think we're chasing our tail
here," Tony said.

"This is definitely the right kind of neighborhood," Alex replied. "If this isn't the right one, let's
call it's a day and start again tomorrow."

"Feel like catching a bite when we're done?"

"Sure. Where you wanna to go?"

"We're pretty close to that barbecue place on
Whitlock."

Alex groaned. "No, I hate that place. Pick somewhere else."

Tony laughed. "Sorry, forgot. What's up with
that anyway? You love barbecue."

Alex ground his jaw. He'd been determined to make it through the day with no reminders. "I just don't care for it, all right? Forgive me if I want to eat a meal without being bombarded by Alabama paraphernalia."

Alex turned onto another road where the houses were spread farther apart, and the sizes matched the description they were looking for.

"All right then," Tony said. "The diner it is."

Alex made one last turn onto the street they'd been searching for. They scanned the mailboxes, and came to the address on the list. It was at the very end of the street, technically in a cul-de-sac, but it was set back from the road, with several trees guarding the edge of the lot. There was no way to see the house without entering the driveway, so Alex turned in.

"Keep an eye out," Alex said. "This could be it."

"Secluded. End of the street." Tony slapped the dashboard. "Damn. This might actually be the house."

Alex pointed to the papers in Tony's lap. "What else was in that description?"

"Trees lining the road. Check. Three-car garage. Check. Pool in the back. You see a pool?"

Alex stopped the car in the driveway. The hair on his neck stood on end. If the guy came home, they'd be burned before they ever got started.

"Let's head up the street and walk back for a closer look," Alex said, moving the car into reverse.

After parking several houses away, Alex and Tony crept down the driveway and around the side of the house. Situated at the back underneath another large tree, was the three-car garage. Alex looked around to see if any neighbors were about, but he couldn't see any other houses from this angle. He continued over to the fence separating the driveway from the back yard, lifting himself up on his tiptoes to look over the top.

"Bingo," he said. "Pool in the back yard."

Tony came from the front of the house. "Curved staircase leading up to the front door matches the description as well." He put his hands on his hips and looked around. "I think we found it."

"Let's get some pics and get out of here."

Alex snapped a few pictures of the garage and the side of the house, while Tony got a few of the front. Then they walked back up the hill to Alex's government car, and headed over to the Marietta Diner.

6.

TONY HUNG UP HIS PHONE AND TOOK A LONG gulp of his beer. "The owner is Roman Jonkovic, a Professor over at KSU who's owned the house for seven years and his citizenship for twenty-six. Apparently he came to the US with his parents in 1976 from Czechoslovakia."

"Anything promising with his criminal history?" Alex asked between the last of his fries.

"Craig said the most he could find was a traffic ticket for running a red light. He was virtually invisible online. A short bio on KSU's website. No social media accounts to speak of. No apparent relatives in the country. Squeaky clean."

"That's going to make a search warrant just about impossible."

"Speaking of that, you know we're breaking in a new Assistant US Attorney? So there's no telling how she runs her cases."

"*Her* cases? Not another female AUSA." Alex gulped down the last sip of his water.

"What do you have against females?"

Alex shrugged. "Nothing most of the time. But remember how Julie was?"

Tony grinned, a gleam coming into his eyes. "Man, do I. She was something."

Well that figured, Alex thought. "That's not what I mean. She was a good attorney, but it was like she was always out to prove something. Just seems like the females get off on the chance to boss us around."

"Well, Julie can boss me around anytime."

Alex couldn't help but chuckle. "Yeah, it was all fun and games till you had to start taking your cases to Frank."

Tony shook his head. "No kidding." Tony shuddered as if the memory made him sick. "Totally not worth it."

Alex's phone vibrated on his waist. It was Craig. "I got something, maybe," Craig said.

"Shoot."

"Did you hear about the kid that went missing from Six Flags on Halloween?"

"The Gomez kid, right?"

"Right," Craig said. "Well, Roman Jonkovic got his traffic ticket the day the kid went missing. Guess where the intersection is where he ran the light?"

Alex pinched his nose between his fingers. He hated guessing games. "Where?"

"About two blocks from Six Flags."

That could be promising toward their probable cause. "Have you contacted the officer that pulled him over?"

"It was one of those automatic cameras. Sent him the ticket in the mail."

"Is there a picture of the vehicle?"

Craig sighed on the other end. "Nothing but the plate and a blurry image of the back."

Alex thanked him and hung up, explaining to Tony what Craig had found. "The suspect in Australia said this guy manages the website, and that a requirement to gain access was video proof of contact with a child."

Tony shook his head. "So maybe Jonkovic took the Gomez kid. Any leads on locating the kid? Maybe we can connect some dots here."

"That's quite a leap to make. But I'll put in a call to Cobb County police and the FBI if they're in on it. We'll get a rush on the surveillance, and first thing tomorrow I'll go brief what's-her-name on what we have so far."

Tony grinned. "Richards says she's hot."

Alex chuckled before downing the last of his beer. But his thoughts quickly returned to the possibility of finding the missing boy. If Jonkovic did take him, the chances he was alive were dwindling fast. And even if he was alive, well, he didn't want to think too hard about what that meant either.

7.

CARRIE HUNG HER LAW DEGREE FROM THE University of Alabama on the wall behind her desk and stepped back to admire her office. It was small, but she was thankful to have a space all her own. Taking a seat, she turned to the stack of files on her desk and shuffled through them. She'd spent the previous day reading them in depth, and she was sure she knew them backwards and forwards. Unfortunately, only two cases had anything to do with child exploitation, and only one of those was promising. All the rest were menial cases of traffic tickets at the VA or some idiot letting his dog take a dump on federal land.

She'd asked around, and every AUSA had to work the crappy cases, but she suspected being the new kid had landed more than usual on her desk. All the same, she needed to get them organized, and put together a plan for prosecuting the best ones. Flipping through several, she made notes in her calendar, and shot off emails for updates on the status of others. She was just hitting her stride when there was a knock on her door.

"Come in," she said, expecting her supervisor, or a colleague. She was definitely not expecting the tall stranger that strode over to her desk.

"Hi, I'm Alex Walker." He offered his hand, and when she shook it, she couldn't help but notice the muscles in his forearm. "I'm a Special Agent for HSI, the Child Exploitation and Human Trafficking group. I understand you'll be handling a lot of our cases from now on."

"Oh, sure! Have a seat."

He lowered himself into the chair and glanced around the office. "You getting settled in?"

"Trying to. I'm already loaded down with cases, so I guess they're throwing me right into the deep end."

He frowned, his dark eyebrows mashing together. "I see you went to Alabama."

"Roll Tide." She laughed, expecting some friendly banter about whatever team he cheered for.

His mouth remained tight. "I'll try not to hold that against you."

Her laughter faded to a smile, though she suspected his affront to her school was more than just traditional hatred of a rival. "You a Georgia fan?"

"Nope."

"Tech?"

"Nope."

"Ah." She nodded. "So you just have a deep-seeded hatred for Alabama then."

He cleared his throat and shifted in his seat. "I wanted to run a case I'm working on by you to see if you're interested in pursuing it."

She noted the subject change, and it made her wonder what his issue was with Alabama. But it couldn't be that big of a deal, so she let it slide. She grabbed a pen off her desk and poised it over her notepad. Then she looked up and met his gaze.

"All right, shoot."

She scribbled furiously as he described the information he'd received from Australian police, a house he'd found that met the description, and the squeaky clean record of Roman Jonkovic, other than the traffic ticket. As she finished writing down the last of the information, she dropped her pen, leaning back in her chair. She studied Agent Walker for a moment, wondering what kind of investigator he was. From what she'd heard, they came in all different ego sizes and abilities. Was he a team player?

"I know it's not much to go on right now," he said, "but I think we might have enough probable cause to get a warrant for a tracker on the vehicle, especially if we can get the suspect in Australia to verify the photo of the house."

"No, there's definitely not enough probable cause yet. You're going to need a lot more than this to go on if this case is going anywhere."

"It might be enough if—"

"Come on, Agent Walker. It's not enough and you know it. Just because I'm new around here doesn't mean I don't know what I'm talking about."

He met her gaze, his hazel eyes boring into hers. "I didn't mean to imply that you don't know what you're doing. I just think a tracker would speed things along. I'd think that with a possible connection to a missing kid, we might at least *try* to obtain the tracker."

Her blood warmed, stirring a hint of anger inside of her. Did he think she was some emotional female that would throw logic and reason, not to mention the law, out the window at the mere mention of a child?

"You have what," she asked, "a questionable source in Australia, a house you identified based on this source's memory from months ago, and a traffic ticket? You think that *might* get you a warrant? Are you serious?"

His face flushed. "I know it's a long shot, but my gut tells me this is huge. If there's even a remote possibility that the Gomez boy is in that house, we have to do everything we can to get to him. You do understand what goes on in cases like these? What happens to these kids?"

Of course she did. Better than he could know. She regretted letting her mouth run away with her, but she never seemed to catch it in time. Obviously he was passionate about his job and wanted to rescue the kid. That she could understand. But they couldn't just dismiss the law. She tried to soften her tone.

"That's precisely why we have to do this the right way. You have absolutely nothing that points to anything illegal going on with that car, and nothing illegal tied to the house. You basically have nothing."

He sighed and pushed himself up from the chair. "So what? You want me to forget the whole thing?"

"No, I'm not saying that." Carrie leaned back. "I think this could be something. You're just going to have to get your probable cause without your tracker for now. Get me something real I can work with, and then we'll go after this guy and the whole sick network he has going on."

"Fine." Alex huffed. "I'll get a pole camera set up and see what I can find."

"Now you're talking."

"Thanks for your time. Nice meeting you."

He turned and left without another word. She watched the door close behind him and wondered what in the world had crawled up his behind.

"Guess he'll be a joy to work with." Carrie sighed and returned to her casework.

8.

A FTER SEVERAL DAYS OF NOTHING INTEREST-
ING from his pole camera, Alex began to
think the case was stalling before it even got
out of the driveway. Jonkovic left each morning at seven, and returned home in the evening at
seven-thirty. And thanks to Miss Reynolds, he had
no idea what Jonkovic was doing while he was
away. No other cars visited the home, and the only
person Alex could see moving around the house at
all was Jonkovic himself, who simply walked to and
from his black Mercedes.

He came into the office on Monday morning
with high hopes that the professor had given him
something to work with over the weekend. But
when he finished the footage from Friday night, he
dropped his head into his hands and swore under
his breath.

As the footage from Saturday began to roll on screen, he also pulled up the available information of the missing Gomez boy. He sifted through reports, trying to find something that jumped out. Samuel Gomez had gone missing from Six Flags when his sister had gone to the bathroom. His dad had tried to watch Samuel at the arcade while standing outside the women's bathroom. He had no idea how or when Samuel disappeared.

When Alex clicked on the next page, an image of the little boy popped up. His dark hair fell across his face, and he was giving a thumbs-up to the photographer. He was standing on the bridge overlooking Splash Water Falls. Alex looked at the information on the photo and saw the boy's dad had taken it the day his son went missing. Samuel was only nine years old. His dad must have gone crazy. Alex knew that kind of crazy, the kind that changes the world forever, changes you forever.

He clicked back over to the footage of Jonkovic's house. Something in his gut told him he was on the right track, but he was hitting a dead end. As he scrolled through the images before him, he found himself praying for help, something he'd sworn he'd never do again. But he'd be willing to give it another try if it meant bringing this boy home to his family.

Then Alex caught sight of another car in the video from the pole cam. He slowed it down and watched as a dark truck pulled into the driveway. A man in a baseball cap got out and went around the back through the fence that led to the pool. Alex jotted down the license plate and kept watching. Within minutes, another vehicle pulled into the driveway; a light-colored Honda. Another man got out and went around the back as well. The last vehicle was a dark Civic, and like the others, it was driven by a man who entered the house through the back. Alex jotted down the tag numbers and then sped through the rest of the footage. The men stayed long into the morning hours of Sunday, leaving about three o'clock.

He did a quick search on the tags and printed out the reports generated. Grabbing the papers, he headed over to Tony's desk. "We got three more possible leads."

Tony looked over the papers. "Derrick Lyons, Brian Meeks, and Mark Johnson."

"They paid a visit to Jonkovic's house Saturday night. Why don't you take Johnson and Lyons. I'll get Meeks. I have a surveillance set up for tomorrow night on the Banks case, so I have to go coordinate that with Craig. Want to hit Brady's later and go over everything?"

"Sure." Tony turned back to his computer, and Alex started to leave. "Hey," Tony said, turning back around. "What did you think of the new AUSA?"

Alex shrugged. "She's all right. A bit on the arrogant side."

"But is she hot?"

Alex shook his head and laughed. "Yes, but like I said. Arrogant."

"Nice." Tony grinned and turned back to his work.

9.

lex and Tony grabbed a table at the Irish pub by the airport and waved to some agents from the Counter Terrorism group across the room. Drinks had become a regular habit for them after work at least once a week. Alex loved the atmosphere of the pub, not so loud you couldn't carry on a conversation, but not the quiet restaurant feel either. Plus, the service was quick, and several of the waitresses were easy on the eyes.

As soon as they took their seats, Deborah sauntered over with a big smile. He liked it when she waited on them. She could carry on intelligent conversation, but she could joke around as well. And she always got their orders right. She stopped at their table and rested her hands on it. Then she leaned forward just enough to tease their imaginations.

"What can I get you boys? The usual?"

Alex appreciated that too, the familiarity of someone knowing what he liked. "Works for me," he said.

Tony placed his order. Deborah winked at them and headed back toward the kitchen. Alex realized they were both watching her walk away, and he chuckled.

"So, what did you find out about our guys?"

"Not much useful," Tony said. "Mark Johnson's a firefighter over in Woodstock. Pretty clean so far. No social media pages yet. No record of anything except a speeding ticket when he was nineteen. He's married and living in a nice neighborhood. Nothing that ties him to Jonkovic or the Gomez kid. Lyons is a pediatric nurse over at Wellstar on East-West Connector. Lives alone over in Austell. Found some possible social media accounts, but haven't narrowed it down yet. What did you get on the other guy?"

"He may be our best one to look at," Alex said. "He delivers pizza in the Smyrna area, and he has a couple of dings on his record. One for DUI about a year ago, and another one for possession of pot about eighteen months ago. He seems like the weakest link. Plus, he has a Facebook page with some photos of him with some kids. Nothing incriminating, but it's a start."

Alex was about to continue when he saw Carrie Reynolds standing at the door, looking around like she was searching for someone. "Great," he muttered.

Tony turned and followed his gaze, and then his hand shot up and waved at her. Her face brightened, and she headed straight for their table.

"Hope you don't mind," Tony said. "Thought we should get to know her if we're going to be working cases together."

"You invited her?"

"Of course. Why?"

Alex didn't have time to explain his distaste for her before she reached their table. He stood and offered her his chair, pulling another one over for himself.

"Thanks," she said.

"Sure." He avoided eye contact and instead waved Deborah over to take Carrie's order.

He took the opportunity while the women spoke to shoot daggers at Tony with his eyes. But his friend only grinned and winked back at him.

"So, what were we talking about?" Carrie asked after she'd placed her order.

"Well," Alex said. "We were just talking about the Jonkovic case."

"Really? So you guys work all day and then come out for the evening to talk about work some more?" She shook her head, looking amused. "All right then. So fill me in."

Tony jumped right in with the names and occupations of the men, including the pizza guy's record. "Alex thinks we should focus on Meeks."

She looked at Alex and wrinkled her nose. She had tiny little freckles spattered across its bridge and down onto her cheeks. "What do you mean by 'focus' on him?"

"I mean pay him a visit. We do a knock-and-talk and see if we can get him to cooperate as a confidential informant."

She shook her head. "You don't have enough evidence for that. You'll blow the case before you even start."

"Excuse me? I've been working CP cases for two years now, and I've probably conducted a hundred knock-and-talks. I know what I'm doing. I don't blow cases."

Tony cleared his throat, and Carrie stared at him with wide eyes before dropping her gaze. Tony leaned onto the table and gave her an apologetic smile. "You'll have to forgive Alex. He doesn't play nice with girls."

Alex shot more daggers at him, but they went ignored. Deborah brought their drinks, and Alex downed three quick gulps of his beer while Carrie and Tony went through the usual pleasantries of getting to know each other. He half listened as Carrie talked about growing up in the suburbs of Atlanta, running cross country for her school and eventually for a small college in Tennessee. By then he'd nearly finished his drink. When she started talking about law school at Alabama, he decided he needed another one, so he excused himself to go to the bar. Behind him he could hear Carrie ask in a low voice, "What's with him?"

Alex stepped up to the bar and ordered another beer. Then he noticed the young woman beside him. He'd seen her in the pub several times. She was a redhead with nice eyes and smooth porcelain skin. He smiled back and introduced himself.

"I'm Sherrie," she said.

"I've seen you in here before. You work nearby?"

"I work at the airport for Delta," she said. "Ticket counter. You?"

"I'm a Special Agent with Homeland Security." He thanked the bartender and handed over some cash.

"Ah, so you're special, huh? Just what do you do that's so special?" She let her eyes wander over him.

"Many, many things," he said, grinning. "You busy tonight?"

She shook her head.

"Feel like getting out of here?"

"Sure."

He downed a large swig of his beer. "Let me just say bye to my friend over here."

She picked up her purse and coat and followed him to the table where Tony and Carrie sat laughing. Of course Tony would get along with her. Alex took his coat off the back of the chair where he'd been sitting.

"I'm heading out," he said, tossing some cash onto the table to cover his part of the food he wouldn't eat.

Tony started to protest, but then he caught sight of the woman standing just behind him. Tony smiled. "Sure thing. Be safe."

Alex took another swig of beer. "Carrie, it was good to see you."

His eyes met hers again. She studied him in a way that made his skin squirm. "I hope I didn't run you off," she said.

"Nope, just trying to add some excitement to my evening."

Her eyes found the girl behind him too. He realized he'd already forgotten her name, and guilt started to work its way through him. Guilt over what? He offered a goodbye and turned to the redhead, putting his hand on her back and guiding her out the door.

10.

"WAS IT SOMETHING I SAID?" CARRIE asked, leaning over the table toward Tony.

He looked over his shoulder as Alex opened the door for the redhead. When he turned back around, he shrugged. "No idea."

"He seems a bit touchy."

"Nah, Alex is a good guy. Great investigator. He does a thorough job, and gets more arrests and convictions than anyone else in the entire office. He'll keep you busy."

She was surprised to hear that. "I figured he was more of the loose cannon type."

Tony chuckled. "He can be that guy too. But he gets the job done. You'll see. Don't sweat the moody stuff. Every once in a while he seems to go somewhere dark, gets kind of quiet and keeps to himself. But who doesn't in this line of work?"

Carrie sipped on her soda and thought about that. She could understand better than anyone. Had almost lost herself completely a time or two. But she'd climbed out of the pit and put her life back together. So she could understand if there were days when Alex was withdrawn or needed to blow off steam. But that didn't seem to be what was bothering him. In fact, it seemed like *she* was bothering him, with no idea why.

If she was going to work with him, she'd have to find a way to get him to trust her. Maybe it was time to do a little research and see what made this guy tick.

11.

THE REDHEAD TOOK A SEAT ON A BAR STOOL at his kitchen counter while Alex poured her a glass of wine. He was still racking his brain, trying to remember what she'd said her name was. Charlotte? Sandy? It was something with an "S".

He handed her the glass. "You hungry?"

"Not for food." She smiled and took a sip of the wine.

His insides stirred. But so did his conscience. He'd been down the road of the one-night stand too many times in the past, and it had always made him feel like a jerk. So what was he doing bringing this girl home? He downed his glass of wine and came around the counter. Taking her hand, he helped her down off the bar stool, leading her to the sofa in the living room.

"You have a nice place," she said. "You live here alone?"

"Yep. Just me and Mutt."

She giggled, and it grated his nerves. "You named your dog Mutt?"

"Sure, why not?"

"Seems a little impersonal is all." She shrugged and looked around the room, fingering the sofa pillow as if evaluating his decorating style. "So where are you from?"

"Down on the coast. Brunswick." Now he remembered why he hated dating. The questions.

"You been in Atlanta long?"

"About two years. You?"

"All my life." She finished off her wine and set the glass on the table in front of her. "Anything else I should know?"

"Like what?"

She shrugged and leaned closer to him. "I don't know. Any ex-wives lurking around or kids sleeping in another room?"

"No," he said.

She leaned in closer, and he caught the smell of her perfume mixed with the sweet smell of the wine. He reached up and pulled her face to his, letting the warmth of her lips rush over him. She pushed him back until she was almost lying on top of him. Slowly, she unbuttoned his shirt and slipped it off his shoulders. Then she kissed his chest, and he closed his eyes. He could shut out everything if he just let himself feel this moment, and nothing else.

Her lips moved along his collarbone and over to his shoulder. "What's this?" she breathed.

"What?" He was trying to focus on her skin beneath his hands, shutting everything else out.

"This scar." She pulled back and ran her fingers over his right shoulder. He shuddered involuntarily. "Is this a gunshot? Were you—"

"It's nothing."

"Oh my goodness, you've been shot. What happened?"

She looked almost gleeful, which made his stomach turn. People thought gun fights and car chases were exciting. Too many movies. Too much television. Not enough real life.

"I don't talk about it," he said, hoping the finality in his voice would convince her to drop it.

She rubbed her fingers over the scar again. "You must be very brave."

He could see her little brain working out a dramatic scene, probably complete with his life being saved by a handsome doctor yelling orders across an emergency room. But his mind was full of the real images, and had her to thank for it. *Dammit.*

He pulled her mouth back to his, forcing the images out, feeling only this moment. Only this moment. She wasn't Lily. She wasn't Adrian. He didn't know who she was, and he didn't care. Didn't want to know. Only this moment. And he plunged into it with everything he had.

He would have kept going, would've poured out every ounce of the ache in his chest. But through all the noise in his head, all the images he couldn't shut out, he heard a small voice.

Don't do this.

He tried to silence it. He dug his hands into her back, tasted her skin. *Don't do this.* He pushed up her shirt as he ran his hands up her torso. *Don't do this.* He stopped. Pushed himself off the sofa, letting out a guttural moan. Not again with the voice.

"What's wrong?" she asked as she sat up. "Are you okay?"

"I can't do this."

"You...can't?"

"What? No! Of course I *can*! I just...I'm not ready."

She pulled her shirt closed over her chest. "Oh, I see. Do you want to talk about it?"

He ran his hands through his hair, wanting to pull it out. Was he crazy? "No. I don't want to talk."

"Maybe I should go."

"That would probably be best."

Abruptly she buttoned her shirt, then gathered her things and practically ran out the front door. He wanted to apologize. But really, what was there to say? *Hey, you're really a great girl, even though I don't remember your name.* He stood in the doorway and watched her car tear out of the driveway. He and Tony would have to find a new pub.

He closed the door and turned the lights off in the living room and kitchen. He let Mutt back inside, and then crashed onto his bed—clothes, shoes, and all. Pulling a pillow over his head, he yelled into it as loud as he could. Then the room went silent. The darkness crept in on him, covering him with the certainty that he was completely alone in the world, and always would be. Because this was the best he could hope for.

After a long time of tossing and turning, he finally drifted off into a fitful sleep and the nightmare that had haunted him for three years, of gunshots and blood—and Adrian's eyes—her cold, green eyes that seemed to take pleasure in torturing him.

12.

ALEX SPENT THE NEXT DAY HOLED UP IN HIS
cubicle trying to put together anything that
would constitute probable cause against the
group that had gathered at Jonkovic's house. He
went through the pole cam footage from Monday
night, but as usual all he got was a documentary on
squirrel behavior.

He scrolled through the possible Facebook pages
Tony had gathered, trying to eliminate obvious
mismatches. Finally, he found an account with doz-
ens of pictures of a male nurse fitting the description of Lyons. Most of the images were of young
patients posing with him for selfies, all of them
with Lyons' arms around them in some fashion.
Alex noted that each patient was about eight to
twelve years old, and each patient was a boy.

His stomach churned. Not one of the pictures showed anything illegal, but Alex knew from experience what he was looking at: a bright array of red flags. He did one more search through the page, noticing that Lyons had only a few friends over the age of twelve, one of whom was Brian Meeks.

"Hello, Pizza Guy," Alex muttered.

Picking up the phone, he put in a call to Carrie Reynolds. He wasn't thrilled to have to talk to her, but he needed to try to smooth things over with her, and he needed her to be on board with his investigation. He was just going to have to swallow his pride.

Unfortunately, he only got her voicemail. He hung up and typed a quick email letting her know he wanted to speak with her when she was back in her office. Within minutes, he got a reply.

Won't be back in the office today. Running errands and heading home. How about a bite to eat in about an hour?

That was probably a bad idea. He replied.

If you're willing to risk it again, I suppose I could meet you somewhere. Name the place.

She gave the name of a quaint restaurant not too far from his house. He supposed he should make the effort to be polite. They were going to have to work together on a regular basis, after all. After agreeing to a time, Alex logged off his computer.

The drive alone would take nearly an hour at this time of day.

13.

ALEX FOUND CARRIE ALREADY WAITING AT A round bar table in the corner of the restaurant. He offered a polite smile and noticed the light blue sweater made her eyes stand out even more. She smiled back, but hers seemed genuine, and he was ashamed he'd been so rude to her before. She was probably a perfectly nice woman, and he'd just let his own hang-ups taint his image of her.

He sat down and wasted no time making amends. "Listen, first of all I want to apologize for being a jerk last night. That's not who I am, and I shouldn't have reacted to what you said the way I did."

"Wow," she said. "That certainly wasn't what I was expecting. But thank you. I accept your apology." The waitress came over and asked for their drink orders. Alex motioned for Carrie to start, and she ordered a salad and a Diet Coke.

He ordered a burger and a beer, and the waitress took off. "You don't drink?" he asked.

She shook her head. "Hey, I should apologize as well. I shouldn't have talked to you like you didn't know what you were doing. Sometimes I just don't think before the words come flying out."

"It's okay. No harm done."

"Tony speaks very highly of you," she said.

"Really? What did he say?"

"Just that you're very good at your job. That I should ignore your mood swings and trust you to make a great case for me to prosecute."

She gave him a wry smile, and he couldn't help but smile back. Still, the air between them felt rife with tension. He couldn't understand why she made him so uncomfortable. He tried some small talk about the weather, but that was just painful. He was grateful for the arrival of their drinks, but soon afterward the conversation just died. For at least a good five minutes, all he could do was watch the basketball game on the television over the bar, which again made him a jerk.

She finally broke the ice. "So you wanted to talk to me about the Jonkovic case, right?"

"Right." How could he have forgotten? He explained everything he'd found on Lyons' and Meeks' Facebook pages.

"Sounds promising, but still not exactly what we need," she said.

"I agree. If these guys are doing what I'm sure they're doing, they've managed to cover their tracks extremely well."

"What amazes me," she said, leaning onto the table, "is that they're congregating at all. This isn't typical behavior for guys who are into CP. They're loners. They hole up in their basement and look at this stuff in complete secrecy. They connect online, sure, but I've never seen them willingly share their true identities with each other."

Alex leaned back and studied her more closely. "So I take it this isn't your first experience with Child Exploitation."

"Unfortunately, no. Like you, I've been around it for a couple of years now. I was at the State's Attorney's office for three years and mostly covered child exploitation for the last two."

He caught something in her voice, a change in her tone. "You don't like the job?"

"I'm not sure *like* is the right word. How can anyone like doing this?"

He nodded in agreement. "So why do you stick with it?"

She grasped her hands in front of her and started running her right thumb over her left palm. Alex could sense her discomfort growing. The food arrived just as she was about to answer. They ate a few bites in awkward silence before she continued.

"For me it's personal. I, um...well, let's just say the subject hits close to home. I know all too well how abuse can destroy a young life. I want to do everything I can to help the families and especially the kids get their lives back."

Alex wondered just how close the abuse had touched her life. But he wouldn't press her. He understood the need to keep the past where it belonged. He was glad she'd told him though. They shared a common goal, and it shifted his perspective of her. She wanted the best case possible, because she wanted to make sure of a conviction. That, he could respect. He might disagree on the path to get there, but he was sure they had the same end in mind.

"What about you?" she asked after finishing another bite. "Why do you stick with it?"

He'd wondered that himself more than a few times. The images he had to sift through were the stuff of nightmares, and they'd haunted his dreams more than he cared to admit. But at the root of it, he knew what kept him going.

He shook his head and put down his burger. "It's the kids, really. They have the most horrific things done to them, things I'd never have imagined before I started this job. They deserve justice. I can't let them down."

"This job can be tough on the heart and mind. Do you ever, you know, talk to anyone about it?"

"You mean like a counselor or something?" He chuckled at the idea. "No. I don't do shrinks. That's not my style."

"Wait, so you've never spoken with a counselor? Ever?"

He leaned back in his chair and eyed her. She'd said that like she knew something. "No, why do you ask?"

She looked down at her food and pushed it around the plate with her fork. "Look, it's probably none of my business, I just would've thought with your history, that you would've talked to a counselor before."

"What history?"

She sighed and gave him an apprehensive look. "You were involved in a shooting, right? Three years ago?"

"How do you know about that?"

"Well, if we're going to be working on cases together, and you're going to be testifying, I figured I needed to know more about you. I did a little digging. Nothing a good defense attorney couldn't find and use to discredit you."

Alex felt his face flush warm and his pulse speed up. "I was completely cleared."

"I know. That's why you were able to get hired as an agent."

He looked down at the burger, his appetite suddenly gone. "I've caught you up to speed on everything for the Jonkovic case. You enjoy your dinner."

He stood and tossed his napkin onto the plate. Then he signaled the waitress for the check.

"I didn't mean to upset you," she said, looking dazed.

"I'm not upset. I'm just not going to discuss my history with you."

"You don't have to discuss anything you don't want to. All I was saying was—"

"All you were saying was that if I shot and killed my ex-wife, I must be a lunatic who needs counseling."

She put a hand over her mouth. "Wait. She was your ex-wife?"

Alex waved impatiently at the waitress again. Could this get any worse? He turned his gaze back to Carrie, trying not to lose his temper. "I said I don't want to talk about it! All right?"

She nodded.

The waitress finally approached with the check. He handed her a wad of cash, told her to keep the change, and blew out of the place as quickly as he could.

14.

ON THURSDAY, ALEX WAS GOING THROUGH a couple of tips sent to the group from Perverted Justice, when he recognized the name of Brian Meeks. He'd posted on an obscure message board known for attracting men sharing their encounters with children. Everyone on the board seemed to speak in code that he couldn't completely break, but given the right lens to look through, it wasn't too hard to figure out what was being said. Alex called Tony over to his cubicle to see if he came to the same conclusions he'd drawn from Meeks' posts.

"That's our guy, all right," Tony said. "He talks about moving to Florida to stay near the family of his favorite boy, and then later on he mentions moving back to Atlanta when the kid got too old for him. That matches up so far with his known addresses. Looks like he's been back in Atlanta about a year and a half."

Alex scrolled down to another post. "Check this one out."

Tony read it to himself before commenting. "Is he talking about what I think he's talking about?"

"Unfortunately, I think so. But just to be clear, what do you think he's talking about?"

Tony rubbed his brow and sighed. "He's excited about a pizza delivery. Looks like a boy came to the door with his mom, and when she left to go find a pen to sign the ticket, he got the kid to give him a hug."

Alex pushed down his disgust and focused his thoughts on putting together the pieces. "So we have evidence of actual contact here, and pretty strong evidence linking these comments to Meeks, and linking Meeks to Jonkovic."

"Still pretty weak, man. There's nothing illegal discussed explicitly in these posts. Technically, it's not illegal to get a hug."

"I know. I'm obviously getting desperate."

Tony peered closer at the screen, scrolling through the posts. "You okay? This one seems to be getting to you."

"I'm fine."

"If you say so. Just seems like you've been a little on edge. Carrie thinks you can't stand her."

Alex sighed and leaned his head against the back of his chair. "I said I'm fine. And Carrie and I just don't click. She's just so..."

"So what?" Tony turned around and grinned at him.

"Look, I'm sure she's good at her job, I just don't care for her on a personal level, all right?"

Tony's grin grew wider, and he turned back to the screen. "Whatever you say, man. But you've been weird the last several days."

"It's just the case. I get a little anxious to get guys like this off the street. I think about that mom who's just turning her back for a minute to get a pen. She has no idea some creep's touching her son."

Tony just nodded. Alex usually avoided any serious discussion about the nature of their investigations. It was best to stay as detached as possible. Getting emotional about the case just made him a less effective investigator. But still, he couldn't completely turn it off.

He racked his brain for any way to turn this information into something actionable, but Tony was right. It was weak. And it gave him nothing on Jonkovic. "Well, I guess we file this under 'possibly useful later' and move on. You got anything new today?"

Tony shrugged. "Dead end right now. The ID on the house from our suspect in Australia was inconclusive. He said it looked like the house but couldn't be a hundred percent sure."

Alex flipped his pen across the desk. "So now we just sit on our hands and wait for something to break our way."

15.

ALEX SPENT THE REST OF THURSDAY AND Friday trying to chase down leads on his other cases and catching up on paperwork, but his mind kept spinning over the Jonkovic case, even through the weekend. Something about it wouldn't leave him alone. He was sure if he could just get a warrant for the guy's house, maybe even one for his vehicle, he'd be able to bring down the whole ring of predators, and destroy the network they were using to communicate. He just needed that one domino to fall his way.

Monday morning, he sat at his desk scanning through the video from his pole cam for the weekend. The same vehicles had gathered at the house on Friday night, but it was maddening not to be able to find out what was going on *inside* the house.

Cataloguing vehicles was pointless if that was all he was going to be able to do.

"Walker, you got a minute?" Craig yelled from behind him. "I think I got something for you."

"Sure," he yelled back. He walked over to Craig's desk. "What is it?"

"I've been calling around several police departments over the past week, asking for them to check their reports over the last year for anything related to your ring of guys. Finally got something."

"What is it?"

Craig spun around and read from his computer screen. "Apparently your guy Jonkovic was involved in a scuffle a few weeks ago. Seems he was lurking around at Six Flags and some dad caught him taking pictures of his kid. Dad freaked and punched him."

Alex's pulse quickened. "What's the date on the incident?"

"October 29th."

Alex clapped a hand on Craig's shoulder. "That's some great work right there. That's just what we need. Send me that report."

"Sending it your way right now."

Alex returned to his desk and opened the forwarded message from Craig. He read through the attached Cobb County police report, and for the first time in years, he actually thanked God. He picked up the phone and called the police department.

"May I speak with Officer Campbell?"

"He's out on patrol right now," a female voice answered. "Would you like to leave him a message?"

"This is Special Agent Alex Walker with Homeland Security. I wanted to ask him a few questions about a report he filed on an incident a few weeks ago. Would you please tell him to contact me so we can arrange a meeting as soon as possible?"

Alex passed on his contact info and hung up. This had to be the break he needed.

It had to be.

16.

ALEX PLACED HIS FOOD ON THE TABLE AND took a seat across from Officer Martin Campbell. "So explain to me what you saw when you arrived on scene."

Officer Campbell set his hat on the table, revealing a shiny bald head. "Your guy, Jonkovic, was sitting in a chair at the security station with a nasty black eye coming on. The other guy, Mr. Thomas, was pacing back and forth a few feet away. There were a couple of security guards keeping the two of them separated."

"Did you talk to both men?"

"Sure did. Jonkovic claimed he was assaulted, which was verified by a few other bystanders. But when I talked to Mr. Thomas, he explained that he caught Jonkovic taking pictures of his kid."

"Did he?"

Campbell shoved his burger in his mouth and chewed for a bit before answering. "I couldn't find any on his phone, but it sounds like they were erased before I arrived." He took a sip of his soda. "It boiled down to one man's word against the other as far as the pictures were concerned. Thomas said he noticed the man following them for a ways. Then, when they stopped at a vendor near the log ride, he stepped over to the counter to get napkins and condiments, and when he turned around, he saw Jonkovic snapping a picture of his boy."

Alex shook his head. He really needed the actual photos for this to be solid probable cause. "And you're sure no one saw the actual picture itself?"

"Look, when I spoke to the dad, he was pretty adamant. He snatched the phone from the guy after belting him. He said it was there, but he demanded the guy erase it. Said he wasn't thinking straight."

Alex leaned back and swore under his breath. "I really needed that evidence."

"Look, if it helps any, when I talked to Jonkovic, I got the definite sense he was shady. He was angry at first and wanted to press charges for assault, but once I started asking him for personal information, he backtracked and said he just wanted to be left alone. I asked him if I could search his phone, but he said no. And from that point on it was clear that all he wanted was to get out of there as soon as possible."

"So what did you make of the guy?"

Campbell shook his head. "The guy's a creep. I had no doubt he was doing what the dad said, following them around and taking pictures of his kid."

"Did you guys ever look at him for the Gomez kidnapping?"

"Honestly, I don't know. I wasn't on that case. But I can find out whose case it is."

Alex handed over his business card. "If you think of anything else that might help, give me a shout."

"Absolutely," Campbell said, his eyes going dark for a moment. "I got a kid too, about that same age. Can't say I wouldn't have done the exact same thing."

17.

ALEX TOOK A DEEP BREATH OUTSIDE THE OFFICE of Carrie Reynolds. He'd tried reaching her by phone and email, but she hadn't responded. He figured she was pissed, but she should still be able to do her job. That was the reason he'd hated working with Julie. So emotional.

He was going to have to apologize to Carrie. Again. But he had no desire to discuss his history with her, and apologizing was like flinging the door wide open on the subject. He needed to keep the conversation as short and direct as possible. No personal stuff.

He knocked and stuck his head inside. "You busy?"

She looked up from her desk, and surprised him by smiling. "Come on in."

He held the affidavit in his hand toward her and laid it on the desk. "Been trying to call you. Finally got something we can move on. Well, if it gets approved that is." He was having a hard time making eye contact, so he let his gaze wander over the bookshelves.

She came around from behind her desk and picked up the papers. Then she leaned on her desk in front of him while she looked them over. "Yeah, sorry about the phone. I've been slammed all day." She read for a moment. "This should definitely be enough for a tracker on Jonkovic's vehicle, but that's probably all you'll get. Nothing on Meeks or any of the others yet?"

"Nothing we can use." He stood to leave, finally looking in her eyes and taken aback by the unexpected kindness he saw there. It made him pause. "I, uh, I'm sorry about the way I left things the other night."

"It's all right," she said. "I told you I have a habit of blurting things out without thinking them through. I hope you'll forgive me for the intrusion, and I hope you don't think I was snooping just for the fun of it."

"No, I just wasn't prepared to talk about that time of my life. I prefer to leave it in the past."

She stood from the desk and shuffled the papers. "Well, thanks for bringing the affidavit by. I'll look it over more closely, but it seems like everything's in order. You should be able to get your tracker on the vehicle by Friday."

"I'll get out of your hair and let you get some work done," Alex said, heading for the door. "Let me know if you need anything more."

She nodded and watched him leave. But he stopped at the door, feeling an uncontrollable need to explain himself. "And listen, I've testified in several cases so far. No one's brought up the shooting. I explained the whole situation to the SAC before he hired me, and he seemed to think it wouldn't be an issue. It was ruled as a justified shooting."

She set the papers down and took a step toward him. His pulse raced to life. "I know. You don't have to explain anything to me you don't want to. And I swear I'll keep it to myself."

He dropped his gaze to the floor, suddenly feeling very tired. Walls were necessary, but they sure took a lot of energy to keep up. "I, um, I appreciate that."

She pushed a strand of hair behind her ear. "Do you go to church anywhere around here?"

He definitely needed to get out of there. He reached for the door handle. "Uh, no. Not my style. I did the whole God thing a few years back, and it didn't really work out for me."

She angled her head. "What does that mean?"

"Look, I should get going." He glanced down at his watch. "It's getting late. I'm sure you have plans.

I have plans. I'll get with you on Friday, and we'll figure out the next step in the case."

He was almost completely out the door when she called out to him. "Alex?"

"Yeah?"

"You're welcome to come with me anytime."

He nodded, and let the door close behind him. He didn't need to ask what she was referring to. He knew what she meant.

He'd been *saved* by a woman once before, and it didn't take. He sure wasn't going down that road again.

18.

THE TEACHER STOOD IN THE DARK BEDROOM watching through the bathroom door as the boy stepped out of the bath and dried himself off. He'd been holding onto this one for too long, but only because he was special. There was something soothing about him. Something that calmed the darkness raging below the surface.

It was the eyes that did it. They were such a rich, deep brown. He got lost in them. And that accent. The trill in the boy's Latino accent drove him mad.

But it was time. He could see the boy's body changing, the small hairs growing in new places. Such a shame that boys had to grow up at all. Especially this one. This one had been so compliant.

The Teacher took a deep breath and watched him finish putting on his shorts. The boy stepped into the bedroom, the bathroom light spilling around him like a cloak. The boy looked at him with the same question in his eyes that had been there every night for a while now.

"Here?" the boy asked. Even his voice was different, growing deeper.

The Teacher shook his head. "Not tonight. Downstairs."

"Are you...unhappy with me, Maestro?"

He smiled and walked over to the boy, wrapping an arm over his shoulder. "No, of course not. I'm just tired this evening, and I have many things to work on. Maybe tomorrow night."

He kissed the boy on top of the head and followed him down the hallway to the door that led down to the basement. The boy stopped at the top of the stairs and looked back at him with apprehension in his eyes, those beautiful dark eyes.

"I don't like it down there. Can't I sleep with you?"

He was tempted for a moment. But that would make the separation that much harder. It was time. He needed to make a phone call to begin the arrangements. It was best that the boy didn't hear them.

"You'll be all right," he said. "You're a big boy. There's nothing to fear. Now go on. I have much work to do."

The boy turned away, his shoulders slumping forward as he descended the stairs. He closed the door to the basement and locked the deadbolt, as well as the doorknob. He'd make sure the boy's next home was a good one, with someone gentle. He deserved someone full of love for boys. Just as he was.

He would miss him terribly, but it was time to make that call.

Part Two

The Monster

19.

IT WAS AFTER ELEVEN O'CLOCK FRIDAY NIGHT when Alex parked his car a few houses away from Jonkovic's. It was risky to install the tracker while the group of guys were inside, but he was anxious to get the ball rolling on this case. He checked the tracker one last time to make sure everything was working properly.

"You doing this, or am I?" Tony asked. He leaned forward in the passenger seat and surveyed the surrounding area.

"I got this," Alex answered. "You keep an eye out." He opened the door and stepped out, glancing around for anything out of the ordinary. Then he leaned down and grinned at Tony. "If I'm not back in five minutes, just wait longer."

Tony chuckled. "Wow. You need some new material."

Alex closed the door and began making his way down the street, trying his best not to look suspicious. He'd hoped for some cloud cover, but to his dismay the brightest full moon ever known to man was lighting up the entire neighborhood. He reached Jonkovic's driveway without spotting anyone, paused and looked around one last time, then slunk along the edge, stepping as lightly as possible. His shoes on the gravel sounded like fireworks filling the quiet of the night. He reached the house and slid down behind the back bumper of Jonkovic's Mercedes, only then noticing the car had been altered with ground effects.

Alex swore under his breath. It was hard enough on newer cars to find something metal underneath to secure the magnetic tracker to, but with this car's body so low to the ground, he might not be able to attach it at all. He sprawled onto his back and slid his left arm under the vehicle, just behind the rear tire, feeling around for a suitable surface. He could barely move his arm, and the edge of the car dug into the front of his shoulder, while the pavement scraped the back of it.

The longer it took to feel around, the more his nerves made his palms sweat. He finally found a spot that might work, but just as he was about to slap the tracker on, it slipped out of his hand and clanged beneath the vehicle. Alex dropped his head back and let out a deep sigh. This was already taking way too long.

He lowered his hand onto the ground, grazing over the cement to find the tracker. But the sound of a sliding glass door made him freeze. A voice came from somewhere near the back of the house, speaking in rapid bursts. At first he couldn't make out any of the words, but once he made sense of the accent, maybe Russian, he began to catch a few phrases, especially when the voice moved closer.

"...Yes, yes, I understand. He's very special."

It sounded like the voice was moving. Alex hoped the guy was just pacing as he talked, but he soon realized he was getting closer to the car. Alex's heart sped up, thundering in his ears. Of course, just when he needed to be absolutely still, his body began to itch.

"He will do a good job and make you very proud," Jonkovic continued in his thick Slavic accent. "He will be a good fit there."

A drop of sweat rolled down the center of Alex's back, tickling like crazy. He scolded himself for being weak. What had happened to the tough guy who'd pushed through all the long days of training for the Marines on Parris Island? One particularly sinister drill instructor had forced them to stand outside bare-chested at dusk while the sand gnats fed on their blood. No one was allowed to swat a single gnat. If he could master his mind over sand gnats, he could do it over a few drops of sweat.

Jonkovic moved closer again. "...Sure, sure. I'll send you pictures."

Pictures. Of who? Someone who'd be a good fit. Probably a kid. He knew it. He'd had the right house all along. And Jonkovic was about to move the Gomez kid. Time was running out.

The gate opened, and Alex heard footsteps getting closer. He turned his head to the side and could barely make out the shadow of Jonkovic moving along the other side of the vehicle. If he found Alex lying on the driveway with his hand under the car, what would he do? The case would be blown to bits. How long was this guy going to talk?

He tried to balance his deep desire to exit the premises without being discovered, with his equally deep desire to overhear Jonkovic reveal something useful. The shadow on the other side of the vehicle stopped, and the back door of the car opened. Alex held his breath. Jonkovic rustled something in the back seat. Then the door closed and the shadow continued past the car, Jonkovic's voice moving further away. He went to the front of the house, maybe up the curved stairs, and into the front door.

Finally Alex heard a slam, and the voice was gone. He let out several long, slow breaths, settling his heart rate. Mercifully, he found the tracker and slapped it into place. Then he crept back to his car. Once inside, he let out the first real breath he'd taken in nearly twenty minutes.

"So, how'd it go?" Tony said.

"Perfect. Without a hitch. What did you expect?"

20.

ALEX MONITORED JONKOVIC'S MOVES OVER THE next couple of days, disappointed by the lack of helpful information they provided. He'd finally gotten the domino he needed, or at least he'd thought he had, but waiting for it to pan out was like waiting for grass to grow in the winter. The guy seriously did nothing more than drive to work each morning and drive home each afternoon.

Knowing he was preparing to move the Gomez kid only made it that more infuriating. Of course, Miss Perfect AUSA still needed more evidence before he could get a warrant for the residence. Forget the fact that a kid was living a nightmare at that very moment, while they stood around discussing proper procedures.

By Wednesday night Alex needed to blow off some steam, so he and Tony headed for a bar downtown that had become one of their favorites in the past few months. It was crowded and fairly noisy, but not so bad they couldn't hear each other, especially if they found a place near the back.

Alex hung his jacket over a chair and set his beer on the table. "Anyone else coming?"

Tony sat down across from him and took a swig of his beer. "I think Richards is coming later. Craig said he'd try." They shared a knowing look, but neither of them said what they were both thinking. No way Craig was coming. "I invited Carrie too. Hope you don't mind."

"Why would I mind?" Alex asked, even though he did. He'd hoped to relax, and Carrie just set him on edge.

"You don't seem to care for her much." Tony took another drink before continuing. "Or maybe it's just the opposite."

"What's that supposed to mean?"

"I don't know. Maybe she gets under your skin because deep down you really like her." Tony grinned. "She is hot."

Alex couldn't help but laugh. "Okay, I give you that. She's nice-looking." Tony raised an eyebrow, and Alex threw his hands up. "Okay, she's very attractive. Any guy in his right mind would feel that way. But there's nothing else there. I'm not interested."

Tony smiled like he could see right through him. "I get it. She's hot, but you have to work together. But just because you have to keep your hands off her, doesn't mean you can't enjoy the view."

"Is that what you told yourself with Julie?"

"Oh no. I threw all wisdom and discretion out the window for that one. I never kidded myself into thinking I wouldn't go for it."

Alex shook his head. "But you said yourself that it wasn't worth having to take your cases to Frank. That guy wouldn't have prosecuted Jeffrey Dahmer."

Tony rolled his eyes. "Good lord, that man has no balls. None!"

They were still laughing when Carrie found them and slung her purse over the back of a chair. "What's so funny?"

Alex stopped laughing, and his eyes met hers. Her mouth tipped into a curious smile, and a tiny jolt ran through his chest. He leaned back in his chair and looked her over. Her fitted skirt and boots revealed long legs without looking like she was trying to show them off. Subtle, but effective.

"You look like you're ready for some fun," Alex said.

She pulled out the chair and took a seat, glancing between the two of them. "That's the idea, right?"

Alex noticed Tony's eyes taking her in as well. He was definitely enjoying the view. "Let me get you a drink," Tony said as he stood.

"Oh, I'll get one in a minute."

He waved her off. "Nonsense. I'm heading over to the bar anyway. What do you want?"

"I'll take a Diet Coke."

Alex laughed out loud when Tony wrinkled his brow at her like she'd spoken another language. Tony sputtered. "Did you just say Diet Coke?"

"Yep."

He shrugged. "Okay then. Diet Coke it is."

Carrie turned back to face him, and Alex caught a glimpse of Tony signaling him from behind her. He mouthed the words, "Go for it," and then headed for the bar.

Alex chuckled and shook his head. "I guess you get that reaction a lot."

"Sometimes. Not too often. I actually don't hang out in bars very much anyway."

"So what made you come tonight?"

She shrugged and looked away. "Just thought it would be nice to get out and have some fun."

He leaned onto the table toward her so he could lower his voice. "I haven't been able to get anything on the vehicle tracker yet."

"No, no," she said, wagging her finger at him. "No work tonight. You're just Alex. I'm just Carrie. We're just hanging out with our friend, Tony."

"Yes, ma'am," he said. "You're the boss." She laughed, and his shoulders relaxed. "So, 'just Carrie', what do you like to do for fun when you're not hanging around with us dopes?"

She leaned onto the table and put her chin in her hand. "Let's see, I like to go hiking or rock climbing. I love skiing, but I haven't gone in a very long time. Oh, and I love to cook! Big huge meals with all the foods that are the worst for you, but are the best to eat."

Her whole face lit up when she smiled, and Alex found himself being drawn to her. "Sounds great. I hate cooking. I keep the restaurants around my house in business just in my takeout orders alone."

She sat up straighter and brightened even more. "Then it's settled. Saturday evening, I'm cooking you dinner."

His heart raced forward. "I, uh...I don't know."

"Oh, come on! I never get to cook for anyone. It's just one meal."

She looked so hopeful. How could he say no? He *needed* to say no. "Okay."

She clapped her hands in triumph just as Tony reappeared with drinks. He looked between them with a curious smile. "So what did I miss?"

"Alex is letting me cook dinner for him Saturday night."

Tony arched an eyebrow. "Really?"

"You should come too," Alex said.

"Yes! The more the merrier." Carrie looked like a little girl asking for presents from Santa. The more apparent it became that this dinner meant so much to her, the more Alex felt the need to bolt.

Tony plastered on his disappointed face. "Aw, that sounds like fun, but I already have plans." He snuck a wink at Alex. "But you two should definitely go for it."

Alex glared at him. Was Tony seriously suggesting that he hit on their AUSA and jeopardize their biggest case ever? Tony needed a dose of reality, maybe in the form of a good punch to the head.

21.

ALEX WAS PRETTY SURE THAT DINNER AT CARRIE'S place wasn't the best idea, especially when she opened the door and saw the flowers in his hands. He saw the flicker of concern in her eyes, the question that undoubtedly ran through her mind of whether he'd gotten the wrong impression. He'd thought the gesture would be polite, but maybe he'd just made the awkwardness between them even worse.

He thrust them toward her and tried to think of an easy explanation. "I, uh, just wanted to say thanks for dinner." She took them and lifted them to her nose. Her eyes closed as she smelled them. He had no idea what type of flowers they were, but she looked pleased.

"I would've brought wine," he said. "But I remembered you don't drink, so—"

"They're beautiful," she said.

He took a deep breath to relax. It had been a long time since he'd felt so nervous around a woman. That was a bad sign. Of all the women in the world, she was exactly the wrong one to be thinking about. He did a quick mental shake of his head, reminding himself that this dinner was just to smooth out the bumps in their working relationship. No more.

She closed the door after he stepped inside and headed through her small living room. As she rounded the corner of what he assumed was the kitchen, she called out to him. "Come on. I have a few more things to pull together and then we can eat."

He followed her around the corner, noting the stark contrast in her smaller apartment and his house. There were pictures on every surface— Carrie smiling and laughing with so many different people; he didn't think he saw the same person twice. He stopped just inside the kitchen to take a closer look at what appeared to be a graduation photo.

"These your parents?" he asked.

She came over beside him and followed his gaze to the nook just inside the kitchen. He caught a quick whiff of her perfume. Just a hint of something sweet.

"Um, yes," she said. "Those are my folks. That was graduation from law school."

He straightened and looked around the cozy kitchen. It was warm, inviting. And the salty-sweet smell of something good in the oven made his mouth water. "You have a nice place here," he said.

"Thanks. I've only been here about a year." Crossing over to the oven, she checked on whatever was inside. Then she leaned back against it and crossed her arms. "It's so funny how I'm nearly thirty years old, and I'm just now getting to the point where I feel like a real grown up."

"Why is that?"

She shrugged. "I've been close to my parents for a long time. They're pretty protective. I think I'm still trying to prove I can make it on my own. Maybe that's just a girl thing. I bet you were out on your own pretty early."

Alex leaned onto the bar that separated the kitchen from the tiny dining area. "Yep. I was out the door the week after graduation and never looked back. Happy to get out of there."

"You weren't close to your parents?"

He tried not to laugh. "Uh, no."

She watched him closely for a moment, but didn't press. "Listen, I just want to make sure you understand that I didn't invite you here to hit on you or anything."

"Well, why not?" He held a serious face long enough for the blush to creep into her cheeks.

Then he grinned, and she let out a nervous laugh. "Am I not good enough for you?" he continued, still grinning.

She smiled back at him. "You're definitely not good enough for me. I only date doctors or geniuses."

"I'll have you know I'm an investigative genius."

She shook her head. "That remains to be seen."

"Hey, all you have to do is approve my search warrant and I'll show you just how good I am. The Gomez boy's in that house. I *know* it."

A pained expression crossed her face. Maybe he shouldn't have brought up work. The playful banter had been a nice break from the tension between them. She walked over to the counter on the opposite side of the bar, looking him right in the eye.

"Alex, I believe you. That's what makes this so hard. And it's why we have to do everything we can to make sure we have the best case possible against this guy."

"We've got enough evidence to go in there. Once we hit the house and get the boy, you'll have the case. I just don't understand how we can leave him there, knowing what's most likely happening to him."

She took a deep breath, gripped her hands, and rubbed the palms. "Then get the evidence. That part is your job, and if you're as good as Tony says, you'll get what you need for your warrant."

He sighed. "The other night, you said this hits close to home. Were you talking about yourself?"

She dropped her gaze and nodded slightly.

"Then you know," he said. "You know what happens to these kids."

Another nod.

"How do you—?"

The buzzer on the oven interrupted him, startling Carrie. She flew into action, grabbing a pot holder and pulling a large pan out of the oven. Alex could see it was a roast, and the heavenly smell filled the entire room. She checked the meat and the vegetables. Then she turned back to him with the smile that had faded earlier.

"It's ready!" she said. "Hope you're hungry."

22.

CARRIE KNEW SHE SHOULDN'T HAVE SAID anything as soon as she uttered the words, "Do you mind if I give thanks for the food?" The conversation had almost returned to normal, at least normal for them. He'd even smiled at her a few times, and seemed eager to dig into the meal she'd prepared. But the atmosphere of her cozy kitchen suddenly went cool when she offered to pray. Alex's smile dropped from his face, and he leaned back in his chair as if he suddenly remembered why he didn't like her.

"Sure," he said. "Go ahead."

She bowed her head and closed her eyes, feeling his gaze on her. "Lord, thank you for this food, and for the company to share it with. Amen."

She looked up again, and he was indeed staring at her. But she'd expected contempt in his eyes, and instead she saw sadness there, maybe even pain. His face went blank almost immediately, and he picked up his fork.

"Careful," she said. "It's hot."

He paused with the fork in mid-air. His eyes met hers, and for a moment it sounded like her heart was in her ears. Then he gently blew on it before taking a bite. He swallowed, and his smile returned.

"It's fantastic, Carrie."

She let out the breath she'd been holding. "Really? You like it?"

He blew on another forkful before shoveling it in. "Absolutely."

She relaxed again as the tension evaporating, and watched him eat several more mouthfuls, relishing the compliments after each one. Then she concentrated on her own plate, satisfied that she hadn't ruined the evening.

"I was afraid you were going to hate it after I made such a big deal about cooking the other night. I figured I'd jinxed myself."

He wiped his mouth and took a sip of his beer. "Seriously. This is the best roast I've ever had. Nothing to worry about."

She took several more bites herself, and it was indeed the best she'd ever made. It had been a couple of years since she'd tried this recipe, but she hadn't lost her touch. Hopefully that success would carry over into dessert as well.

"Is your mother a good cook?" she asked.

"She's decent. That wasn't really her thing when I was growing up. She worked a lot."

"You got any brothers or sisters?"

"A sister." His whole body seemed to tense as he said it.

"Are you close to your family?" she asked.

"Not really." He rested his fork on his plate, looking at it thoughtfully. "I know I've been a bit of a jerk with you, and I am sorry for that. I don't want to offend you or anything. You seem like a perfectly nice person." Then he looked up at her, and she saw that pained sadness again. "But I don't talk about my family."

"I see," she said quietly. She continued eating, not sure what to say next. It seemed like no matter what she said, it was the wrong thing. "Are you like this with everyone?" she finally asked.

"Like what?"

"Closed off. Every time I try to talk to you about anything, you act like I'm either interrogating you or questioning your ability to do your job. You know, sometimes I'm actually just trying to make pleasant conversation."

She stood and took her plate over to the sink, her appetite gone. She scraped the remains of her roast into the garbage disposal. Alex remained at the table, staring down at his plate.

"Yes," he said, so quietly she almost didn't hear him.

She stopped scraping. "What?"

He looked up at her then. "Yes. I'm like this with everyone. It's not because of you. I'm just...I'm a jerk. Okay?"

She set the plate in the sink and leaned onto the counter. "It's not okay."

He let out a deep sigh. Then he picked up his plate and brought it over to the sink. "This probably wasn't a good idea. I should get going."

"No." Heat rushed through her body. "Quit running away from me. Just talk. Like a normal human being. It's called conversation."

He crossed his arms over his chest and leaned against the counter. "Fine. What do you want to know? I already told you, I'm clear to testify. None of my past is Giglio material, but if you think you need to know it in order to properly prosecute your cases, go ahead. Ask away."

She stepped back and took a deep breath. "I wasn't asking because I thought you'd be a liability on the witness stand. I was trying to be a friend. I just...wanted to get to know you. Obviously something happened in your past that troubles you deeply, but that doesn't give you an excuse to treat me like the enemy. Believe it or not, I might actually understand. I don't exactly run around telling everyone I was sexually abused as a child."

He dropped his head and rubbed the back of his neck. She waited for him to respond, but he just stood there in silence, refusing to look at her. Finally he took a deep breath and blew it out, turning to face her.

"You're right. I'm sorry. I didn't mean to lash out at you." Another long pause. "Look, several years ago, my wife and I lost our son in childbirth. She couldn't handle it, and she left. I thought she was just angry with me, and I tried to reconcile with her for a while, but she just got more and more hateful. We finally got divorced after she moved to New York. I thought that was the end of it."

Carrie braced herself, sensing something awful coming.

"I started seeing someone else. Thought I'd finally gotten it right, girl of my dreams and everything. She helped me heal, made me think it was possible that God loved me, and that everything would be all right. But then Adrian, my ex-wife, showed up with a vengeance and tried to kill us all. Me, Lily, and Lily's ex. It was like something out of a horror movie. I wound up having to shoot Adrian."

Alex stood there with his arms over his chest like a shield. He told his story like he was giving a report. No emotions for all his loss.

"I don't talk about it because, obviously, it's a difficult subject. And I can't change anything. I can't bring back my son. I can't bring back Adrian. I don't want to keep going over that night in my head again and again. I made the best decision I could, and it ended Adrian's life."

Carrie wanted to reach out for him, to sooth the hurt somehow. But she didn't want to make things worse between them by making him even more uncomfortable. "What about the girl?" she asked. "Lily?"

His expression darkened. "After all that talk of being in love with me, of a loving God who had protected us from Adrian, she ditched me for the ex-boyfriend."

"What?" Carrie couldn't help her surprise. "After you saved her life?"

He shook his head and almost grinned. "Well, if I'm being honest, I guess he really saved her life too. He jumped in front of a bullet to save her. The jerk." Then he did smile, a relieved half smile. "I guess everything happened as it should've. They loved each other. Just wish she'd figured that out before getting me involved."

Carrie wasn't sure what to say. He'd obviously suffered more loss than anyone should ever have to endure. No wonder he was distant.

"Thank you for telling me," she said. "It sounds like you did everything you could. I understand why you don't like talking about it."

He met her gaze, and she realized she'd moved closer as he'd been talking. Her hand rested on the counter, only inches away from where he leaned against it. Before she could talk herself out of it, she reached out and touched his arm.

She felt a tingle run along her own hand and up her arm as the hair stood on end. He unfolded his arms, and moved away from her. Heat and shame crept over her face, and she stepped back as well.

"I'm sorry," she said.

He pressed his brow into a frown as he looked down at her. She couldn't say a word. All she wanted to do was to crawl into a hole and never come out. What was she thinking?

"Carrie," he said, his voice low and full of doubt. "I don't think it would be a good idea to—"

"No, no! Absolutely. I didn't mean anything."

But he took a step closer, and her head swam. She tried to take a step back, but her body moved forward instead. He was only inches away. She longed to turn her face up to his, but she shouldn't. He took in a deep breath, just above her ear, and warmth shot down her torso and legs. His cheek touched her temple, and her face tilted up as if it had a mind of its own.

Their lips met, and he cupped her cheeks in his hands. Her body turned to liquid, and she opened up completely to his kiss. For a brief moment everything stood still, and she drank him in.

The blaring of a cell phone jolted them apart, and Alex turned away from her immediately. He pulled the cell up to his ear. She stood there watching his back as he talked, wondering what had just happened, and what consequences lay ahead. But she didn't have time to ponder it long.

Alex turned back to her with wild eyes. "It's Meeks. He's been arrested."

23.

A LEX BLEW INTO THE NORTHEAST COBB
COUNTY precinct and asked the duty officer
where he could find Special Agent Sparks
with the DEA. The hefty officer looked back
at him with an annoyingly vacant expression. Alex
dropped his hands onto the counter a little too
forcefully, and anger flashed in the man's eyes.

He whipped out his badge. "I'm Special Agent
Alex Walker. An Agent Sparks with DEA called me
about forty-five minutes ago saying he was bringing in a suspect for questioning. I just need to
speak with him about it."

The officer managed to lift himself out of the
chair. It groaned with relief as he stood and walked
over to the counter. "I see," he said. "I'll check it
out. In the meantime, you can wait over there." He
lifted a huge sausage finger and pointed behind

Alex to a set of chairs near the front. They were peppered with lowlifes with whom he had no interest in mingling.

He nodded at the duty officer and made his way over to the wall across from the chairs. There he paced back and forth for what seemed like hours, trying not to get carried away with the idea that his case could break wide open tonight. He just needed to get his hands on Meeks.

After a few minutes, a tall gangly man in jeans and a sweatshirt walked toward him. "Are you Agent Walker?"

Alex extended his hand. "You must be Agent Sparks. Thanks for the call."

"Sure, but you didn't have to come all the way down here tonight. I'd be happy to send you a copy of the report on whatever we get out of him."

Alex shook his head. "I need to speak with him tonight. He's key to an international child exploitation case."

Sparks folded his arms, and his expression hardened. "I don't think you're going to be able to speak with him tonight. The call I made to you was simply a courtesy call."

Alex got an uneasy feeling things were taking a turn for the worse. *Damn DEA.* He hated trying to work any cases that involved them. They had a perpetual stick up their collective ass.

"Look, I just want to be part of the interview. I don't see what the big deal is."

Sparks pressed his lips into a thin line. "Agent Walker, this is a Drug Enforcement issue. If we develop any kind of Homeland Security issue, I'll give you a call."

Alex gritted his teeth and pulled out his cell phone. "Don't move," he said to Sparks. He hit Carrie's number and lifted the receiver to his ear, never taking his eyes off Sparks. When she answered he launched into a brief explanation.

"Miss Reynolds, I have a conflict with an Agent Sparks from DEA over our suspect, Brian Meeks. He doesn't seem to understand the seriousness of the situation. I was wondering if you could contact the US attorney and clear this up."

"Certainly," she said. "I'll get him on the phone right now." Alex hung up and tried not to grin in satisfaction.

Sparks rolled his eyes. "Sure, run to Mommy 'cause the mean old DEA agent won't play nice," he huffed. "What's she going to do? Tattle on me to my daddy?"

Alex had never wanted to strike another agent as badly as he wanted to pummel this one. But within a minute, Sparks' phone began to buzz. Alex leaned toward him.

"That'll be Daddy," he said.

Sparks eyed him with disdain and answered. "Yes, sir," he said, frowning. "I understand." He listened for a moment longer before hanging up and dropping his phone back into his pocket. "Looks like your phone call to Mommy worked. You can go talk to the suspect, but I want to be in there during the interview."

Alex smirked. "Look, this is a Homeland Security issue. If I develop any kind of Drug Enforcement issue, I'll let you know." He relished the surprise that crossed the jerk's face. Then he followed the duty officer through the hallway and into an interview room.

Meeks was seated on the other side of the table, hunched down in the chair with dark circles under his eyes. "Where'd the other guy go?" he asked.

Alex went right to work, not giving him a moment to think. "You have one shot right now," he said, pressing his fists into the table. "You can take your chances with Agent Sparks and go to prison for twenty or thirty years—hell, maybe the rest of your life if you had a kilo on you—or you can cut a deal with me and do a lot less time behind bars. Your call, but you gotta make a decision now."

Meeks withered even more. "I don't...understand. Who are you?"

Alex pushed down the disgust building inside of him and tried not to think about the words he'd read on the message board from this pervert. "I'm Agent Walker. I work for Homeland Security. I'm offering you a chance to become a confidential informant and work off some of your charges. If you cooperate, and if you get us something we can use, you have a good chance of reducing your sentence."

Meeks shook his head like he was clearing the cobwebs. "Homeland Security? You mean you want me to be an informant against...who? Terrorists?"

Alex took a deep breath and resisted the urge to reach out and smack the guy. "No. You have some pretty shady friends you've been hanging around with. Do the names Roman Jonkovic, Derrick Lyons, or Mark Johnson mean anything to you?"

The color drained from Meeks' face. "Wait." His eyes widened. "You mean *those* friends...are terrorists?"

Alex pushed away from the table and pulled a chair over to him. "No! Get off the terrorist thing. I'm talking child pornography here. You like kids, right? That's your thing. You get your kicks from touching little boys."

"No!" Meeks shook his head vehemently. "No, no. I don't know what you're talking about, man."

Alex threw his hands up. "Hey, look. We have pretty damning evidence that says otherwise. But like I said, if you want to take your chances with the DEA and see if you like the idea of spending the rest of your life hanging with the Bloods and Crips, well then..." Alex leaned across the table and lowered his voice. "And we all know just how much they love child molesters in prison."

Meeks actually let out a whimper and dropped his head into his hands. Alex could've sworn he heard the guy mumbling prayers. As if God listened to guys like him. He pushed himself up to standing and tapped on the table.

"All right, so I guess you want to take your chances with the DEA then? So I'll be seeing ya." He turned to go.

"Wait." Meeks whispered. Alex turned back to face him, sickened by the weakness looking back at him from across the table. "I'll do it."

Alex leaned onto the table again. "Good call. Now let's get out of here."

24.

ALEX PRACTICALLY DRAGGED MEEKS OUT OF the police station, throwing a satisfied smirk at Agent Sparks as they passed. Sparks leapt out of his chair and followed them to the door.

"What do you think you're doing?" he yelled.

Alex turned and put a hand on Sparks' chest. "I'm taking my suspect over to my office for an interview."

Sparks pushed Alex's hand away, his mouth dropping open. "You can't just come in here and take a suspect out of my custody! He sold nearly a kilo of heroin to an undercover agent tonight. He's going down for that."

"I guess we'll see, won't we?"

Alex grabbed Meeks by the arm and pulled him out the front door. He shoved him into the back of his personal car, hoping that small detail wouldn't come up later. Then he raced across town toward the Homeland Security offices. He glanced back at Meeks every couple of minutes just to make sure the guy wasn't up to any funny business. Meeks sat slumped in the seat, his head resting against the back and his eyes closed. He might have been asleep, except Alex could make out the faint movement of his lips.

When they pulled up to the office, Alex took pleasure in yanking Meeks out of the car and "gently" guiding him through the empty hallways to the interview room. Only a few emergency lights were on, creating an eerie glow to everything. That was exactly what he needed. He'd take every advantage he could get to put the fear of God into this guy.

He closed the door behind them and pointed to a chair on the other side of the table. "Have a seat."

Meeks looked at him like a frightened mouse. "Where are we? Why isn't there anyone here?"

"I'll be asking the questions. Now sit."

Meeks slid over to the chair and sat down, resting his arms on the table. He looked around the room, pausing at the corners of the ceiling. "Are you recording this?"

"Nope. Just you and me talking things out."

Meeks ran his hands through his greasy hair and returned them to the table. "So what happens next?"

Alex took the seat across from him and also laid his arms across the table. Mimicking the suspect was a subtle way of gaining trust. It said, *I'm just like you; you can tell me anything.*

"I'm going to lay all my cards on the table," Alex began. "Then you're going to tell me everything you know. After that, we'll see if you have anything worth my time and effort to get your sentence reduced." Meeks nodded, so Alex pressed on. "We've been investigating a global ring of child predators who use the dark web to communicate. There's a group operating here in the Atlanta area, and you happen to have met them. So you should be familiar with their work." Alex paused to let this sink in. Meeks stared at the floor. "Lucky for you, we're after a bigger fish, but if you can't give us anything we can work with, then we still have plenty of evidence to put you away."

Meeks glanced up at him. "Do I need a lawyer?"

"I'm not looking for evidence to use against you. I already have that in spades." A little fudging of the truth never hurt. "You only need a lawyer if you decide not to cooperate, and are charged with a crime. If you agree to be a confidential informant, you walk out of here tonight, go home and sleep in your own bed, and we work out a plan to bring down your friends."

"They are *not* my friends," Meeks groaned.

"Okay, sure. But the choice is still the same. Go home to your bed and work with me to get these other guys, or I take you back to Agent Sparks and let the DEA have you. What's it going to be?"

Meeks dropped his head into his hands and groaned again. He pushed his hands through his hair and then leaned back in his chair, staring at Alex with contempt. The feeling was mutual.

"You think you know so much about me, don't you?" Meeks asked. "The disgusting pervert who's turned on by little boys. I'm the scum of the earth to you, right?"

Alex returned his gaze, but refused to acknowledge the question. "What'll it be?"

"You think I'm scum, but guess what? You can't possibly think any worse of me than I already think of myself. I *am* the scum of the earth. I *hate* what I am. It's like some monster that lives inside me that I can't ever get rid of. All I can do is try not to let it out."

Alex nearly rolled his eyes, but he kept his gaze focused on Meeks. He wasn't buying the sob story, but maybe it would work to his advantage to let Meeks think that he was. "I'm sure it's hard to live that way."

Meeks' mouth twisted in agony. "Ahhh," he moaned, "don't patronize me! I know what you're thinking. But all those things you said would happen to me, all the awful things that might happen to me in prison...I deserve every one of them! I am a sick, sick human being."

Meeks dropped his head into his hands again and started to sob. Alex had to steel himself against the obvious pain the guy was going through. The pervert did deserve it. He *deserved* it. But it made Alex wonder if he had deserved his pain too. Maybe that was all any of us deserved. Pain. Unimaginable, inescapable, soul-crushing pain.

Meeks lifted his head, tears streaking down his face. "I'll do it. I'll do whatever you want. But I need you to know I never touched a kid...in *that* way. I never wanted to hurt them. Most of us love the boys we're attracted to. We don't want to hurt them. But that older guy, the professor. He's different."

Alex leaned in. "How?"

"He enjoys that part the most."

25.

LEX TOOK A SEAT IN NICOLE'S OFFICE ON Monday morning, prepared for the lecture he knew was coming. He watched her pace around the office, breathing like Darth Vader and throwing her hands into the air as she mumbled to herself about all the other jobs out there she could be doing. She was a wreck. He could already see the sweat seeping through the back of her shirt.

She finally took one long breath and turned to face him. "What you did Saturday night was completely irresponsible. We've worked very hard to maintain a good working relationship with other agencies—*especially* DEA—and you just decided to blow it to hell and back." She leaned onto her desk and narrowed her eyes at him. "Alex, I cannot deny that you do excellent work, *when you're working*. You're damn good at your job. But...*but*...no matter how good you are, you are not above the policies that have been put in place to keep things running smoothly around here, and to keep everyone from doing stupid crap like the stunt you pulled the other night!"

"The stunt I pulled? Are you kidding? I finally got a break, a major break, in getting something actionable on these guys. Do you know how many kids we're going to save by taking them down?"

She rested her hand on her desk, and the furrow in her brow smoothed just a bit. "I realize what this means—"

"Then I won't apologize for doing my job." He pushed himself forward and pointed his finger into the top of her desk. "This is huge, Nicole. Did you read my report? Do you know what Meeks said is going on in that group?"

"Yes," she said, sighing and falling into her chair. "It's awful, I know. And I understand why you went after Meeks as a CI. I just wish..."

"What?"

She gave a half-hearted smile. "That you would simply walk over bridges rather than racing across them just before blowing them up."

Alex chuckled and pushed himself up from the chair. "So can I get back to work? I practically have to gain approval from God himself to use this guy as an informant."

"Go!" She shooed him out like a naughty child.

Alex headed through the maze of cubicles toward his own, sharing grins and even a high five along the way. He'd retold his encounter with Agent Sparks to a captive audience just before being called into Nicole's office. Now that his customary scolding for the week was behind him, he had to focus on the mountain of paperwork necessary to get the ball rolling with Meeks.

On the way to his desk, Craig gave Alex a rare smile. "There's a very special delivery for you at your desk."

Alex smiled back, wondering what he could mean. He rounded the plastic wall and was greeted by Carrie waiting for him in his chair. She popped up and straightened her gray suit, pushing her hair behind her shoulders. She cleared her throat as if preparing to make a formal speech.

"We need to talk."

Alex almost cracked a one-liner, but he could see she was serious, and good sense told him to curb his humor. "Sure," he said. "I was planning on coming over to your office this afternoon to get all the details worked out for Meeks."

Glancing around, she lowered her voice. "Is there somewhere a little quieter?"

He stepped back into the walkway and gestured for her to follow. Then he wound his way toward the break room. He could feel her moving behind him, her quick, clicking steps behind his long strides. He hoped to keep the conversation on the business at hand, but he was getting a bad feeling there was more on her mind than work.

He opened the door to the break room and let her walk in ahead of him. No one else was around, which may or may not have been a good thing. He went over to the fridge as she took a seat at the small table in the middle of the room.

"Want something to drink?" he asked.

She shook her head. "Thanks. I'm good."

He pulled out a bottle of water and grabbed a granola bar from the cabinet. Then he hopped up onto the counter. "So what's up?"

She looked up at him with incredulous eyes. "What's up?"

He shrugged. "What do we need to talk about?"

She shook her head and tapped her fingers on the table. "Let's start with how we're going to mend fences with DEA."

"Not you too," Alex groaned. "I've already had my lecture this morning, thanks. So what else do we need to discuss?" He tipped back his water to avoid her angry stare.

"I don't appreciate you dragging me into a situation that I'm going to have to fix later on. You should have been patient and waited for—"

"Patient? Where the hell is patience going to get me? Besides, that smug little twerp deserved what he got."

"Meeks?"

Alex grinned. "Well, him too. Both of them, actually."

The corner of Carrie's mouth twitched. "So how do you plan on using Meeks exactly?"

"He'll wear a wire and a camera while he meets with the others. He should be able to get us enough for a warrant on the house."

"Look, Alex, he's simply no good as a witness. So you're going to have to get evidence he doesn't have to testify to."

Alex lowered his chin and tried not to take offense. "I know what I'm doing, okay? This isn't my first rodeo."

She stood and moved toward the door. "Just get me the paperwork ASAP. Getting approval to use an admitted pedophile as an informant is going to be tough. In fact, it looks like you're going to have to get DOJ headquarters to sign off on it, maybe the Attorney General himself. I just hope Meeks can deliver what he says he can."

"Oh ye of little faith," he said, amused at her surprise. "Trust me. It's going to work out just fine."

Carrie raised an eyebrow. "It better." She reached for the door handle as if to leave, but then stopped and turned back to him. "Listen, the other night...we should talk about that."

"Talk about what?" He couldn't help the small pleasure he took in watching her squirm.

She blushed, which gave her an almost girlish quality. "You kissed me."

"Oh, that," he said. He hopped off the counter and stepped close enough to look down into her eyes. "You didn't like it?"

Her face flushed even deeper. Her breathing changed, sped up just a bit. She rubbed her hands together. "No, it's not that. It's just, you know...it's against the rules. Not to mention just a bad idea all the way around."

She was right about that. It was best not to jeopardize their ability to work together. But ever since he'd practically kidnapped Meeks, he felt like he could do anything. What was the harm in one little kiss?

"Look, Carrie, I like working with you." She sputtered out a half-laugh, half-cough, and Alex had to smile. "Mostly. I mean, you can be a real pain in the ass, and a little nosy about my past, and you seem to love telling me how to do my job..." He looked up at the ceiling. "Wait, where was I going with that?"

She laughed, and the tension evaporated. "You were telling me how much you enjoyed working with me."

"Oh yeah." He smiled and met her gaze. "Seriously though, this case is important to me. I'm not going to do anything to screw it up. So relax. No more kissing."

For a moment she looked like she didn't believe him. He was a little unsure of whether he believed it himself. He'd tried not to think about her all weekend. The sudden turn of events in the case had helped. He'd spent all Sunday writing and re-writing reports. But, he had to admit, that had been one hell of a kiss.

Still, he didn't need any complications right now, and it was best to forget the whole thing ever happened. "Really, you have nothing to worry about. I wouldn't kiss you again, even if you begged."

He winked, and she rolled her eyes. Then she pulled the door open so it nearly hit him in the face. "I want the paperwork by this afternoon," she called over her shoulder.

He stepped out of the room and watched her walk away from him. Yes, definitely one hell of a kiss.

26.

ALEX FASTENED THE HIDDEN CAMERA THAT looked like a button to Brian Meeks' shirt. Well, actually it was Alex's shirt. He'd told Meeks no less than three times he'd have to wear a dark shirt with black buttons, but he'd shown up at the meeting point with some powdery blue t-shirt. Alex had nearly lost it right then and there. Instead he'd composed himself and whipped out the spare he kept in the surveillance van.

"Let me just make sure the video and audio are coming through," he told Meeks, then signaled to Tony in the front seat with his laptop and head-phones. "Say something."

Meeks cleared his throat. "Um, okay. Hello?"

Tony put his thumb up.

"Got it." Alex faced Meeks again and scanned him closely. "Looks good. No wires out. You're all set."

Meeks eyed him warily. "Derrick will know I'd never wear this shirt."

"You'd be surprised how little people actually notice. You'll be fine."

"I think I'm going to be sick."

Alex pinched his nose between his fingers. He'd already had enough of this guy. He'd wanted to send him into Jonkovic's house right away, but the asshole had been so jittery about getting caught, they'd had to start him on someone a little less intimidating.

"Let's go over this one more time, just so you're sure," Alex said. "Go in there like it's a perfectly normal evening. Just hang out like you always do."

Meeks nodded his head. "I got it. I got it. Really. We don't have to go over it again. I'm fine."

"You're sure?"

Meeks nodded again and let out a long breath. Alex wanted to knock the nerves right out of him. He'd done everything he could to get this in motion, and he wasn't about to let this jackass screw it up.

"Just make sure he shows you the images," Alex said, curbing his irritation. "We have to see them on camera. And find out when the next group meeting's going to be. We need video of the others as well."

"Got it."

"All right then. Showtime."

Alex shoved the back door open and took a quick look around. The parking lot was clear, so he waved Meeks to come on out. "Good luck," he said, closing the door.

Alex climbed into the driver's seat and waited for Meeks to pull out into traffic. He followed the red Honda for several miles before they turned into the right neighborhood. Three more turns and they were on the street where Derrick Lyons lived. Alex stopped the van down the street from the duplex and watched Meeks turn into the driveway. He shut off the van just as Meeks walked toward the door.

"You think he can pull it off?" Tony asked.

"He'd better. If he doesn't give us anything to work with, this case is dead in the water."

Tony chuckled. "He looked awfully nervous."

"No kidding," Alex said. "All right, here we go."

Tony turned up the volume on the laptop, and the two of them watched as Lyons opened the door. Right away Alex could tell there was a problem. Meeks sounded like he was about to hyperventilate.

Alex shook his head. "Breathe, you moron."

Meeks took a deep breath, as if he'd heard Alex, and the camera raised and lowered slowly. Lyons didn't seem to notice and invited Meeks into the house. The two men headed for the sofa, where Lyons had a video game on pause. Alex recognized the game. It was like the calling card of pedophiles. That, and a cat.

"You want to play?" Lyons asked.

Meeks agreed, and they spent the next hour engrossed in the game. Alex settled into his seat and waited them out. It was boring, but maybe it was helping Meeks to relax. So Alex sipped on his soda and waited.

After finishing the game, Lyons and Meeks spent the next thirty minutes stuffing their faces with chips, crunching so loudly Alex wanted to walk right in there and punch both of them. But finally they seemed to be getting around to relevant conversation. Once the chips were gone, Meeks asked about Lyons' job at the hospital. This led to questions about his latest pictures on Facebook. Alex had suggested that line of conversation to lead into the incriminating part, and to his surprise, Meeks pulled it off like a champ.

"You remember the one boy I told you about?" Lyons said. "The one whose dad left his mom just after he was diagnosed?"

"Yeah, sure," Meeks said.

"He's really been warming up to me this week. I played Xbox with him for a while every day, and yesterday he sat on my lap while we watched television. I think he's almost ready for something more."

Alex's gut tightened. He met Tony's gaze. They were thinking the same thing, and had discussed it numerous times on other cases. Busting someone too early meant jeopardizing a bigger fish. But waiting to move in on a target left vulnerable children in their reach. That was the part that kept Alex up at night.

"Dude, you have got to lighten up," Lyons said on camera. Alex realized he'd zoned out for a minute. Had Meeks already blown his cover?

"I'm fine," Meeks said. "I'm just not in the same place as you."

Lyons stood and moved toward the kitchen with an empty dish, his voice fading as he walked away. "You have to accept who you are, Brian. There's nothing wrong with you. I don't know why you torture yourself over something you can't control."

Lyons disappeared for a minute before he came back around the corner and continued his pep talk. "Besides, the kids like the attention. I mean, take my sweet little Charles. No dad in the picture. Mom's having to work to pay for his treatments. I'm basically all he's got. He loves me. I make him happy. He makes me happy. There's nothing wrong with that."

And that's exactly why every one of you deserves to rot in hell, Alex thought.

The camera shifted with Meeks as he leaned forward. "If there's nothing wrong with us, Derrick, then why all the secrets and lies? Why are we so afraid of the cops?"

"Easy," Alex murmured.

"That's because society's screwed up, not us," Lyons answered.

The room went quiet, and Meeks leaned back again. Lyons shut off the video game and stood. "I know what you need. Come on."

They went down a dark hallway and into a cramped office where the glow of the computer screen made the entire image go white for a moment. Lyons turned on a light, which helped everything come back into focus.

"This is it," Alex said. "We're finally going to get some real evidence."

Lyons sat down at the keyboard and started punching in keys. "Here's some new stuff."

The two of them stared at the images that flashed across the screen, Lyons clicking through them slowly. They were disturbing, grotesque depictions of sexual acts with children. Alex's stomach churned as he watched, but this would definitely be enough for a warrant on Lyons' place.

"That's the best one," Lyons mumbled in a voice that was heavy, almost intoxicated.

"Can I get a copy of those?" Meeks' voice was tight. He shifted his weight constantly, making the camera shake.

"Sorry, dude. We're not supposed to share images until Roman says we're in the clear. Some idiot in Australia got himself arrested and set the kill code in motion."

Alex rolled his head back against the seat. Of course Lyons wouldn't just hand over the evidence. That would make things too easy.

"That's not good," Tony said, giving Alex a worried glance.

"Tell me about it." Alex pushed himself up from the driver's seat and paced the back of the van. "If they won't hand over hard copies, Meeks is going to have to meet with every single member of the group and get video evidence of the images. There's no way that scared little creep can pull this off."

27.

WHEN THEY RETURNED TO THE REMOTE PARKING lot, Alex pulled Meeks into the back of the van. He did his best to hide his disgust while he retrieved his button camera and shirt. "What's this business about a kill code?"

Meeks slid his t-shirt over his head and smoothed his hair back. "They have...rules."

"Yes, we've been over the rules. But you seem to have left this part out. Can you get access to the images or not?"

"Not right now."

Alex pointed his finger right in Meeks' face. "You lied to me."

"I did not lie!"

"You said you had access to the images. You're no good to us as a witness. There's no way you're getting on the stand."

Meeks went pale. "I didn't know about the guy in Australia—"

"What's the kill code?"

"It's a process that goes into play if someone in the network gets arrested," Meeks said. "They take down the entire site, move it to a new location on the dark web, and everyone has to be given new access codes. That way, if you're arrested and the cops break you, they can't gain access to the site."

Alex sighed and glanced at Tony, who sat in the front of the van shaking his head. Then he turned back to Meeks. "Let me guess. You haven't gotten access to the new site yet."

Meeks dropped onto the bench on the side of the van. "There's a blackout period. No access for at least four weeks."

"Then what were you and Lyons looking at?"

"Stuff on his hard drive from before the blackout."

Alex leaned down until they were eye to eye. "This means you have to meet with every one of the members of the group and get footage of them looking at this stuff."

Meeks shook his head. "I can't do that again. Someone's going to figure it out. He'll have me killed!"

Alex straightened and closed his eyes. "What did you just say?"

"I can't do it again." Meeks' voice shook. "You saw how nervous I was. I can't do this."

"That's what I thought you said." Alex opened his eyes and took a step back, controlling his desire to level the guy. "You know what this means, Brian. This means prison. For life. I told you already if you didn't deliver what you promised—"

"I know what you said!" Meeks looked up at Alex with anguished eyes, full of watery sorrow. "If one of these guys figures out what I'm doing...Do you have any idea what they'll do to me? The last guy who tried to snitch, they found a couple of his fingers on a plate in his apartment. Nothing else. Just fingers! I'll just have to take my chances in prison."

Tony cleared his throat. "I'm not sure you comprehend what's going to happen to you in prison."

Alex leaned back against the side of the van and crossed his arms. "You know all that footage you like to watch of what your friends are doing to those little boys? Have you ever heard them cry, or scream? You remember that sound. Because that's going to be you. Every day. For the rest of your life."

Meeks looked up, tears streaking down his face. "I know. I deserve every bit of it. I'm a monster. An actual, real-life monster. And nothing will ever change that."

For one second, Alex felt sorry for the guy. But only for that one second. There was no way in hell he was about to try to convince a pedophile that his life was worth something, that he could somehow make amends for all the suffering he'd helped to create. But he also knew that if he didn't do something, he was going to lose his only means for getting to El Maestro and rescuing the Gomez boy.

He glanced over at Tony, who shrugged as if to say he had no idea how to proceed. Alex took a deep breath and summoned every ounce of patience in his bones. "Brian, I understand what you're saying, and I know you're scared. But if something inside of you has any desire to change the direction of your soul, this is your chance. You want to pay for what you've done? Then help me put the worst ones away for good. You said yourself, you never wanted to hurt them. Right?"

Meeks nodded, but wouldn't look up.

"You said the leader, this El Maestro, is the worst of the worst, right?" Another nod. "He's out there taking these precious kids and tormenting them. He's the one who deserves to end up in prison for life. And you can still make that happen."

Meeks shook his head and spoke into his hands. "I can't. I can't."

Alex threw his hands up. "Fine. Get out."

Meeks looked up in confusion. "What? Just go? You're not going to arrest me?"

"Not tonight. Go home. Sleep. We'll talk tomorrow after I figure out what to do with you."

28.

CARRIE WAVED AT ALEX AS HE SURVEYED THE Chinese restaurant from the front entrance. Her stomach took a dive when he caught sight of her and smiled. She felt his lips on hers for a split second, but pushed it out of her head. *Not worth my job. Not worth my job.* He strode up to the booth and slid onto the seat, a slight waft of soap and peppermint following him.

"So last night was a mess," he said, tossing his keys onto the table.

"You want to grab some food before we get into this?" she asked.

"Good idea."

A waitress nearby took his drink order, and the two of them proceeded to fill their plates with an assortment of items from the buffet. Carrie spooned some sweet and sour sauce onto her chicken before wondering if she should scale it back a bit. She didn't want to look like a complete pig. So she skipped the fried rice and opted for some steamed vegetables instead. But she couldn't help letting her eyes linger on the sesame chicken. Just a little wouldn't hurt.

Once they were settled back into their seats, Alex wasted no time getting down to business. "Meeks is a bust," he said between bites. "He says he doesn't want to wear a wire anymore, and he'll take his chances in prison."

She lowered her fork and sighed. "You're kidding. Did you try to explain things to him?"

"Of course I did. I was very clear about what happens to guys like him in prison. But he fell apart. Thinks he's some kind of monster that deserves what he gets. Hard to argue with him on that."

"You need to talk to him again. Convince him he can do this."

He looked up at her like she was nuts. "I already tried. The guy's a basket case. He's no good as a witness, and he can't get us any hard evidence because of some kill code put in place by Jonkovic."

"A kill code?"

He leaned forward. "Look, here's the bottom line. Meeks can't get any hard evidence, and he refuses to wear a wire anymore. I say we use the video evidence we got of Lyons last night, arrest him, and see if he'll cooperate. Maybe he'll wear the wire."

"Well, whatever we're going to do, we need to do it quickly. We've got agents all over the world putting together a ton of evidence in their respective countries. The guys in the Netherlands want a raid of all the sites on the same day."

"The same day? That'll be tough to coordinate. I suppose it's the best thing to do. Give the bad guys less time to react and move everything to a different site."

"We're catching heat from the Attorney General to get some results. They want El Maestro."

Alex nodded. "I know. Headquarters wants him too. Seems like this has turned into an international press opportunity. Guarantee you all the bosses are sitting around in a room in DC salivating over a chance to show the world we're cracking down on child porn and saving all the little children."

Carrie paused at the cynicism in his voice. "I thought you believed in what you're doing. I thought the kids were the whole reason you stick with it."

"Absolutely. I'm just not naive enough to believe the big boys won't take advantage of it. I couldn't care less about the press opportunity."

Alex went back to eating and seemed to wander off into his thoughts for a while. Carrie took the chance to finish her own food. But her stomach didn't seem to want to cooperate. Why did he make her so nervous? She needed to keep talking, keep her mind on the job.

"I still think Meeks is our best and quickest way to get these guys," she said. "So what do we do to get him back on board? What's got him so freaked out?"

Alex took a sip of his water and leaned across the table. "He's afraid that Maestro's going to have him tortured and killed for ratting them out."

"Do you think the concern's warranted?"

"It's never out of the realm of possibility, but I'd say it's unlikely. I think our first concern has to be the kids, especially if Jonkovic, or El Maestro, or whatever the hell he calls himself is as bad as Meeks says. Apparently he likes to keep one special child for a while."

"And you think that's the Gomez boy."

"Yes. So our focus is on saving the kid, and we'll do our best to protect Meeks. If the world loses one more scumbag, so be it."

Carrie set down her fork. "Alex, you can't mean that."

"No, of course not. It's never good for an informant to get killed. But don't tell me you feel sorry for him."

She paused, not sure how she felt. "Everyone's broken in some way. Don't we all deserve a little bit of compassion?"

He studied her for a moment, his intense gaze sending goosebumps down her arms. "So you think Jonkovic deserves compassion? A guy who keeps one special child to torture for a couple of years, until the kid gets too old for him?" He shook his head. "I don't buy that."

"Look," she said. "I'm not saying I feel sorry for them, or that I don't think they should be punished for their crimes. I wouldn't even have this job if I believed that. But I don't want to go so far as to hate them or wish them harm. That just puts me on their level."

He tilted his head and gave her a curious smile. "Fascinating. So if the guy who hurt you was sitting right here, right in front of you, what would you say? Would you forgive him?"

Her chest tightened, and for a second, all the air in room evaporated. Her heart skipped. She took a deep breath, and it slowed again. She glanced at the door. Glanced to the sides. She was safe. She was *safe*.

Alex wrinkled his brow. "I'm sorry. I shouldn't have brought it up."

"It's okay," she said, letting out her breath. Then she had an idea. "Listen, I'm going to invite you to something, and you're going to say no. But I want you to think about it."

He rolled his eyes and laughed. "Okay, let's hear it."

"There's a gathering this weekend at a small church not far from where I live—"

"I don't do church—"

"Let me finish," she said. He pressed his lips together. "It's a small group of families that have all gone through some form of child abuse. They support each other and provide a place for the kids to play together where it feels safe. My parents started it a while back. It's how we were finally able to deal with everything. I like to spend time talking with the kids and mentoring them." She leaned back in her seat and waited for some kind of response. It was a long shot, she knew that. But she couldn't help letting her hopes rise just a bit.

"Look," he said, his eyes softening. "It sounds like you and your parents are doing a great thing for those families. But what would I do there? I don't think it's for me."

"You'd get a chance to see the families you work so hard to help. You'd see that their lives aren't defined by their tragedies."

"Ah, I get it. So you think I need to see these people triumphing over their circumstances. Because I need to move past my own circumstances."

"I'm not saying that at all. I just think it would do you some good to come. I'm asking nicely. Please?"

He let out a defeated sigh. "Okay! I'll come. But I'm not promising I'll stay long."

She clapped her hands together, unable to control her smile. "You are going to love it!"

29.

ALEX PULLED HIS CAR INTO THE PARKING LOT of Grace Community Church in Smyrna and shut off the engine. He'd almost turned around several times along the way, and he thought about bailing once again as he sat in the quiet car. What was he thinking? This was a bad idea on several levels, and yet somehow he'd ended up right where he'd said he would never set foot again. Right in hope's path.

He glanced over at the front doors and saw Carrie standing under the awning. She was waiting for him, ever the patient savior. She'd learn soon enough what he'd figured out long ago. There was no salvation for him.

He let out a deep sigh and pushed the door open. It was a beautiful fall Saturday, with a crisp breeze rustling the trees as he passed by on his way to the front entrance. Carrie smiled at him, that hopeful smile of hers that cut right through his chest. He hated it. He loved it.

"You're right on time," she said. "I thought you might bail."

"Honestly, I thought about it."

"I would have understood."

He met her gaze and knew she meant it. Maybe she did understand, more than he'd given her credit for. His nerves eased just a bit. "So, let's get this show on the road, Reynolds."

She laughed and motioned for him to follow her. "Come on. We've already started."

He followed her through a foyer and a couple of hallways, then out a side door to a large playground. A group of younger kids were playing on the equipment, while teenagers lounged around the picnic tables. The parents were gathered around a table outside the fence, and they sent Alex a few curious glances. They looked tense. He wondered if these parents had been at ease a single day since learning their child had been harmed.

Carrie waved at some of the kids as she and Alex made their way across the playground. As they approached the gate, an older couple walked through it with tentative smiles. These had to be her parents. The woman looked like a shorter version of Carrie. Same eyes. Same freckled cheeks. The only difference was in the hair color. Carrie's was golden

brown and flowed loosely at her shoulders, but her
mom's was dark and cut short. Carrie shot him a
nervous smile before introducing them.

"Alex, this is my mom, Katherine, and my dad,
James. Mom, Dad, this is Agent Alex Walker."

Alex shook their hands, feeling like he was about
to take Carrie out to the prom. "It's nice to meet
you," he said.

"Carrie mentioned you work together," Mrs.
Reynolds said. "We're glad you could make it today."

Mr. Reynolds put an arm around Carrie's shoulder and squeezed her. "This is a very special group
of families, as I'm sure Carrie's told you. They mean
the world to us. Especially the kids. You're a big
part of giving these families a chance to heal."

"I didn't have anything to do with these cases,
Mr. Reynolds."

"I know that, son. I just meant that your work is
important. We know it's painful and can be difficult
to shoulder at times. You don't have to do it alone,
you know."

"Dad," Carrie said. She stared at him with some
hidden message Alex could only guess was meant
as a scolding.

Mr. Reynolds smiled and put his hands up. "I'm
not pushing. I'm just saying, our doors are always
open."

Alex fought the sudden urge to flee. "Thanks. I
appreciate it." He didn't want to insult them, but he

was certain this was a one-time deal. No way he'd come here and bare his soul to perfect strangers.

Mrs. Reynolds took her husband's hand. "Well, we're glad you're here today. You're in good hands with Carrie. We'll be breaking for lunch soon, so why don't you two mingle for a bit?" She tugged Mr. Reynolds away, leaving Alex with an unnerving sense that he would be studied from afar.

"They seem...nice," he said.

Carrie grinned. "They're out to save the world, one sad case at a time. They mean well."

"I'm sure." Alex looked around again, unsure of his real purpose. "So what are we doing?"

She shielded her eyes and looked around the playground, settling her gaze on a boy near the back corner. "Ah, I think Reggie would be a great place to start. Follow me."

They stepped away from the playground equipment and crossed over to the grassy section near the back of the church. A boy who looked to be about nine sat crossed-legged on the ground, resting his chin on his fist. On the ground in front of his legs, he spun a football with his free hand.

Carrie walked up and took a seat in front of him in the same position. "What's up, Reggie?"

The kid looked up and smiled. "Hey, Miss Carrie. I wanted to play football, but nobody else wanted to."

"You see this nice man beside me? This is Agent Walker. He rescues kids and people in trouble. Kind of like a real-life superhero." She smiled up at Alex, and he rolled his eyes.

"Really?" Reggie asked.

"Yep. And I bet he knows how to play football. Just look at him." They both turned their gazes to Alex, and his face warmed.

"Do you play football?" Reggie asked.

"I used to play when I was in school," Alex said.

"Do you...want to play now?" Reggie peered up at him with just a hint of fear in his eyes.

Carrie jumped up and dusted off her pants. "Come on. I'll play too. You two try to score, and I'll play defense."

Reggie grabbed his ball off the ground and jumped up as well. "Okay! The trees over here are the end zone."

Alex couldn't help but grin at the smile on Carrie's face. "You're playing defense?"

She put her hands on her hips. "Yep. Why? You scared?"

He shook his head and walked to the other side of the playground from their end zone. Reggie looked up at him with wide brown eyes, like he was about to play the game of his life.

Alex pointed to the ball. "You want to play quarterback or receiver?"

"I'll be the receiver. That all right?"

"Sure." Alex kneeled down in the grass and took the ball from Reggie. "You know how to run a post route?"

Reggie's eyes lit up. "Of course! I played football for three years. I can run a post route or a fade or comeback or a slant—"

"Whoa! All right!" Alex laughed. "Let's start with a post. Look back for the ball after about ten to twelve strides. Got it?"

"Yes, sir."

Alex stood as Reggie jogged a couple of paces away. He held the ball out in front of him, locking eyes with Carrie, who was about ten feet in front of him. She bounced her weight back and forth from one foot to the other.

"Down. Set. Hut!"

Reggie took off and ran the route perfectly, blowing past Carrie and catching the ball just beyond her. She chased him for a few strides before doubling over with laughter. When he reached the end zone, Reggie turned around, and Alex put his hands in the air, signaling a touchdown. Reggie spiked the ball and celebrated.

Next, they ran a fade route, and then a slant. Reggie never once dropped the ball. And each time he scored, he did a little dance in the end zone. Alex couldn't help the small ache that squeezed his heart. He pictured his own son catching the ball. Wondered if Evan would've played football, or maybe baseball. What would his laugh have sounded like?

Reggie raced across the grass toward Alex, stopping just in front of him. He panted through his huge smile. "That was awesome! Let's do it again!"

Alex looked over his head at Carrie standing just a few yards beyond. She smiled with such peace and joy. It was like the sun shone right out of her. How did she do that? Especially knowing all she did about the world, about the possible evil lurking around every corner. How could she be around all these kids who would be scarred for life, and still find joy?

A whistle sounded from near the entrance to the church. Reggie's face fell, and his shoulders slumped. "Ah man! Time for lunch."

Carrie walked up behind Reggie and patted him on the back. "Sorry. Guess we'll have to try this again another time."

"You'll come back again, won't you?" Reggie looked at Alex with hopeful eyes.

Alex looked at Carrie and shook his head. "You did this on purpose."

"Oh, come on. How can you say no to this face?" Carrie put her face next to Reggie's, and they looked up at Alex with their best pouts.

"Please, Alex!" Reggie said. "I need someone to play football with me. My parents won't let me play for my other team anymore, so all I get to do is throw the ball around with other kids. None of these kids play."

Alex felt that need to flee creep back into him. Had Carrie really brought him here to trap him into coming every week? "I don't know, Reggie," he said.

Carrie straightened and gave Reggie another pat on the back. "Go on inside and get washed up for lunch."

Reggie took off running for the door, and Carrie turned to Alex. "I'm sorry. That wasn't fair. You don't have to come back."

"You're right. That wasn't fair." She dropped her gaze to the ground. "Just give me some time, okay?"

She looked up at him again. "So you'll think about it?"

He shrugged. "I'll think about it."

Her smile returned. "You hungry?"

"Starving."

He fell into step beside her across the playground, wondering what was coming over him. Was he actually thinking about coming back here? That seemed crazy.

He followed her along the hallway to a large room with several tables spread out and a kitchen off to his left. Mrs. Reynolds was filling up cups with ice and setting them on the counter. She waved at Carrie and Alex as they came into the kitchen.

"What can we do to help?" Carrie asked.

"Um, can you go around to the back door and help your father bring in the pizzas?"

"Sure."

They rounded a corner in the back of the kitchen, heading for the open door where her father stood. Mr. Reynolds had several boxes in his arms, and as he turned toward them, Alex caught sight of the delivery guy standing in the doorway.

It was Brian Meeks.

30.

A S HER DAD TURNED TO PLACE THE PIZZA BOXES on a nearby counter, he asked Carrie to pay the delivery guy. He handed her a wad of bills, and she shuffled through them. She reached the open door and looked up at the young man before her.

"How much is it?" she asked.

He didn't say anything. Just stared past her as if he was seeing a ghost. She turned and looked over her shoulder at Alex, who was staring at the open doorway with a face as hard as steel. What had she missed?

"Miss Carrie!" Reggie came running around the corner. "Can I help?"

Alex stepped in front of him, blocking his way to the door. He narrowed his eyes, and she could've sworn he actually bowed up. She turned to take a closer look at the young man at the door. He still hadn't said a word. His mouth hung open, and he took a step backward.

"Excuse me, sir. How much do we owe you?"

He finally looked at her, but the fear in his eyes remained the same. "I, um, I'm not sure." He pulled out the ticket and looked it over. His hands shook. Behind her, she could hear Alex mumbling something, and Reggie asking why.

"Not now," Alex said. "We'll bring them around front and you can help then. Just go back."

Carrie felt her stomach start to crawl. She looked at the nametag on the guy's shirt. *Brian.* What was up with Alex? She felt him come up behind her, felt his tension wrap around her like a shield. He placed a hand on the wad of bills.

"Let me take care of this," Alex said.

"What's going on?" she asked.

Her dad came back to the door. "Are there any more boxes? I thought I got them all."

"Alex," Carrie said, pulling the money out of his hand. "What's going on? Who is this?"

He looked from her to the delivery guy, who had taken another step backwards. "Carrie, this is Brian Meeks."

It took a moment for the name to register, but her heart thundered as soon as it did. *Brian Meeks.* The guy who delivered pizza in the Smyrna area.

The one who tried to get kids to hug him when their parents weren't looking.

Alex reached for the money again, and this time she let him take it. He stepped between her and Meeks, so she couldn't see him anymore. Her heart beat so loud, she couldn't think for a moment. She felt a hand on her shoulder and jumped.

"What's going on, honey?" her dad asked.

She had no idea how to explain that they had inadvertently let a predator so near their precious group. But if anyone would know what to do, it was him. She took a deep breath, and ran through the quickest explanation she could.

His face paled. "You said he was working as an informant?"

She nodded.

"So you think he wants to change?"

"It's possible, from what Alex has said about him. Do you think you could help him?"

"I don't know," he said, frowning as he looked past her into the parking lot. "Why don't I talk to him?"

Her dad moved past her, and she fell in behind him. She could make out some of Alex's words as they approached. Meeks had backed all the way to his car, and Alex was positioned in front of him, his feet spread wide and his arms crossed over his chest.

"I should arrest you right here," Alex said as she and her dad came near.

"I don't think there's any need for that," her dad said.

Alex stepped back, opening his stance to them. He mashed his eyebrows into a determined frown. "Sir, with all due respect, I don't think you understand who this guy is."

"Carrie just filled me in."

Her stomach took another dip as Alex turned his frown on her. "Still," Alex said. "It's best if I handle this."

"Agent Walker, I have no doubt you're great at your job. But I'm pretty good at mine too. I'd like to speak with Mr. Meeks for a few moments if you don't mind."

"What?" Alex looked absolutely baffled.

Carrie held out her hand. "Come on, Alex. Let Dad talk to him for a minute."

Alex shook his head before glancing back at Meeks. "You don't set a foot inside that church, you hear?"

Meeks stared back at him with contempt. "I got it. Relax. I ain't going near anyone."

Alex finally turned away, and Carrie led him back into the kitchen. She closed the door behind her. Alex walked over and spread his hands on the counter, dropping his head. It almost looked like he was praying.

"What could your dad possibly say to that man?" he said.

Carrie leaned against the door. Her pulse had finally slowed enough to clear her thoughts. "He's probably talking to him about Jesus."

Alex snorted. "You guys are a trip."

"What's that supposed to mean?"

"It's just so ridiculous how quick you are to forgive these scumbags. That man out there gets off on watching someone hurt little boys. Do you get that?"

"You said yourself that he doesn't want to hurt anyone. That he's sickened by what he is."

"That doesn't change what he is!"

"But what if he could change? What if there's a chance he could turn his life around? Shouldn't we try to offer him some hope?"

"No! No." Alex took several steps toward her. "These guys do not change. I've seen it first hand. There's been study after study. Not only do they continue to prey on children, they get more and more violent. They don't get better. Once they go into the darkness, there's no coming back."

"Your studies are all well and good, and maybe they're true. But it doesn't mean that *this* man is completely without hope. If he doesn't want to be this way, then maybe God can—"

"You're deluding yourself, Carrie. That's what all this God nonsense does. It puts blinders over your eyes to reality, and it just leads to more pain and suffering when real life comes knocking."

She closed her eyes and asked for wisdom. He was filled with so much anger. She opened her eyes and moved over beside him. "Alex," she said quietly. "I know your past is filled with pain. I know you don't think God can save you. But if you'll just open your heart and listen to him—"

"If I've learned one thing, it's that no one's going to save me, especially God. I do my own saving. Like you said earlier. I'm practically a superhero."

Before she'd thought it through, she reached for his arm. His muscle tensed beneath her hand, and her stomach tightened. The urge to soothe him nearly overwhelmed her.

She forced herself to step away.

31.

A LEX STILLED HIS RACING THOUGHTS AS Carrie took a step back. They were on a train headed for a major crash, and from the look on her face, she knew it too. He took a step toward her, heat rushing up his neck.

"Carrie, I think we should—"

"You should go." She crossed her arms and hugged her chest.

He dropped his arms to his side. "Yeah. You're right." He took a couple of steps toward the door and grabbed the handle. "Do me a favor though." He waited for her to meet his gaze. "Do not let Meeks anywhere near these kids."

"This isn't my first rodeo, Agent Walker. I'm not in the business of handing out crack to addicts either."

He lifted a hand as a goodbye, and then he walked out the door. Several yards away, Mr. Reynolds leaned against Meeks' car beside him. They looked deep in conversation, and Meeks' eyes were bloodshot. For a fleeting second, Alex had to wonder if it was possible for a guy like Meeks to find redemption. But he couldn't see it. Couldn't see anything but the endless videos of tortured little boys that Meeks was drawn to. Impossible.

Mr. Reynolds saw Alex coming toward them and pushed away from the car. "I better get back inside. Thanks for coming out today, Alex."

"Thanks for having me." Alex shot a glance at Meeks, who was sliding around to the driver's side of the car.

Mr. Reynolds paused before he got to the kitchen door and looked at Alex once more. "Please come back any time," he said.

Alex could see he meant it, but the past few minutes had only confirmed that he didn't belong here. He turned back to the car just as Meeks slammed the door. Bending down, Alex knocked on the passenger side window. Meeks slammed the steering wheel and rolled down the window.

"Can we talk for a minute?" Alex asked.

"You gonna arrest me?"

"Not today."

Meeks pressed the unlock button on his side. Alex pulled the door open and took a seat. The car smelled like musty pizza and a faint hint of dope. What a loser.

"What did Mr. Reynolds have to say?" Alex asked.

Meeks dropped his head against the back of the seat and exhaled. "Look, I didn't do anything. I'm just doing my job. I can't help it if some Jesus freak group orders pizza and you happen to be there."

"What did Mr. Reynolds say?"

Meeks let out a cynical laugh. "He just wanted to pray for me. Then he gave me the name of a counselor who works with guys like me."

Alex shook his head. "Guys like you?"

"Yeah, guys like me. Who have monsters living inside them. Guys like me. Who'd rather die a thousand times than live like this."

Alex couldn't buy what he was hearing. "So you think that's it? You can just go talk to a counselor who's going to offer you some magic formula so that you don't like little boys anymore?"

Meeks pressed his head into the steering wheel. It was so quiet in the car, Alex's thoughts seemed to scream at him. If this guy could find peace, some kind of forgiveness for what he'd done, but he, Alex Walker, could find none...what did that mean?

"Do you think Maestro will kill me?" Meeks' voice was small, full of doubt and fear.

Alex knew he owed Meeks the truth. "It's possible he'll try."

"Will you even care?" Meeks looked over the top of his arm at Alex. "Will you even try to protect me?"

"Yes."

"Why?"

Alex shrugged. "It's my job. And I'm damn good at it."

Meeks turned his face to the window. "I'll do it. I'll wear the wire."

Alex couldn't believe what he was hearing. "Are you serious?"

"Yes."

"What changed your mind?"

Meeks turned his tortured gaze on Alex. "Either Maestro kills me, or some sick bastard in prison kills me. Either way, I'm dead. And I don't want to be this man. If there's even the slightest chance that I can make things right, if there's even a tiny grain of hope for me, then I have to do this." He directed his gaze out the window again. "I want to face God knowing I fought this monster inside me till my last breath."

32.

THE TEACHER HUNG UP THE PHONE AND leaned back in his leather sofa, pondering this latest development. If Derrick was right, Brian was growing a conscience. He'd known Brian was struggling, and the others had been trying to help him accept who he really was. It didn't seem to be working. That could lead to all kinds of unfortunate consequences. He hated dealing with consequences.

He pushed his tired body up from the sofa and went to the door that led down to the basement. He'd been trying to keep his distance. Best for both him and the boy. But he needed to relax.

He turned the dead bolt and descended the stairs as quietly as he could. Then he stopped at the door at the bottom and pressed his ear against it, hearing nothing. The boy must be asleep. Good.

He'd been afraid the visitor upstairs would wake him, possibly encourage him to make noises for attention. That had only happened once. The painful lesson that had followed had hurt him as much as it had the boy, though he'd hidden it well. And the boy had never made a sound since.

He turned the lock on the door and eased it open. The room was dark except for the tiny light plugged into the wall near the boy's bed. He crept toward the light and stood beside the bed.

The boy's face peeked out from under the covers. So peaceful. The Teacher reached over and, as gently as he could, pulled the covers back and laid them at the boy's feet. Then he slid onto the bed and watched the boy's chest rise and fall. Rise and fall.

Several buyers had expressed interest in him, but finding the perfect fit would be difficult. Would someone else appreciate all the boy had to offer? Would he be loved the way he deserved? Cared for? Nurtured, as he himself had been? He needed more time.

In fact, maybe this was the perfect time to start over. The small group of followers he'd amassed was ripe for trouble. He always advised against such gatherings. In his experience it was only a matter of time before someone pointed the finger at his friends. And taking care of those fingers was a nasty business he preferred to avoid.

Take that idiot in Australia, Collin Drake. He'd kept his mouth shut for all of five minutes. At least he'd kept his wits enough to initiate the kill code. But what a mess. Starting from scratch would slow everything down. Maybe this was the perfect opportunity to leave for a while.

Once the boy was settled in his new home, he could travel abroad for the winter. Procure a new companion. The authorities in other countries were so much more understanding than in the States. It made the initial training so much easier.

The Teacher looked over at the boy for another long moment, wishing he could get lost in his dreams. But he resigned himself to reality, and slid out of the bed as quietly as he'd come. He locked the door as he left. At the top of the stairs, he secured the locks again and went to the kitchen for a last drink before bed.

Brian would need to be dealt with. If he was truly turning away from group, he'd be a threat. There was only one way to deal with threats. Maybe it was time to meet with Brian face to face.

Part Three

The Shadow

33.

ALEX HAD DONE HIS BEST TO KEEP MEEKS calm, but even he had to admit to a few nerves as he and Tony sat in the van. Meeks had handled Mark Johnson well, getting video of his computer images just as easily as he'd gotten Lyons'. But knowing he was heading into El Maestro's home had shaken Meeks again. It was only when Alex agreed that Meeks could bring Lyons along that they were able to get the plan back on track.

Meeks and Lyons walked up the driveway to Jonkovic's house, a meeting Jonkovic himself had requested. Alex could practically hear Meeks' heart thumping behind the camera on his chest. At least the moron had remembered to wear a dark shirt of his own this time.

Meeks rubbed his hands together. "The guy just makes me jumpy, all right? That whole Russian mob thing of his is downright creepy."

"He isn't Russian, you dope."

Meeks' voice shook as he turned to Lyons. "Then what's with the accent?"

"He's Slavic or Czech or something."

"Same thing," Meeks muttered. "Did you know that he's actually El Maestro?"

Lyons stopped walking and faced Meeks. "What? What makes you think that?"

Alex beat his hand on the outside of the steering wheel. "He's going to blow the whole damn thing."

Meeks tried to stammer out an explanation. "I...I'm not sure where I heard it. Maybe Mark? Plus, he's got that place in South America, right? He goes down there enough. Bet that's where he gets the boys."

Lyons pushed the back gate open, giving Alex his first full view of the back yard. There was a large pool with several lounge chairs scattered around it as well as a circular table near the patio. Lyons and Meeks stepped up onto the patio and passed a large stainless steel grill.

"That would make sense, Roman being El Maestro," Lyons said as they approached the door. "He seems to be the one doing everything with the website. And I've heard him speaking Spanish on the phone."

"Do you think he's got a kid in there some-where?"

Again, Alex gripped the steering wheel. He'd told Meeks to keep an eye out for anything that might help them determine if the Gomez boy was in the house, but this was far from discreet. "If this idiot can just stick to the plan, we might actually get some evidence of the kid being here. We could blow this whole thing up tonight."

"I don't think the guys in the Netherlands and Australia will be too happy with that," Tony said.

"Who cares what they think? Cut the head off the snake, and the rest will die too. I'm sure if we get access to the site, we'll be able to get enough info for the agencies in the other countries to move on. We get actual proof the kid's in there, we're go-ing in."

Tony leaned up closer to the monitor as Jonkovic opened the door. His lean frame looked more like a shadow in the doorway. "Dude's creepy," Tony said. "I'll give 'em that."

Jonkovic invited them inside and led them through an immaculate kitchen before reaching an equally immaculate living room. The dark leather sofas and snobby decor screamed "rich bachelor". In the light of the living room, Alex got his first re-al view of Roman Jonkovic. He wasn't especially tall, but he was lean in that way runners or bikers look. Alex wondered how he stayed fit when it seemed he rarely left the house. "Gentlemen,"

Jonkovic said. "Come in and make yourselves comfortable. Can I get you anything to drink?"

Meeks turned to sit on a sofa, and Alex caught
sight of the elaborate entertainment system. A
huge screen hung on the wall, with shelves underneath that housed some pretty expensive-looking
equipment.

"I'll take a beer," Lyons said from off-camera.

"Uh, yeah. A beer for me too." Meeks sank onto
the sofa, and Jonkovic left the room.

Lyons leaned toward Meeks and lowered his
voice. "If this dude is El Maestro, he should have
some great videos."

"Cool."

A moment passed before Jonkovic returned with
the beers. "Sorry, gentlemen," he said. "But I don't
have anything I can show you this evening. Unfortunately, the kill code was initiated a couple of
weeks ago, and you know the drill. No site for at
least two more weeks."

"You don't keep anything in your personal collection?" Lyons asked.

Jonkovic stared at Meeks before he answered.
"No. Nothing I can show you tonight."

"Then why ask us to come?" Meeks asked.

Jonkovic cleared his throat. "Just to touch base. I
had a chat with Derrick a couple of days ago. He
seems concerned about your state of mind."

Meeks turned toward Lyons, who shrugged his shoulders as he spoke. "Sorry, man. Just worried about you."

"It seems Derrick thinks you might be leaving our group," Jonkovic continued. "Are you unsatisfied with the experience you've had with us, Brian?"

"No, no." Meeks' breathing sped up. "I'm very happy with my experience."

"Derrick says you're questioning the...how do you say it? The *morality* of our lifestyle."

Alex didn't like the direction this was headed. Not only were they not going to get any video of images, Meeks was a breath away from blowing his cover. Despite his disgust for everything about this group of men, Alex found himself pulling for Meeks. He just had to hold it together a bit longer.

"I have had some moments of doubt," Meeks said. "I don't want to...I just can't...I—"

"You've let the expectations of society make you doubt who you really are. You have to listen to the man inside of you. He will tell you what is right. You yearn for a connection, just like everyone else. Who has the right to tell you who to love?"

"Exactly what I've been saying," Lyons added.

"You're right," Meeks said. "I, um...I just need to accept who I am."

Jonkovic seemed to study Meeks for a bit too long. Alex ran through the exit scenario in his mind, imagining every complication he could think of. He'd promised Meeks he'd protect him.

Meeks stood and excused himself to the bathroom. Probably a good move. He walked down a narrow hallway and turned right into another. Then he stepped through a door on the right and closed it behind him.

"No idea what to do," he whispered. "No video." He looked in the mirror and gave Alex a view of his face. Then he wiped his hand across his brow and whispered again. "What do I do?"

Alex knew Meeks couldn't hear him, but he answered anyway. "Stay calm. Get what you can and get out."

Meeks let out a deep breath. He washed his hands. Then he stepped out into the hallway again. He took a couple of steps toward the direction from where he'd come, but then he stopped and turned around.

Alex leaned closer to the monitor. "What are you doing?"

Meeks stopped at the end of the hallway. He stood frozen in place for a full minute. Alex looked over at Tony. "What the hell is he doing?"

Tony shrugged. "You told him to look for evidence of the kid. Maybe that's what he's trying to do."

Meeks reached for the doorknob on his left. It was locked. "Damn," he whispered. Meeks turned around. Jonkovic was standing behind him.

Alex headed for the back of the van. "If we have to go in after him, I'm going to kill him myself."

"Just stay calm," Tony said.

The deep Slavic accent filled the front of the van. "What are you doing, Brian?"

Meeks didn't answer.

"Come on," Alex shouted. "Think of something!"

"I...I was in the restroom," Meeks said.

"Yes, but this is not the restroom. What are you doing here?"

"I guess...I just always wondered, you know. The guys say you have some pretty interesting things back here. I was just curious."

A grin spread over Jonkovic's face, but it wasn't happy. "You want to see something special, yes?"

"Yes," Meeks said.

Jonkovic came over and wrapped an arm around Meeks' shoulder. "I tell you, I have many special toys. But tonight, this is not for you. You still have much to learn. You need a few lessons before you are ready for this door."

Alex let out the breath he'd been holding. He fell onto the bench in the back of the van and wondered how he'd gotten himself so turned around as to be scared for the life of a monster

34.

CARRIE STUFFED THE FILES SHE'D NEED INTO her briefcase and took a deep breath to push down the uneasiness building inside her as the top of the hour approached. She wished, just for a moment, that she could down a glass of wine. But she didn't let the thought get far. A run after work would be much better. She took another deep breath, and her nerves settled a little more. "You all right?"

She jerked her head up to see Alex in the doorway of her office. He frowned as he looked her over, and her heart sped up again. *He's not worth my job.*

"I'm good," she said. "I was about to head over to the conference room. You need something?"

"I just wanted to talk to you for a second before we start prepping for the Williams case." He came all the way into the office, pushing the door nearly closed, but not all the way.

She cleared her throat and motioned toward the chair on the other side of her desk. "You want to sit down?"

"No thanks. This won't take long."

"Okay, well then, spit it out. We're supposed to be in the meeting in five minutes."

He raised an eyebrow and almost grinned. "Do I make you nervous or something?"

"Of course not. Why would you ask that?"

"You rub your hands together when you get anxious."

She pulled her hands apart and shoved them into the tiny pockets on her pants suit. They were only there for decoration, so just the tips of her fingers fit inside, but they'd keep her from fidgeting. "I'm fine. What did you need to talk about?"

"I emailed you an affidavit for a warrant this morning for a key logger on Jonkovic's computer. I wanted to see if you got it and if everything looked good."

"Yeah, I got it. It should be fine. You're all set."

"Thanks." He rocked on his heels, looking into her eyes until she had to look away.

"Is that it? That's all you wanted to ask?"

He drew closer to her desk and lowered his voice. "I got a little bent out of shape last weekend. I shouldn't have. In fact, I should have just followed my instincts and not come. I think it's best if we make sure our relationship is strictly professional from now on."

"I agree." She heard the words come out of her and knew she meant them. So why did it feel like her insides were melting?

He frowned again. Then he stepped around her desk and planted himself right in front of her. She hadn't realized she was rubbing her hands together again until he put a hand on them. "You're nervous."

"No, I'm not." The air warmed. His smell surrounded her. Soap and peppermint. Such a strangely pleasant combination.

"Then look at me."

She forced her eyes up to his. Her stomach swam, but she held his gaze with as much confidence as she could muster. *Not worth my job.*

"Might be a little tough," he said.

"What might be tough?"

He'd moved closer. Now his face was only a few inches away. "Keeping it professional."

She closed her eyes and repeated to herself, "Not worth my job."

She felt his finger on her chin, and she opened her eyes. "You're right," he said. "I'm not worth your job."

He stepped back and went around to the other side of her desk. It was as if he'd sucked the air right out of her. She took a deep breath and grabbed her briefcase. "You're just messing with me now."

He grinned, a mischievous grin that dared her to play with fire. "Guess we'll never know."

Walking around her desk, she headed for the door. "I hope you're done playing around. This Williams case is serious, and I need to make sure I'm caught up on everything."

"I thought Frank was handling this one?"

"He is, but since I'm still getting my feet wet around here, he thought I should assist. And since I'm coming to the party late, I don't want to miss anything important."

Alex shook his head. "I don't get you sometimes."

"What is that supposed to mean?"

"You seem so driven to put these guys away, but at the same time you want to take pity on them. Doesn't make sense. Especially this guy. Have you read the case file?"

She pushed down the flare of anger at the implication of his question. "Of course I read it."

"Then you know. This guy's as bad as they come. Straight up evil. So don't go trying to take it easy on him."

She couldn't argue with him there. She'd read the case file earlier in the week, and it had been the stuff of horror movies. Tom Williams had raped at least six kids from the ages of two to eight. And videoed himself doing it. The worst part was, he had HIV and knew exactly what he was doing. She was glad Frank was the lead prosecutor on this one.

"I won't be taking it easy on anyone, Agent Walker. I do believe in compassion, but I believe in justice too." She shook her briefcase at him. "These kids deserve justice for what Williams did to them."

"Glad we're on the same page."

There was a knock on her door, and Kevin Sanders, who handled mostly ATF cases, poked his head inside. "Hey, Carrie! Just wanted to see if you want to come out with Jonathan and me after work for drinks. He's bringing his girlfriend, so it would really help me out if you'd pretend to like me. She thinks I'm a loser."

Carrie laughed. "Of course. Just come get me before you leave."

"Thanks!" Kevin winked at her before continuing down the hallway.

She turned back to Alex. "You ready?"

He was frowning again. "You're going out with that clown?"

"Yeah, why do you care?"

He shrugged. "I don't. I just think you can do better."

"Well, at least he won't get me fired."

35.

ALEX TOOK A SWEEPING GLANCE OVER
Jonkovic's front yard, hoping no one happened to be out walking a dog or something.
After two days of holing up in his house, Jonkovic
had finally gone out for a while. And after two full
days of surveillance, Alex was anxious to get in the
house that had eluded him for weeks. Of course,
that all depended on Craig being able to pick the
lock, and so far that was proving to be a challenge.

Alex glanced over Craig's head and caught Tony's gaze, who frowned. "Sometime today would be
great," Alex said.

Craig angled his head and looked up at Alex.
"Look, this is no ordinary lock."

"But you're supposed to be an expert, which
means you can open locks that us regular folks
can't."

"Give him a break," Tony said.

Alex sighed and looked down at Sean Richards, who was waiting a few steps below and already sweating through the t-shirt beneath his police vest. Richards needed to get out in the field more often. Get out of the computer forensics room and see some real action.

Alex tapped his hand on the iron railing of the stairs as he watched Craig fumble with the lock again, his patience running thin. The team following Jonkovic had reported he was at the grocery store, so there was no telling how much time they had.

"Let's just try another entry," Alex said.

Craig dropped his hands from the lock and let out a frustrated sigh. "Fine. Whatever." He gathered his tools, and the four of them headed around the side of the house, checking the ground-floor windows. Not only was each one sealed tight, but they also had decorative bars in place to keep intruders out.

They tried the gate to the back yard. Locked. Alex entwined his fingers and bent his knees, looking at Tony. "Come on. Up and over."

Tony chuckled and shook his head. "You first."

"Nah, come on. You're the lightweight around here. Get over the fence and then let us in."

Tony gripped the top of the fence and put his foot in Alex's hands. "All right, but don't hurt your back, Grandpa."

Alex lifted Tony in the air, and he swung his leg over the top of the fence. There was a thud on the other side, then a click before the gate opened. Tony bowed and gestured toward the back yard. "Welcome to my humble abode, gentlemen."

Alex pushed past him and headed straight for the back door, giving Tony a little shove as he went by. Of course, the back door was locked. The men spread out and checked the windows, which were all sealed tight. Alex was about to give up when Craig called them over to a window near the far side of the house.

"I think I can jimmy this open," Craig said.

He pulled out a pocketknife, slid it between the panes, and pushed the lock open. Then he stood back and looked at Alex with a satisfied smile.

Alex clapped his hands twice. "Awesome. Now climb your big ass through there and open the door for the rest of us."

Craig opened his mouth to respond, but then closed it again. He huffed as he moved toward the window, but Alex put his hand on Craig's chest and laughed. "I was just kidding! Sheesh!" Alex pushed up the window and took a quick look around. Dining room. All was quiet. He slid his upper body through, followed by his waist. As he swung his leg into the room, he knocked a plant off the table beside the window.

"Damn!" Pushing the rest of the way through, he stood, and surveyed the mess.

Tony stuck his head inside. "What happened?"

"Plant." Alex returned it to the table and tried to straighten it as best he could. "I'll let you guys in the back."

He took a quick survey of the room, following the wall to where it opened up into the large living room he'd seen on Meeks' video. Still clear. Moving over to the back door, which led out from the kitchen onto the patio, he let the others inside. He half expected the alarm to sound when he opened the door, despite Richards having already disabled it.

They swept the first floor quickly in pairs; opening each door to make sure no one was around. Two doors were locked—what appeared to be a door down to the basement, and the door Meeks had tried two nights ago.

Alex glanced at Craig. "Think you can pick this one?"

Craig shrugged. "Probably. But, not *legally*. And you know it. The warrant is to install the key logger, not to search the house."

"Hey, we have to make sure no one's inside, right? And we haven't found the computer yet. It's probably in there."

"This isn't the time to screw up a case over a technicality."

Alex sighed. Normally he'd agree. But this case was getting under his skin. There was something behind that door, something big. "Look, there's no telling how much time we have. Tony and Sean are clearing the second floor. If they find the computer, great—we lock this back up and head upstairs. If they don't, then we save time by having it ready for entry."

Craig raised an eyebrow. "Is that what you'll testify to in court?"

He was right. Alex pinched his nose and waited. They were wasting time. Two minutes passed before Tony and Sean appeared behind Craig in the hallway. "No computer upstairs."

Alex looked at Craig. "Now, please." Craig went to work on the lock, popping it open in less than thirty seconds. "That's more like it," Alex said.

Alex looked around the room, knowing exactly what he was looking at. The walls and floor were painted white. In the far corner was a photographer's background stand holding a canvas depicting a blue sky. In the next corner were three umbrella lights and a box of various toys and stuffed animals. The shelves were lined with cameras and more toys. To an average person, this might look like the studio of an innocent photographer. But Alex knew from experience, there was nothing innocent about it.

"Here we go," Sean said from behind him.

Alex turned around as Sean headed for the computer. "It's a studio."

"This is where he makes his videos," Tony said, looking around the room.

Alex walked over to the background stand and studied it. "Something's familiar about this." The lower left corner had a rip that went in a jagged line about six inches across the bottom, and the top had a thick crease that cut through two of the clouds.

Tony walked up beside him. "Too bad we can't flip through these and check them against any of the known images we already have."

Alex turned in a circle. "Surely there's something in plain view that'll get us our search warrant?"

Craig's phone buzzed with a text message. "We got incoming. Grocery shopping's over."

"Um, fellas?" Sean called from the floor behind the computer tower. "We have a slight problem."

Alex crossed the room to take a look. "We don't have time for problems."

Sean looked up from his back at Alex. "See the back of this tower? All the plugins are black or gray."

"So?"

"Here's our key logger." Sean flashed a bright purple thumb drive.

Craig's phone buzzed again. "He's definitely headed back this way. We have ten minutes, tops."

Alex couldn't believe what he was seeing. "You mean to tell me the best the United States federal government can do is a neon purple key logger?" He turned to Tony. "We really are the Keystone Cops." They looked around at each other in desperation. "Damnit!" Alex yelled. "Let's think of something, now!"

"I have some black electrical tape," Sean said.

"Go! Wrap it up the best you can." Alex turned to Craig. "Tell Murray's guys to go to Plan B."

Craig started typing, but before he could finish, he let out a string of curses. "They lost him."

"What?" Alex marched over to Craig and grabbed his phone. He pressed the radio button. "Agent Murray, what's going on?"

The radio crackled. "We lost Jonkovic. But we believe he's heading home. You should get out of there ASAP." Alex closed his eyes and tapped his forehead with the phone. Then he pressed the radio button again. "Go to Plan C."

Craig wrinkled his brow as Alex handed his phone back. "What's Plan C?"

"Traffic stop."

Sean sat up from behind the computer. "Got it. We're all set."

Alex stepped over to him and surveyed the back of the computer. The device still stood out, but hopefully only because he knew it was there. "That'll have to do. Let's go."

They filed out of the room. Alex took one last glance at the background with its peaceful blue skies. No telling what horrors were filmed in front of that background. Something about it still tickled the back of his mind, so he took a quick photo of it with his phone.

Locking the door behind him, Alex headed for the dining room. Checked the plant one last time. Secured the window. Then he slid out the back door and locked that behind him too. The last door he secured was the gate around the back yard. Finally, the men crossed the front yard and slunk along the trees lining the driveway.

Alex half expected to see Jonkovic pull into the driveway as they were jogging along the edge of the road. The van was parked two blocks away. Once they were a couple houses down, Alex took out his phone and called Murray. "What's our status?"

"Local cops stopped the vehicle two streets away from you. They're still running the tags. You have three to four minutes."

Alex hung up and breathed a sigh of relief. One step closer.

36.

CARRIE FORCED HERSELF TO CONCENTRATE ON Frank Hunter's opening statement in the Tom Williams case. She straightened her back, held her pen at the ready to jot down anything important, and studied the jury, gauging each member's reaction to Frank's remarks. Anything to keep her mind off the fact that Alex was seated right next to her, bouncing his leg under the table right next to hers.

Each time Alex shifted in his seat, she went through the same process. Jolt to the stomach. Repeat the mantra. *He's not worth my job.* Refocus on Frank's words. Write down something. Anything. Look at the jury.

It was downright ridiculous. She was a competent attorney who'd let herself be reduced to a middle school girl with a crush. And not just any crush. One that could end her entire career. She needed to get ahold of herself.

By the time both Frank and Williams' defense attorney had finished their routine objections to each other and their opening statements, Carrie was exhausted from the effort to control her thoughts. When the judge issued a fifteen-minute recess, she exhaled and leaned back in her chair. It also helped that Alex stepped out of the courtroom.

Frank stood and straightened his suit. "You nervous?"

She could kick herself for giving off the impression she wasn't ready for this. "Not at all."

"Good. This case is a slam-dunk. It's a good time to get your feet wet. I think you should question Agent Walker."

"Sure. I can handle that." She sat up again and searched through her notes. So she was going to ask Alex a few questions on a case that was a slam-dunk. No big deal.

"Great," Frank said, and excused himself to the restroom.

Carrie took a deep breath. She wasn't nervous about questioning Alex. She could handle that with no problem. So why did she feel like she'd swallowed a live wire? Another breath did the trick, and the pace of her heart slowed. She found her notes and glanced over them once more. This case wasn't about Alex, and it wasn't about her. It was about justice for those six precious babies. It was about forcing evil to face its consequences.

Alex came around behind her and took his seat again. "Frank says you're running the show."

"Yep." She kept her gaze on her notes.

"'Bout time I got to see you in action."

She glanced over at him. He smiled and winked at her. Her cheeks warmed, and she couldn't help but smile. "Don't even think about messing with me today."

"Wouldn't dream of it."

Judge McEntire re-entered, and the rest of the room moved back into order. He looked over the bench at both tables and frowned. "Are we ready to proceed?"

The attorneys affirmed they were ready, which meant it was time for Carrie to prove she wasn't an immature girl with a silly crush. She pushed herself up and made eye contact with Judge McEntire.

"Your Honor, the prosecution calls Special Agent Alex Walker."

Alex stood and moved across the room like he'd done this a thousand times. He took the oath to tell the truth, and then took his seat. When he met her gaze, she could see nothing of the playful laughter usually there. It bolstered her with a shot of confidence.

"Please state your name."

"Special Agent Alex Walker."

Easy enough. She looked down at her notes. "What's your occupation?"

"I'm an investigator for the Department of Homeland Security."

"How long have you been at your current position?"

"Two years."

"And before that? Where were you employed?"

"I was a detective for the Glynn County Police Department in Glynn County, Georgia for four years, and before that I was a United States Marine for four years."

The comfort of familiarity took over, and before she knew it, Carrie was moving through the questions they'd rehearsed with barely a thought. Alex was a machine. Answered every question thoroughly and professionally, without a hint of impropriety.

By the time they'd wrapped up his testimony, she was certain she could handle a little flirtatious banter with Alex and still do her job.

37.

ALEX SAT AT THE PROSECUTOR'S TABLE DO-ING his best to keep from showing the jury how anxious he was to get out of there. He'd hardly slept the night before after searching for hours through a catalogue of child pornography, looking for the image he knew he'd seen some-where before. That sky-blue background with the fluffy clouds wouldn't leave his mind alone.

On the stand, Sean Richards was explaining to the jury exactly how they'd been able to conclude that Tom Williams was the man in the video cen-tral to their case. "At first," he said, "the image was too blurry to make out the tattoo on the man's leg."

"And where was the tattoo located on the man in the video?" Frank asked.

"Just below his right knee."

"And how were you able to identify the tattoo?"

"I was able to enhance it enough for us to clearly see the skull and the number twenty-one."

Alex was only half-listening at this point. His mind was already back on the Jonkovic case and how they were going to extract the key logger in a few days. The warrant had specified it was for ten days, but he'd received word from Nicole that time was running out. The agents in Australia, the Netherlands, and Guatemala had all reported that they were set to go on their take-downs. The entire operation was waiting on one single search warrant. His.

In front of him, Frank continued to question Richards. "Agent Walker testified that you were able to identify five other victims. How?"

"We looked at hundreds of known child pornography videos, and found five that had similar scenarios to the footage we had in our possession. We were able to identify the tattoo in each one."

Alex remembered the endless search through video after video. He'd nearly made himself sick watching so much torture. He'd tried desperately to identify the kids, but so far they hadn't found one. And the scum at the other table wasn't talking. He remembered the video of the youngest victim, a two-year-old girl crying and screaming the whole time. His stomach knotted. He'd let himself imagine his own version of justice for Williams too many times, and he didn't want to go there again.

So he turned his thoughts back to Jonkovic and that damned background.

Frank took a seat while the defense attorney made a shoddy attempt to discredit their identification of Mr. Williams. Alex leaned forward and jotted down some notes about Jonkovic's house. They couldn't count on the same window being loose enough to open again, so he wanted to have several backup entry points. Maybe Craig would have better luck with the front door the next time.

Carrie pushed a piece of paper in front of him. *What are you doing?*

He wrote down his answer and pushed it back. *Planning entry into RJ's house again. Have to get key logger.*

She scribbled again. *Watch out for plants.*

His face did not betray his amusement. *That was a rare species of low-flying plant. Came out of nowhere.*

She smiled briefly and turned her attention back to the trial. He studied the graceful curve of her jaw, the gentle arch of her brow. How to make her smile again? He slipped the paper back in front of her.

Want to grab dinner afterward?

No.

He stared at her answer, a bit surprised. *Why not?*

PROFESSIONAL.

That was good enough. He was under her skin, and though he didn't want to risk either of their jobs, he took small satisfaction in making her squirm. His thoughts returned to his entry plan, picturing each window and door in his mind. The studio window would probably be quickest. In one room and out the same. He tried to remember what kind of window it was.

He saw sunlight stretching a long shadow of a cross on the white floor, with a decorative swirl on the ends. It was unusual. Not a window they'd be able to open. But the swirls on the end...

Meeks. Lyons. They were looking at a picture of a boy on the floor with the sun draped across him, and the elongated cross on the floor. Behind him were clouds, with a rip across the bottom of the background. The picture was on Lyons' computer when he and Meeks were looking at images. That was it! He nearly jumped out of his seat. He scribbled out a note and passed it to Carrie.

I have the evidence we need for the search warrant! I've had it all along!

38.

S SOON AS THE JUDGE'S GAVEL CAME DOWN to end the day, Alex pulled Carrie aside. "When Meeks and Lyons were looking at images at Lyons' house, they looked at a picture that was taken at Jonkovic's house."

"Are you sure?"

"Absolutely. I saw the background hanging in Jonkovic's studio when I was there. I knew I recognized it from somewhere. I saw it on the video from Meeks."

She frowned. "Please tell me you have pictures or something and not just your memory."

He pulled out his phone and scrolled through the photo album until he came to the one from Jonkovic's studio. "See the rip across the bottom and the crease in the clouds up top? That's in the video from Meeks."

"Alex, this is great! So we finish this trial up tomorrow, get the search warrant the next day and—"

"Are you crazy? I'm writing the affidavit for the warrant tonight, and we're getting that baby signed first thing in the morning."

"Tonight? That will take you hours."

He shrugged. "Got nothing better to do, especially since I'm eating alone."

She smiled and shook her head. "I'll probably regret this later, but why don't we grab some takeout and work on the affidavit at my apartment? I can review it right away so it's ready to be signed first thing in the morning."

Alex grabbed his notebook from the table and shoved it into his briefcase. "Oh no. You rejected my offer for dinner. Now I have something interesting and you want to jump on board the Alex train? No, thank you."

"Did you just say the *Alex train?*"

He started for the doors. "Yes, ma'am. Come on, though. I'm insulted, but I'm not stupid. With you there to review the affidavit, I might actually get some sleep tonight." She stared at him for a moment, unmoving, unsure of whether he was serious or joking. "Come on." He nodded toward the door. "We'll even splurge for some Chinese. That's your favorite, right?"

She finally moved toward him and followed him through the doors. As she passed him, she put a finger in his face and grinned. "All right. But no funny business. *Professional.*"

Alex couldn't help but smile down at her tiny finger. "Yes, ma'am."

39.

A LEX LEANED AGAINST THE WALL OUTSIDE
Carrie's apartment while she unlocked the
door, his arms loaded with Chinese takeout
boxes. "This really isn't necessary."

"Yes it is." She pushed open the door. "Now stay
right there. I'll come get you when I'm done."

He chuckled to himself and called after her. "I
don't care if your place is a mess!"

"But I do!" she called from inside.

He heard her scurrying around, her footsteps
fading and returning multiple times. She finally reappeared at the door, just a bit out of breath. "Okay,
you can come in now."

He stepped through the door and took a quick
look around. Seemed to be in good order. In fact, it
was cleaner than his place would ever be on its best
day. "Well, I definitely can't work in this pigsty."

Her eyes widened before she let out a laugh. "It's the best I could do in a pinch."

"So what did you do? Throw everything in your bedroom and close the door?"

"Maybe."

"So what makes you think we won't end up in the bedroom?"

He held a straight face for as long as possible, but the shock in her eyes was too much. When she stammered something about keeping things *professional*, he nearly doubled over.

"Carrie, relax. It was a joke. I promise, no matter how much you beg, I will keep my hands to myself."

Her face flushed pink. "You sure have a high opinion of yourself."

"Look, if you're so worried about the mess and that I might take advantage of you, then why are we here? We could've done this in your office. Or is that a pigsty too?"

She took the food from his arms and headed for the kitchen. "I'm not hanging out in my office for hours with no access to food. And heaven knows what's in your fridge."

He followed her through the kitchen over to the table, helping to spread out the containers. Then he pulled out his laptop and set it on the table. While she spooned food onto their plates, he pulled up the video from Meeks' visit to Lyons' house.

She pushed a plate over to him and moved behind his shoulder. "Did you find it?"

He slowed the video down at the point where he thought he'd seen the image, muting the conversation in the background. "It's around here somewhere."

She slid a chair around the side of the table so it was next to his. "What if it's not in there?"

"It's in there."

Alex watched the video carefully for several minutes, not even thinking about his food until Carrie asked if he was going to eat. He was beginning to wonder if he'd just dreamed up the image in his mind. And then it was there. He hit pause and pointed.

"Right here."

Carrie leaned over and studied the screen. "It's in black and white. How do you know it's the same background?"

"Look at the bottom of it. See the rip? And the crease across the top?" He pulled up the picture on his phone that he'd taken of Jonkovic's studio. "Look."

She looked between the phone and the computer screen several times. Then she sat back and nodded her head. "Tony was right about you."

"How so?"

"You're very good at your job. I'm impressed."

Warmth rushed up his chest. "Wow. A compliment. Bet that hurt."

She grinned, leaning towards him slightly. "You have no idea."

He held her gaze long enough to feel his heart speed up just a touch. "You know...if I wasn't me, and you weren't you, I'd probably kiss you."

She fell back against her chair and dropped her gaze. Then she gripped her hands, rubbing her thumb over her palm. He started to reach for them, but thought better of it. Maybe it was time to stop clowning around with her.

"Why do I make you so nervous?" he asked.

She pulled her hands apart and sat up straight. It took a moment, and obviously some effort, but she looked him in the eyes. "Alex, every man makes me nervous."

Shame crawled all over him. How could he have forgotten? "Still?"

"Still."

"You never told me what happened to you."

She shook her head. "Another time. Let's get this affidavit done and get you the search warrant you need."

Alex fought the urge to probe a little more. "Hey, I didn't mean to make you uncomfortable."

"It's okay. I mean, you make me nervous, but not like...I'm not afraid. I just..."

"Just what?"

She smiled, almost a bashful sort of smile. "You make me laugh. Like, *really* laugh. I love that about you. So don't worry about my hang-ups. Just keep me laughing. Especially when we're doing this." She pointed to the image on the computer screen.

Alex nodded, relieved, and just a bit unsure of what to say. "Well, this affidavit isn't going to write itself."

40.

CARRIE READ OVER THE AFFIDAVIT ONE LAST time, making sure everything was worded exactly right. On the other side of the living room, Alex was sprawled across her sofa, his long legs hanging over the armrest and his elbow resting over his eyes. He'd done a good job. The affidavit was well written, concise, and needed very little direction from her. She'd meant it earlier when she'd said she was impressed. He knew his stuff.

"So?" he mumbled from under his arm.

"Looks perfect. Mac should sign it without any issues."

He pushed himself up to a sitting position, groaning with exhaustion. "What time is it?"

"One in the morning."

She thought about offering him her couch, but that was definitely headed in the opposite direction from maintaining a professional relationship with him. All jokes aside, she was dangerously close to falling for him, and she had to keep a level head.

He ran his hands through his hair, his forearms flexing. She closed the computer and set it aside, willing herself to look away. She stood from her chair, but realized she had no idea where she was going.

"Can I get you a drink or something?" she asked. "Some coffee, maybe?"

He shook his head and pushed himself up to standing as well. "No thanks. I'll be fine."

"Can I ask you about something before you go?"

"Sure."

"I was thinking about Brian Meeks. In the affidavit you don't refer to him by name, obviously to keep his identity safe, but once his friends get their defense attorneys and prepare for trial, they'll have access to this document. They'll know it was him."

Alex frowned. "That's always a possibility."

"Is there any way to keep him walled off?"

"I did the best I could. I didn't refer to him by name, only a number. I used as little description of the scenario as possible. I don't know what else I can do. I mean, I can't lie. At least when the other guys find out, they'll all be in prison awaiting trial. So he should be safe." He moved past her and picked up his laptop, placing it in his briefcase.

She tried not to watch him. Failed miserably. "Thanks for doing your best to protect him. I know we don't see eye-to-eye on things, but—"

"Hey, it's never good under any circumstances for an informant to get burned. I'm just doing my job." He slid the zipper closed on his briefcase. "Besides, maybe you're right about him. He does seem like he wants to change. Maybe he's the one in a million that can actually pull it off."

"Wow, I'm shocked. That almost sounded like optimism."

"Well, let's not get carried away. I'm not saying I'd ever let the guy around my own kids or anything." He pulled his briefcase over his shoulder and started for the door. When he reached it, he turned back to her and smiled. A genuine smile that warmed her heart. "You know, I meant to tell you. You're pretty good at your job too. I know we got off to a rough start, but I've been impressed with you."

She felt the blush creeping into her cheeks and wished she could push it away. So embarrassing. "Thanks."

"I mean it. You know, Frank's a good attorney, don't get me wrong. But he wants you to chase every rabbit down every freaking hole, no matter if it has anything to do with the case or not. Then he'll delay and delay. Motions, more evidence, rewriting affidavits. Takes forever with that guy. I'm glad you're around, and I appreciate the job you're do-ing."

She couldn't help but smile. "Okay, okay. Stop begging. I already told you I'm not kissing you again."

He threw his head back and laughed. "We'll see about that." He reached for the door.

"Can I ask you one more thing?" She knew she should let him go, but something inside her wanted him to stay.

"Sure."

"You said something a minute ago, about not letting Meeks near your own kids." His smile faded, and she hesitated. "Do you...do you still want kids someday?"

He sighed and looked down at his feet for a moment. "Can't seem to help that part of me that wants a family." He looked up at her again, his eyes hardened. "It's just not in the cards for me. I mean, how many chances does a guy get?"

"You're awfully young to be giving up. You don't strike me as a quitter."

He opened the door and stepped outside, and she followed him into the hallway, gripping the doorknob behind her. She needed something to keep her tied to the earth. Alex paused like he was considering her statement.

"I'm not a quitter. Just a realist. I keep falling for the wrong girl."

His smile returned, but it was a sad sort of smile. His eyes drifted down to her waist, and she realized she'd let go of the door and was once again rubbing her hands. He took them in his. Rubbed his thumb over the back of her hand. As heat spread through her hands and up her arms, she stole a glance at his lips. His head bent toward hers.

"You know," he murmured. "It might be worth it, taking my cases to Frank. Just so I can kiss you again."

She put her hand on his chest, feeling the muscles tighten. "Let's give it some time. Finish this case. You may change your mind."

"Hmmm, I doubt it."

His lips were so close to hers. So close. *Just breathe.* She closed her eyes. Felt his breath move across her cheek and up to her forehead. No one would know. If she just tilted her mouth to his. No one would know.

She lifted her face, and his lips came to hers. Just a light touch that sent a wave of electricity down her whole body.

"Carrie," he murmured, sliding his hand under her hair and around her neck. He moved his mouth along her cheek. "You're killing me here."

Her heart thundered so loud, she could barely think. No one would know. She slid her hands up his chest. Wrapped them around his neck. Pulled her mouth up to his. *No one would know.*

He pressed her body against the door, and dug his fingers into her hair.

"You can't stay," she breathed. *Stay.*

"Of course not." He kissed her again. "That would be unprofessional." His briefcase hit the floor. His other hand slid around her waist.

She gripped his shirt. "This is a bad idea." She pulled him tighter.

"Terrible."

"You're not really here."

He moved his lips to her neck, sending chills down her arms. "Left hours ago." He slid his hands around her neck, caressing her cheeks with his thumbs. "I'm actually at home right now. Asleep. Dreaming."

"Great dream."

"Best ever." He kissed her once more. Then he touched his forehead to hers. "I should go."

"Mmm hmm. You should."

He pulled back and shook his head with a mischievous grin. "I'll see you soon." Then he picked up his briefcase again and pulled it back over his shoulder. Her body felt electric. She wanted to pull him back to her again, but she shouldn't. *Patience.*

He touched his hand to her hip. "Goodnight, Carrie."

"Goodnight."

She watched him walk down the hallway before falling back through her door. She was crazy.

This was crazy.

41.

"ALL RIGHT, LET'S GO OVER THIS ONE MORE time." Alex leaned onto the conference room table and looked over his ops plan. "Craig, you're leading a team of eight into Mark Johnson's house at twenty hundred hours. You got the plan in place and all the guys assigned?"

Craig nodded. "Just need a Victim Witness Co-ordinator in case either of his kids have to be interviewed."

Alex glanced at Nicole. "Can you check on that?"

"Sure." She headed for a corner of the room with her cell phone.

"Okay, Carl, you've got a team of eight for Derrick Lyons' apartment. You're speaking with management at nineteen-forty-five and hitting the door at twenty hundred hours. Is your plan and team in place?"

Another nod. Alex pushed a couple of papers away and pulled his ops plan over for Jonkovic's house. "The big hit is at Roman Jonkovic's house. Like everyone else, we go in at twenty hundred hours. We've got two floors and a basement to clear, and the computer equipment is in a studio near the back of the first floor. The front door has a narrow staircase leading up to it, so the back door is our best entry. Tony will clear the back yard and open the gate for us." He winked at Tony, who shot him a middle finger.

"When we cleared Jonkovic's house for the key logger, we didn't see any weapons in plain sight, but be aware of your surroundings. We weren't able to clear the basement, so there's no telling what's down there."

"Are we arresting all three of these guys?" Carl asked.

"Yes. We're taking all equipment that could be used in child exploitation, including computers, video cameras, phones...you know the drill. Do any preliminary interviews you need to, but then the men will be arrested and taken to the detention center nearest their residence."

Alex looked around the room. "Any more questions?"

Sean Richards waved at him. "Why aren't we doing this at oh-six-hundred tomorrow? Seems a bit risky to hit the places when the targets could be up walking around."

Alex sighed. "It wasn't my first choice, but we're coordinating with agencies all over the world and had to find a time where we could get the best chance of getting the most people. Anything else?" The agents looked around at each other, but no one else spoke up. "All right. Grab a bite to eat and meet back here at fifteen hundred hours."

Alex gathered his papers and laptop, shoving everything into his briefcase. Then he followed the crowd of agents out of the conference room. He'd need to finalize a couple more details and make sure Craig got the Coordinator he needed. His mind raced through all the different scenarios they could face at Jonkovic's house, especially with the basement being an unknown. But he was confident he'd covered all his bases.

As he rounded the corner and headed through the maze of cubicles toward his own, he caught sight of Carrie standing outside. He strode up to her and gave his best polite smile. "Hey, what are you doing here?"

She straightened her spine and lifted her chin. "Just checking in. We got a Guilty verdict for Williams. Jury took about thirty minutes."

"Awesome."

"Everything set for tonight?"

It was all he could do to keep a straight face. Her overcompensating was adorable. "Yep. All set." He turned to his desk. "Tony and I are grabbing some food. Want to come?"

He took his keys from his desk and turned back. She glanced around before stepping into his cubicle. "Is there somewhere we can talk in private? Just for a minute?"

He tried not to grin. "Sure." He led her past Tony and Craig at the end of the row. "Hey, where are y'all heading?"

"Pizza," Tony said. "The new place over by Target."

"Meet you there. Get me a pepperoni with pineapple."

Alex ignored the arched eyebrow Tony gave him. He continued past the cubicles for the exploitation group and the drug group, turned down the hall and checked the break room. It was empty. He motioned for her to enter, then closed the door behind him.

"So what's up?" he asked.

Her eyes widened. "What's up? Really?"

He took a deep breath and wondered what in the world he was supposed to say right now. Was she angry? Did she regret kissing him? He leaned against the door. "Are you okay?"

"I...I don't know. I mean, I can't stop thinking about last night. What did we do?"

"I don't know about you, but I had one hell of a dream." He willed her to smile, but she only shook her head.

"Alex, this case is a big deal. If we screw this up, I could lose my job. So could you."

He pushed away from the door and took a seat at the table. He patted the chair next to him. "Come here and sit down. It's going to be okay."

She fell into the chair next to him. "I love my job. I don't want to mess it up."

"You won't. You're a great attorney, and you're going to be fine." He covered her hand with his. "No one has to know anything. This case will be over before we know it. And then I'll take all my cases to Frank."

"You can't stand working with Frank." She pulled her hand out from under his. "Look, I've been thinking about this a lot today, and I don't want to put either one of us in jeopardy. We just have to stay away from each other. No more cases, no more dinners, no more—"

"Kissing?"

She lowered her chin. "Especially that. Or anything else."

He leaned back in his chair, wondering how he could have been so stupid to fall for another chick that didn't want to be with him. He wasn't about to pursue another dead end. He threw his hands up and pushed himself out of the chair. "All right. If that's what you want. I'll stay away from you."

"Don't be mad."

"I'm not mad. Like I said, I'm a realist."

"I just want to do what's best for both of us."

"And now you have." He moved to the door and pulled it open. "If you'll excuse me, I need to eat and get ready to serve this search warrant. Thanks for coming by."

He didn't wait for anything else. Just let the door slam behind him.

42.

"POLICE! SEARCH WARRANT! OPEN THE DOOR!"

Nothing happened. Alex waited the customary thirty seconds. Banged again on the back door of Jonkovic's house. Repeated his command. Thirty more seconds. He stepped back and let another agent ram the door. One hit, and it caved in. Alex led the team inside.

"Police with a warrant! Come out into the open with your hands up!"

Music was coming from the living room. Something classical. Half-sliced vegetables and two steaks were laid out on the kitchen counter. The team moved swiftly into the living room. Alex swept the right side, while Tony cleared the left. Empty.

They headed down the hallway, clearing a bathroom, a guest bedroom, and the studio. Still no sign of Jonkovic. Alex signaled to Tony to reverse course, and they headed back through the living room. Alex took the lead, and five other guys joined in behind. He signaled to Tony to clear the basement.

Alex turned his attention upwards as Tony called for the ram. He moved up the stairs, nodded his head, felt the squeeze on his left shoulder to proceed. He turned left and cleared the hallway. Heard other guys yelling clearing signals behind him. An agent gripped his shoulder and they proceeded to the master bedroom on the right. Alex nodded, felt the squeeze. He pushed the door open and trained his M4 on the left side of the room.

"Police with a warrant! Get on the ground!" He moved along the wall as the other agent yelled, "Clear!" Crossing the doorway that opened into the bathroom, he cleared both sides. Empty.

He came back to the hallway where he met with the other agents. Every room was empty. He motioned for the agents to follow. "Basement."

Alex raised his gun again as he descended the stairs, checking each corner of the living room as he passed. Where was this guy? He had to be here, and the only possibility left was the basement. But he should've heard Tony call out if he had Jonkovic in custody. Something wasn't right.

He led the team down the stairs to the basement. Another door had been rammed at the bottom, and it lay across the floor. "Tony! What you got?"

"Nothing!" he yelled from somewhere around a corner. "We're clear!"

Alex lowered his gun and stepped into the room. Tony crossed in front of a small mattress stained with brownish red spots. Blood. A sofa next to the mattress had a few stuffed animals scattered across it. On the other side was a small table with a television and DVD player.

"Nothing?" Alex asked.

"There's a bathroom, a closet, and this room here. No people though." Tony picked up a stuffed rabbit. "There's some pretty messed-up stuff in the closet. Restraints. Whips. Sex dolls. Nasty stuff."

Alex looked around the dark room, wondering if a kid had been down here when they'd installed the key logger. Was the kid dead now? The blood on the mattress looked old. Maybe there wasn't a kid at all.

"Let's do a secondary search, guys," Alex called out. "Jonkovic has to be here somewhere." He pointed at Richards. "Take Sanders with you and get started on the computer equipment upstairs. Hendrix, take a couple of guys and do a secondary search of the second floor. Every inch."

The agents headed back up the stairs, and Alex took another look around the basement. It was more like a dungeon. Only a single light bulb hanging from the ceiling. "Let's spread out and look for any hidden doors or crawl spaces."

A couple of guys headed into the closet, while Alex followed Tony around the perimeter of the room. They ran their hands along the walls, eyed the ceiling for anything unusual, and lifted the rug. Still nothing.

As they rounded the wall of the makeshift bathroom, Alex noticed a space about two feet wide that led between the closet and the wall of the house. He pointed at it and gave a hand signal to Tony. The two of them slid along the wall, across the doorway of the closet, and paused just before reaching the opening. Tony held up three fingers beside his M4. Counted down to one. They turned into the opening, Tony low, Alex covering high.

"Police! Get on the ground!"

It was full of old parts from appliances, and a water heater took up almost the entire back third of the space. Alex shined his flashlight on the tank and the wall next to it. There was a gap just behind it. He pounded on the wall next to him. Plywood.

He and Tony backed out of the narrow passage and stepped into the closet next to them. The other two agents, Freeman and Tripp, stood in the middle of the closet, looking around at the equipment inside. They were in the drug group, and were obviously not used to seeing the wide variety of tools pedophiles used for entertaining themselves. They looked downright nauseous.

Lightweights.

"Did you guys find a hidden doorway in that back corner?" Alex asked, pointing to the wall between the closet and the passage.

Tripp shook his head. "Didn't see one."

Alex moved to the corner and pushed aside a pile of ropes. Behind them was a safe, right where the gap would be on the other side. "Tony, see if we can slide this out of here."

Tony gripped one side of the safe, while Alex pushed on the other. It was surprisingly light. And behind it was a narrow door. He motioned for Tony to cover low and waited for him to move behind his shoulder. Then Alex yanked the door open and aimed his gun.

Seated about twelve feet away in the corner like a trapped raccoon, Jonkovic held a shaking boy in his lap. The Gomez boy. And he had a knife to the kid's throat.

43.

SHOUTS FILLED THE TINY PASSAGE.

"Drop the knife! Now!"

"Back up or I cut the kid!"

"Drop the knife!"

"Back up! I'm not kidding! I will cut his throat right here if you move any closer!"

Alex trained his M4 on a tiny corner of Jonkovic's head. Was it enough space to slide a bullet by without hitting the Gomez kid? Then he saw the boy's dark eyes, wide with terror, tears streaking his cheeks. Below him, Tony was still commanding Jonkovic to drop the knife, but it was useless.

Alex tightened his grip on the trigger. "Roman, you have nowhere to go. Let the boy go, and let's all walk away from this without anybody getting hurt."

"You will not take me," Jonkovic said, his accent thick and angry. "You will get the hell out of my house, or we will all suffer. I will kill the boy. And take one of you out as well. Then I will die."

"What's your name, son?" Tony asked, his voice calm and steady.

The kid swallowed, his throat sliding up then down beneath the knife. "Samuel."

"Roman," Tony said. "Samuel's a good kid. Let's leave him out of this."

Jonkovic tightened his grip on the knife, and Samuel winced. Alex's chest constricted as blood trickled down Samuel's throat. *Too much talking. Just shoot.* This was about to end badly, and it was going to happen fast. He only hoped Samuel would still be alive.

Roman pulled his feet underneath him to a squatting position, careful to keep his head behind Samuel's. Alex shined the flashlight into Roman's eyes, hoping he'd move his head to adjust.

"I said to get out of here!" Jonkovic screamed. "I will cut his throat now!" He slid his body up the wall, pulling Samuel up off the ground in front of him.

Alex shifted his weight forward. "Put the kid down! This is your last chance. I will shoot you."

He saw the moment Jonkovic made up his mind. Saw the resolve to die. And to take the kid with him. Alex squeezed the trigger just as Jonkovic slid the knife across Samuel's throat. Both of them dropped to the floor.

Tony lunged for Samuel's body, covering his throat. Alex dropped his gun. *Don't be dead. Don't be dead.* Tony pulled Samuel out of the passage and laid him in Alex's arms. Alex covered his throat with his hand. Blood seeped through his fingers. Samuel's eyes were filled with horror as he gazed up at Alex. He gasped for air.

Tony ran over to the bathroom, tossing everything in search of some kind of rag or towel. He returned seconds later with a handful of washcloths, and pressed the rags onto the boy's throat. "Let's get him out of here!"

"Samuel, you hang in there," Alex said, heading for the stairs. "Coming through! Move it!"

Tony ran ahead, clearing a path for them. Alex bolted through the door and ran for Tony's car in the driveway. Someone opened the back door. He dove inside, positioning Samuel across his lap. He pressed down on the rags, praying the bleeding would stop soon.

Outside the car, he could hear Tony yelling at the cops on the perimeter to escort them to the hospital. He popped the trunk, then slammed it a few seconds later. Tony stuck his head inside and ripped open a packet of special gauze that turned to gel on application. Alex withdrew the rags and Tony pressed the gauze in place. Alex met Tony's gaze for an instant.

"Hurry!" Alex said.

Tony climbed out of the back and into the front of the car, gunning it as he pulled out of the driveway and behind two police cars. He flipped on the lights and the siren, and they flew through the neighborhood. Tony radioed to dispatch to let the hospital know they were coming.

Alex looked down at the dying boy in his arms, and he couldn't help remembering the last moments he'd held Evan. He closed his eyes and shut out the pain. Then he focused again on Samuel, not the blood, or the thought of death.

"Just stay calm, son. You're going to be okay. We're almost there. Just keep your eyes on me. Don't talk."

He should have shot Jonkovic sooner. He could have shot him sooner. Samuel's eyes drifted shut. Alex leaned closer to his face. "Hey! Don't go to sleep on me. Stay awake. We're almost there."

Tony whipped the car onto Cherokee Street. They were moments away. "Just hang in there, Samuel." Alex had to keep his own breathing in check as well. His head spun with adrenaline.

Finally, Tony flew into the parking lot at WellStar Hospital, sliding to a stop just outside the emergency room door. There was already a gurney with several staff ready to take Samuel. Alex lifted him out of the car, maintaining pressure on his throat. He laid him on the gurney and leaned into

Samuel's vision. "You're here, champ. You did great. You're going to be okay."

Still dazed, Samuel's eyes floated over to Alex. He moved his mouth, but nothing came out. The team rolled the gurney through the front doors, and Alex dropped to his knees. He couldn't catch his breath.

Tony put a hand on his shoulder. "You all right, man?"

Alex had no words. All he could do was suck in air. He pushed himself up from the ground and headed for the waiting room.

He was going to be there when Samuel Gomez woke up.

44.

THE HOSPITAL WAITING ROOM FLOODED WITH
people. Alex turned his firearm over to Georgia Bureau of Investigation Agent Brody,
who'd be investigating the shooting. He'd explained
the events several times over to Nicole and Special
Agent in Charge Hank Carpenter. If he had to go
through one more explanation, he might lose it.

When an Internal Affairs agent requested a
statement, Nicole stepped in on his behalf.

"Agent Walker has twenty-four hours before he
has to give an official statement. This can wait until
tomorrow."

Alex thanked her and dropped into a chair near
the windows. Nicole sat beside him, but thankfully
asked no more questions. The SAC and other
Homeland Security officials were gathering in a

section a few rows away to put together a statement for the media, who would inevitably show up.

Mr. and Mrs. Gomez arrived within minutes, surrounded by police officers and GBI agents. Once the chaos died down, and Nicole explained the situation to them, things went from bad to worse for Alex. He knew the panic in their eyes; the fear so overwhelming it engulfed every cell of your being. Like he'd lost his son only yesterday. And now he might be responsible for someone else losing theirs.

He leaned forward in his chair, resting his head in his hands. He couldn't watch Mrs. Gomez fall apart in her husband's arms as they learned exactly who their son had been with for the past weeks— and the nightmare he'd most likely endured. Alex couldn't watch. But he couldn't leave. He had to know if Samuel was okay.

Within another half hour, right on time, the parking lot began to fill with media vans and reporters. When Nicole left his side to confer with the HSI spokesman, Tony took her place. He put a hand on Alex's back. "You okay?"

"No."

"Can I get you anything? Something to drink?"

"No."

"Some clean clothes?"

Alex sat back and sighed. "No. I'm fine. But thank you." He heard the frustration in his voice. Tony was only trying to help. "Really, thank you."

The sound of the sliding doors made him look up and he saw Carrie enter the waiting room. She looked around until she saw him. Their eyes met, and it shot another jolt of pain through him. So much for staying away from each other.

She hesitated, raised her eyebrows as if to ask permission. He nodded once.

"Carrie's here," he said to Tony.

Tony stood and offered her his seat. She sat down and gripped her hands in her lap. "You okay?"

How many times was he going to have to answer that? "Sure. I'm fine."

She glanced up at Tony. "How's the kid?"

"In surgery."

"Is he...going to be all right?"

"No," Alex said. "Even if he lives, he'll never be okay. You know that better than anyone."

A blush crept into her cheeks. He shouldn't have said that. He pushed up from the chair and walked across the room to the water fountain. He wanted to wait alone. Why couldn't everyone leave him alone?

He took a long drink then stepped back into the waiting room. He hated hospitals. A doctor approached the crowd gathered around Mr. and Mrs.

Gomez. Alex moved close enough to overhear. Samuel was stable and in recovery.

A wave of relief and exhaustion flooded Alex's body. His knees nearly buckled. He needed to move, clear his head. He turned away from the crowd and headed down the first hallway he came to.

He heard shoes clicking behind him, and he glanced over his shoulder. Carrie. He kept going. No way he could deal with his emotions with her around. He just needed to find a place to breathe. He turned down another hallway, unsure of where he was going. The clicking followed.

"Alex, wait." The clicking sped up.

He stopped and took a deep breath. This wasn't the time or the place to sort their mess out. But he couldn't have her chasing him through the hospital either. He turned around as she caught up to him.

"Where are you going?" she asked.

"I don't know. I just...I can't breathe around all those people right now." The sympathy in her eyes only made him more frustrated. "Why are you here?" he asked.

"Because I was worried about you. I wanted to see if you were all right." She reached for his arm.

He closed his eyes and fell back against the wall. "I don't want to talk."

"It's okay. You don't have to."

He slid down the wall until he was seated. "I almost got that kid killed tonight."

She crouched down in front of him. "He's going to be okay. You saved him from that monster. Now he can heal."

"Is there any way I could have gotten to him sooner? He had to have been down there when we put in the key logger. While we were doing surveillance—the whole time—he was down in that dungeon."

She moved next to him and took his hand. "Don't drive yourself crazy. He's going to be okay. The whole ring of predators has been taken down. Lyons and Johnson are in custody. El Maestro's dead. Even the raids in the other countries have been largely successful. Do you have any idea how many kids were saved tonight?"

For a second, he almost felt better. He squeezed her hand before letting go. "Thanks for coming."

She rested her head on his shoulder. "When I heard the shot fired and all the screaming, I almost lost it right there in front of everyone at the Command Center. All I could think about was that you were dead, and I'd never see you again."

Warmth stirred inside his chest, and he tilted his head over to hers. "Well, we managed to stay away from each other for all of about..." He looked down at his watch. "...Nine hours."

She sighed and took his hand again. "I guess we're just two idiots out to get our asses fired."

He chuckled and laced his fingers through hers. "Maybe not. This case will be wrapped up soon. I can be patient if you can."

She pulled her head back and looked at him like he was crazy. "You? Patient? I doubt it."

He took her chin in his fingers and touched his lips to hers. "For you, I can."

45.

A COUPLE OF DAYS LATER, ALEX SAT AT HIS desk trying to catch up on the mountain of paperwork the search warrants had created. His butt hadn't left the chair in two days, except to go home or visit the restroom. Thankfully, he was meeting with Mark Johnson and his attorney today, so that would break up the monotony.

"Morning, Agent Walker."

He turned in his chair to Carrie standing behind him. His pulse sped up just a notch. "Good morning, Miss Reynolds."

She grinned, but then cleared her throat and forced her lips into a line. "You got a minute before we head into the meeting?"

"Sure. What's up?"

She stepped further into his cubicle and set her briefcase on his desk. He made a concerted effort not to check her out. Failed. She was just too gorgeous. He brought his eyes back to hers and smiled.

"Derrick Lyons committed suicide last night in his holding cell," she said.

Alex shook his head. "Coward."

"So this means Johnson is the only one left to prosecute."

"I still don't get why you're offering him such a good plea bargain. We don't need his cooperation. As soon as all the data is collected from the computers, we can put him away for life."

She sighed. "He's got a family, Alex. Kids. He was a fireman with no previous criminal history."

"Except for being part of a ring of pedophiles that kidnapped kids and made pornographic videos."

"What do you want me to do? If he cooperates and takes the plea, this case gets wrapped up in a matter of weeks rather than months. I thought you wanted that."

He pushed himself up from his chair and grabbed his briefcase from the floor. "Of course I do. I just want to see justice served as well. Samuel deserves that." He looked into her eyes and knew she wanted justice too. How did she have room for mercy as well? He couldn't wrap his brain around it. "Come on, we need to get to the conference room," he said.

She moved a step closer and smiled up at him. "Relax, Alex. This is the part I'm good at. Johnson gets his deal, explains everything, and we wrap all this mess up. Then we finally move on."

He couldn't resist that smile, and he suspected she knew it. He glanced around and lowered his voice. "Think we could do some moving on tonight?"

She rolled her eyes, but her smile didn't falter. "Don't hold your breath."

When they arrived at the conference room, the suspect and his attorney were already there. Mark Johnson sat with his whole body rigid as a statue. He didn't make eye contact with anyone. Introductions were made, and Alex shook hands with Johnson's attorney, James Whitfield.

"All right," Carrie said. "Let's get this started. Mr. Johnson, just to be clear, you are pleading guilty to one count of the production of child pornography, which carries a minimum sentence of fifteen years. Though I can't guarantee the sentence—the judge will decide that—I can tell you that judges do take into consideration your cooperation and willingness to admit your wrongdoing."

Johnson still didn't look at her. He sat at the table with his hands folded neatly together and his mouth pressed into a determined frown.

"In exchange for receiving a lesser charge," Carrie continued, "you will give us an account of everything you know about the group of pedophiles of which you were a member, namely the group headed up by Roman Jonkovic."

She slid some papers in front of him. "If you agree, would you please sign here?"

Mr. Whitfield, a large man who looked like he might keel over from a heart attack at any moment, glanced over the papers. He nodded to Johnson, who then signed them. Carrie slid the papers back into a folder, and Alex took out his folder.

He laid out several pictures across the table—headshots of Samuel, Lyons, Meeks, Jonkovic, and Collin Drake from Australia, who had originally identified the house. "Okay, let's start by identifying all the players. Mark, I need you to tell me who each person is and his role in the organization. Don't leave anything out. Understand?"

Johnson nodded. He leaned up onto the table and began looking over the pictures. After nearly a full minute of silence, Alex grew impatient. He pointed at Jonkovic. "Why don't we start with him? Tell me who this guy is."

Johnson looked over at his attorney, then back at Alex. "Is this everyone?"

"What do you mean?" Alex asked.

"The men you arrested. Are these all the men?" Confusion flickered across his face.

Alex looked at the attorney, who shrugged his shoulders. Then he turned back to Johnson. "These are the men we arrested. Except for this one. He was killed while resisting."

Johnson pushed away from the table and began to pace behind his chair. He pointed a finger at his attorney. "You said he was dead."

Mr. Whitfield looked just as confused as Alex felt. "Mark," he said. "I told you everything that Miss Reynolds told me. Now, just calm down and explain everything to Agent Walker."

Johnson kept pacing and shaking his head. "You said he was dead."

Alex stood and pointed at the pictures. "Mr. Johnson, are these all the members of the group? Are we missing someone?"

Johnson stepped back to the table and looked at Alex with absolute fear. "I can't do this. I have a family. He'll kill them. I can't do this."

Alex sat back down, his head spinning through all the details of the case. Carrie leaned onto the table now. "Mr. Johnson, are you backing out of the plea deal?"

"I won't say another word," Johnson said.

"You do understand that you lose everything we offered. You will be charged with much more serious crimes. Conspiracy to commit kidnapping, production of child pornography—"

"I don't care."

"That's a life sentence," she said.

"I don't care! I'm not saying another word."

Alex came back to the table and pointed at the picture of Roman Jonkovic. "Is this El Maestro?"

Johnson said nothing.

"Mark, is this El Maestro?" Alex tried again.

Johnson looked down at his attorney, who stood. "My client has decided against the proffer. He'll be answering no more questions."

"Then he'll be going back to jail until his trial," Carrie said.

Alex gathered up the pictures on the table, still wrapping his mind around what Johnson had said.

If Jonkovic wasn't El Maestro, then who was?

46.

THE TEACHER SAT IN HIS CAR STARING AT THE dark intersection ahead. The sniveling cockroach should be along soon. He checked his mirrors to make sure no one was around, and indeed the street was empty. That was one reason he'd chosen it. Nice and anonymous. Nearly abandoned.

In the trunk were all of his essentials for a nice long stay at the cabin. It pained him to be going alone, but he had no choice. He'd sold the boy. And Roman, his dear friend Roman, was dead. He'd tried to warn him. Meeting others face-to-face, no matter how small the group, was asking for trouble. And now he'd found it.

He laid his head back against the seat, pushing away the tears that threatened. Roman had made so many mistakes. Too many. Now it was time to tidy up. Mark would take longer. But he also had more to lose. If he was smart, he'd keep his mouth shut. But...Brian. Brian would be easy. He'd take his time with Brian.

He checked his watch. Any minute now. Stepping out of the car, he made his way down the darkened street. He turned into a yard at the end with an empty driveway, went up the stairs, and onto the porch. Off to the side was a large post barely holding up the roof of the porch. He reached into his pocket and felt the handle of his gun. He pulled it out and twisted on the silencer. Then he waited.

Within minutes, the small red car pulled up in front of the house. Footsteps approached. Thundered up the steps. Brian stepped into view carrying a pizza box. He never glanced sideways. As he reached a hand toward the door, the Teacher moved behind him.

"I think that can wait," he said.

Brian started and dropped the box. He turned around with wide, terrified eyes. "Who's there?"

The Teacher remained in the shadows. "You've been up to no good, Brian."

Brian backed up to the door. The full-blown terror on his face was an instant rush of adrenaline. He deserved every moment of his terror.

"Who's there?" he said again, louder this time.

The Teacher stepped a little closer, pointed the gun. "Don't you know me, Brian?"

He shook his head.

"El Maestro."

Brian turned and pounded on the door, screaming. It was beautiful. Like a perfect soprano solo that silenced an entire audience. The Teacher took one more step, and pulled the trigger. Brian dropped to his knees. He clutched his chest and fell onto the ground.

The Teacher straddled him. He lowered himself down to his knees, pressing the remaining air out of Brian's chest. Brian's face reddened as he struggled to breathe. The Teacher placed the gun on the floor and pulled out recently sharpened wire-cutting pliers. He grabbed Brian's hand and pressed it back against the wrist, splaying his fingers wide.

"You took Roman from me. Now I will take something from you."

Brian's eyes rolled.

"No, no," the Teacher said, slapping him across the face to keep him conscious. He placed the pliers just above the lowest knuckle of Brian's pointer finger. "This is for Roman." And he squeezed.

The pitiful cry that escaped Brian's lips was not nearly satisfying enough. So he took another. But that would have to do. The Teacher pushed himself up and reached for his gun again. Although he'd prefer to take more fingers and drown this worthless soul in his own blood, it was best to cut it short and leave. The street might have been mostly deserted, but he didn't want to take any more chances. He pointed the gun at Brian's forehead and pulled the trigger.

Part Four

The Fire

47.

CARRIE LEANED BACK AGAINST THE COUNTER of Alex's kitchen and watched him bend over to open the stove. Nice view. "How's it looking in there?"

"All done." He reached into the oven with a towel over his hands.

"So what are we having?"

"Oh, something very sophisticated." He straightened, holding the sizzling pizza. "I knew you'd be hard to impress."

She nearly spilled her drink from laughing. "That is one sophisticated-looking pizza. I'm definitely impressed. Did you put it in the oven all by yourself?"

Alex turned a mischievous grin in her direction. "Nah, my French maid put it in before she left." After sliding the pizza onto the counter, he took the baking sheet over to the sink, dropping it in with a clank.

"It's good to hear you laugh," she said.

He reached sideways, found her waist, and slid over in front of her. "It's nice to have a reason to."

"Johnson really threw a wrench into everything, didn't he?"

"He has nothing to do with us."

As Alex touched his forehead to hers, Carrie's heart sped up. "Alex, without a plea, that case could take months, maybe as much as a year. Maybe more."

"Craig led the search warrant for Johnson's house. I'll designate him as the case agent."

"You're still a witness. You'll have to testify."

He sighed. "So what are you saying? There's no chance for us?"

"I don't know. Do you really want to wait a year?"

He shook his head. "I can barely wait a minute."

Goosebumps skittered down Carrie's arms, making her realize she'd never felt so connected to her body. She'd shut down so long ago, but Alex made every cell within her come alive. She didn't want to wait either. His eyes took her in like he was starving, a feeling she shared. But what would it cost them to give in?

"Alex, do you really want to risk your job to be with me?"

He met her gaze and seemed to study her before answering. "No. And I don't want you to risk yours."

"Then what choice do we have?"

He wrapped his arms around her, and she buried her head in his chest. How wonderfully simple it was to let him touch her, to feel safe. Such a basic, carefree feeling. How could she walk away from this?

"What if you don't testify against Johnson?" she said, pulling her head back and looking up at him.

"Is that...even possible?"

"You make Craig the case agent. I'm the prosecutor. I can decide who testifies. The computer forensics report will speak for itself."

As Alex cupped her face and pressed his lips to hers, heat spread down her body like fire. No one would know. She could make this work. Case over. No testifying for Alex. They'd be free.

She let go of all her fear, and gave into his kiss completely. From somewhere far away, she heard a phone ring. Ignoring it, Alex pushed her mouth open with his. Her stomach dropped, then soared to life. Another ring.

"Is that you?" she asked between kisses.

Groaning, he pulled his phone out of its holster, checked the call screen, and tossed it onto the counter, then swept it aside as he lifted her up onto the surface. "I'll call him back." Then he slid between her legs and pulled her hips into his.

And she was under again, drowning in a flood of sensations she'd never felt before.

"Do I still make you nervous?"

"Very."

The phone rang again. This time Alex pulled back and sighed. He grabbed the phone and touched the screen to answer. "Hey, what's up, man?" He frowned. "Sure, he's mine. But I'm kind of in the middle of something—What? Are you sure?" Meeting Carrie's gaze briefly, he closed his eyes and pinched his nose. "Okay, I'll be down there first thing in the morning." He hung up the phone and stared at it.

"What's going on?"

He shook his head, dazed. "Brian Meeks is dead."

"What?"

"Cobb police found his body yesterday. He was shot."

Eyes wide, Carrie slid off the counter. "What does this mean?"

"It means Johnson was right to be afraid. El Maestro isn't dead."

"You're not going to turn the case over to Craig are you?"

After a moment's reflection, Alex pounded his fist on the counter. "I can't. This is my fault. I missed him. I missed the one bastard I was supposed to catch."

"You don't know that for sure. Meeks' murder could've been random."

"Carrie, I..." He turned and looked at her with tortured eyes. "I want to figure out a way to be together. I really do."

"But we can't."

"This case is my responsibility. I can't put that on someone else. And if we both agree we shouldn't risk our jobs, then I don't see how this works out."

Her stomach dropped again, but this time it left her feeling sick. Could she really walk away? How long would he wait for her?

Alex reached out and lifted her face until their eyes met. "You asked me if I wanted to risk my job to be with you. What if...what if I said yes?"

Maybe they could pull it off. Maybe no one would realize, if they were smart. But she'd spent so many years working her butt off to get to this job. If someone found out, she could lose everything.

The phone rang again. Alex stepped away and looked at the screen. "It's Tony."

"Look, you have a lot to take care of. I'll just let you do what you need to." She backed toward the hallway, feeling behind her for the entrance. "I'll call you tomorrow and get an update."

"You don't have to—"

"Yes, I do. You need to work. And so do I." She made her way to his front door as calmly as she could, when everything inside of her wanted to run out, screaming. Somehow she kept her composure, and with it, she ensured they'd both have a future.

48.

LEX FOUND DETECTIVE MICHAEL CROUSE AT his desk the following day, situated among a slew of identical desks on the second floor of the Smyrna police precinct. He was an older guy, graying around the edges but still pretty fit, and greeted Alex with a stern handshake and an immediate warning.

"Look, I don't play nice with feds." He plopped into his chair and leaned toward Alex, who took a seat opposite. "You guys always come swarming in and take over a case as if a lowly detective hasn't got the good sense to run a proper investigation. And I'll tell you right now; I already have some good leads I'm working on. I don't need a snot-nosed agent telling me how to run things."

Alex cleared his throat, weighing his words carefully. "I have no intention of taking over your case;

I just wanted to offer my assistance. Brian Meeks was my responsibility, and I let him down. I just want to do right by him."

Crouse studied him with a frown that didn't budge an inch. "And just what do you think you can offer in the way of help?"

"Meeks was my informant. I have reason to believe he was killed by the leader of a group of pedophiles I've been investigating. I thought we'd captured them all. Thought the leader was dead. But if I'm wrong, and he's killed Meeks—"

"Did you say pedophiles?"

Alex nodded. Crouse shook his head and muttered something under his breath. "I've had to deal with some unsavory sorts for informants before, but never a guy like that."

"Just part of the job."

Crouse lifted an eyebrow. "You investigate those cases often?"

"Yes, sir. It's about all I investigate."

"Was this guy Meeks one of the pedophiles?"

Alex leaned forward. "Yes, he was part of the group. But he got busted for drugs and when I gave him the chance to turn in his buddies, he took it."

"So who's this other guy? The leader? What do you know about him?"

Alex sighed. He'd been wondering the same thing. "Not as much as I thought, apparently. I know he goes by the moniker El Maestro online. That he's dangerous. And that he likes little boys."

Crouse picked up a pen on his desk and tapped it a few times. "I don't have a lot to go on yet, but we do have the number of the phone used to place the order for the pizza Meeks was delivering. It was a disposable phone, of course. But we were able to trace its purchase to a drug store a few miles from the scene. Now we're just waiting on the video from the store's security camera."

"Sounds like a promising start," Alex said. "What can I do to help?"

Crouse shrugged. "Maybe some background info on Meeks. Sounds like he was a dopehead with an affinity for kids. Bastard probably got what he deserved."

Alex's blood stirred. "That may be the case, but I promised him I'd do what I could to protect him. He hated what he was, and he was trying to do something right. I owe it to him to find out who killed him."

Alex was surprised by the turn his feelings had taken toward Meeks. He'd been avoiding thinking about it too much. How could he feel sorry for such a creep? Maybe Carrie was rubbing off on him.

"Hey, Crouse!" a short lady from the front of the overstuffed room hollered in their direction. She held up a packing envelope over her head. "You got a delivery!"

Crouse pushed himself up and motioned for Alex to follow. "Must be the security footage."

Alex followed the detective over to the woman with the package, and then down the hall into an interview room with a DVD player. Crouse slid in the disc and eyed Alex with barely muted distaste. "Not as sophisticated as the equipment you're used to, I'm sure."

"It'll do just fine," Alex said.

Crouse pressed a button on a remote and the footage sped up. The silence in the room grew thicker as Alex shifted his weight between his feet. He was used to tension between himself and other agents, but he remembered Nicole's warning after his encounter with Agent Sparks of the DEA, and he was determined to keep this bridge firmly in tact.

"Here we go," Crouse said. He pointed at the screen where he'd paused the video. He let out a puff of air and shook his head. "Figures."

Alex looked at the fuzzy man on the screen, only able to make out a light-colored trench coat and dark fuzzy hair peeking out from under a baseball hat. "What is it?"

"That's Chuck." Crouse crossed his arms over his chest. "He ain't your guy. Chuck's as harmless as a gnat. He hangs around that area of town looking for handouts."

"Homeless?"

"Appears that way, but I've never run him through the system. Never needed to."

"Well, let's go talk to him."

Crouse's eyebrows shot up. "Yeah," Crouse said. "Let's do that. You can fill me in on the details of your case while I drive."

"You sure you can handle it?"

Crouse practically growled at him. Alex imagined he'd shove a finger into his chest and cuss him out given the opportunity. "Of course. I ain't no pussycat."

49.

"HERE HE IS." AFTER CIRCLING A THREE-block radius for about twenty minutes, Crouse finally stopped the car on a small street next to the Smyrna Memorial Cemetery. Following Crouse's pointed finger, Alex saw the same tan trench coat draped over what could have easily been a sack of garbage on a bench beneath a large tree.

Crouse turned off the engine. "He sleeps here sometimes. Talks to the dead, from what I hear."

Alex wasn't sure what to say to that, so he just followed Crouse's lead and got out of the car. They crossed over to the front entrance of the cemetery and made their way toward the center where they'd spotted Chuck. As he neared the bench, Alex could see he was asleep, his head rolled to the side. His hat was draped over his face to block the sun.

Crouse stopped a couple of feet in front of the snoring man and bellowed, "Afternoon, Chuck!"

Chuck jerked awake and grabbed at his hat as it fell off his face. Alex kept his mouth shut, though he thought the tactic was a bit cruel. If Crouse knew this guy, it was better to let him ask the questions.

Chuck squinted up at them through foggy eyes and set his hat back on his head. "I reckon you come to tell me to move along." He began pulling himself together, straightening his coat and picking up a paper sack next to his feet.

"Nah, Chuck. I just need to ask you a few questions is all. You can stay where you are."

Chuck settled back against the bench. Then he pointed up at Alex. "Who's he?"

"That's my good friend, Agent Walker. He's helping me solve a case you might know something about. You mind if we talk for a bit?"

"No, I reckon we can talk." Chuck scratched his long beard with blackened fingernails.

"You remember someone giving you some money a few days ago to go into the store and buy a phone for them?"

Chuck scratched his beard some more. "A phone?"

Crouse clinched his jaw. Then he made a visible effort to relax it. "Yes. A phone. Did someone give you money to go into the CVS and buy them a phone?"

"I can't rightly remember."

Alex could hardly stand it another minute. It was all he could do to keep his voice steady. "Is there anything that might help you remember?"

A smile filled with yellowed teeth spread over Chuck's face. "I reckon a man thinks much better on a full stomach than he does on an empty one."

Alex glanced at Crouse, who rolled his eyes. "All right then. Come on. We'll get you something to eat, and you can answer our questions."

Chuck looked almost spry as he jumped up from the bench. "Ken's place is just right over yonder. They got a mean steak sandwich. I like it with extra onions, and then some of those big ole onion rings."

The vagrant kept up an enthusiastic culinary monologue as Alex and Crouse fell into step behind him. They headed out of the cemetery and across the street again. Chuck stopped in the middle of the road to turn back and ask them which vehicle he was riding in. Crouse shouted and pointed out the car.

The small diner was barely two turns away from the cemetery, but Chuck filled all three minutes with further verbal anticipation of his lunch order. And he wasn't kidding. He went through the front door, climbed onto a stool at the bar, and called over the waitress by name.

"Hey, Miss Maddie! You making me a steak sandwich today? I'm getting me a steak sandwich! You know how I like my sandwich, right? Lots of mayo. Throw on some fresh onion rings too. I don't want any you got sitting around, now. I want fresh onion rings out of the fryer. And a big sweet tea."

Alex and Crouse slid onto stools on opposite sides of Chuck. The waitress, an older woman whose nametag indeed read Maddie, raised an eyebrow at Alex. "Give him whatever he likes. I'll cover it."

Maddie walked over in front of them and leaned onto the counter, her large breasts barely contained in her shirt. "What can I get you two?"

Alex nodded toward Chuck. "Sounds like you have a killer steak sandwich. I'll give that a go."

"I'll have one too," Crouse said.

Maddie placed the order, and a skinny man with a hairnet threw some meat on a grill on the other side of the bar. Alex wanted to ask Chuck more questions, but it was clear he was mesmerized by the sizzling heaven just feet away. It gave Alex a few moments to take in the whole picture.

Chuck was clearly homeless, but not a stranger to helping hands. He didn't seem malnourished. So what was his deal? A mental case? Too lazy to work? Carrie's voice broke into his thoughts. *Everyone's broken in some way. Don't we all deserve a little bit of compassion?*

The thought of Carrie made his chest ache. The look on her face the night before had spoken volumes, and she'd practically run out of his house before he could clear things up. But what would he have said? He had to see this case through.

Maddie shoved a plate in front of him, pulling him back to the task at hand. He took a bite of the steak sandwich. Not bad. Beside him, Chuck chomped down on his sandwich and onion rings. Alex waited a few moments, and enjoyed a few more bites of his own sandwich before attempting any questions.

"All right, Chuck," Crouse said. "You got your lunch. Now tell us what you remember about buying that phone."

Alex nearly gagged as Chuck licked his filthy fingers and turned to Crouse. "He gave me a few bucks and told me to buy him a phone."

"Did he tell you his name?" Alex asked, knowing the answer, but hoping for a miracle.

"Nah, no name. Just said he needed a phone and he'd pay me to go get him one."

"You didn't think that was odd?" Crouse asked.

"Sure. Didn't care."

"What did he look like?" Alex asked.

Chuck took another bite of his sandwich, savoring it long enough to drive Alex nuts. Then he licked his fingers again. "Kinda average, I reckon. He had on sunglasses, so I didn't see his eyes."

Alex caught Crouse's gaze and knew they were thinking the same thing. They weren't going to get anything useful out of this guy.

"What about his car?" Alex asked. "Did you see his car?"

"Sure. He had a dark car."

Well that narrows things down, Alex thought. "What kind of car?"

"Some kinda sedan. It was black. Looked like the kind of car a rich guy would drive. Mercedes or Cadillac or something. Always wanted me a Cadillac."

"I don't suppose you remember seeing the tag?"

"Nope." Chuck took another huge bite and chased it down with some onion rings.

Alex caught Crouse's attention again and motioned to follow him to the parking lot. "This is getting us nowhere," he said, as he reached Crouse's car.

Crouse leaned onto the hood. "I agree. Looks like a dead end. I mean, we can check the businesses near CVS and see if any of them have security cameras pointed toward the street. But that's about it."

"All right. I'll go take care of Chuck's lunch and we can get started on that." As Alex walked back across the parking lot, his phone rang. It was Carrie. His heart sped up a notch.

"Hey," he said.

"Johnson wants to talk," she said.

He'd been expecting something else entirely, so it took a moment for her words to register. "What?"

"I got a call from Johnson's attorney. Apparently his wife got a threatening message, and now Johnson wants to talk with us."

"When?"

"Can you be at the courthouse at three?"

"Sure."

"Great. We'll meet in the conference room where we prepped for the Williams trial."

Alex paused, wondering if she'd say anything about last night. But the line remained silent. "Carrie—"

"See you then." And she hung up.

50.

ALEX STOLE A GLANCE AT CARRIE AS THEY waited for Johnson and his attorney. She tapped a pen on her blank notebook, focusing solely on the conference room door. She'd barely made eye contact when he'd greeted her, and they'd sat silently at the table now for nearly ten minutes. She had to know this was torturing him.

"Stop it," Carrie said, still staring at the door.

"Stop what?"

"Stop looking at me."

He touched the back of her hand, but she pulled it away. He needed to reason with her. "Maybe if you'd talk to me we could put all this tension to rest."

She let out a sigh, her shoulders sagging. "Not now."

Alex shoved his emotions away for the time being. If she was determined to shut him out, then there was nothing he could do. But he couldn't just sit there in silence. "Any idea what this meeting is about?"

She shook her head. "Mr. Whitfield said only that there's been a new development, and his client wants to talk."

"Maybe we can finally get something useful on El Maestro and get this case moving."

The door swung open and Mr. Whitfield walked in ahead of a US marshal, followed by Johnson in an orange jumpsuit and handcuffs, and finally another marshal. Right away, Alex was struck by the change in Johnson in just a few short days. His eyes were framed in dark circles, and his skin seemed to sag from his bones. His mouth was drawn tight, and he never looked up from the floor.

The marshals walked him over to the table, and Alex stood to shake their hands. The large one on the right spoke first. "You Agent Walker?"

"I am."

"Let us know when you're finished here. Till then, he's in your custody." The marshals exited the room and closed the door behind them.

Johnson stood before them with his hands resting against his handcuffs. He studied the floor. Mr. Whitfield stepped forward and offered his hand to Carrie and Alex. "I thank you both for seeing us so quickly. I'm afraid things have taken a rather awful turn."

"Take a seat," Carrie said. "Fill me in."

Alex watched Johnson closely. He'd looked beaten down before, but nothing like this. What could've happened? Had he been raped? He couldn't help the part of him that was sure whatever had happened to him, the pervert deserved it. And if it made him more willing to cooperate, all the better.

"My client would like to know if the previous offer is still on the table," Mr. Whitfield said.

"That depends on what information he can provide," Carrie answered. "If he can give us something useful to track down El Maestro, we'll honor our original deal."

Mr. Whitfield wiped the sweat from his brow and glanced at Johnson, whose gaze remained at floor level. "What about witness protection?"

Alex shifted his attention to Mr. Whitfield. "What? He's in the federal section of the prison. He doesn't get any more protected than that." He looked back at Johnson. "Let me guess, some buddies of yours got too friendly?"

Johnson jerked his eyes up to Alex. "You don't know what the hell you're talking about."

Mr. Whitfield placed a hand on Johnson's arm. "Listen, I can explain what's happened. The protection is for Mrs. Johnson and her two girls."

"Can they testify to anything?" Alex asked.

"I would be the only one testifying," Johnson said. "If the bastard wants to come after me, let him. But not my girls."

Carrie's face softened. "Look, I know you're worried about their safety, but you have to understand how witness protection works. If you can give us definitive testimony that is instrumental in the case, and your life is truly in danger, then we can petition the Marshals for protection. But I would first have to hear what evidence you can offer."

Johnson turned to his attorney with pleading eyes. "Just tell them what happened. I can't."

As Mr. Whitfield cleared his throat, Johnson dropped his head and slumped forward, resting his weight on his knees. "Last night, about eight o'clock, three men broke into Mr. Johnson's home, took his wife from the residence, leaving the two girls there alone. They took Mrs. Johnson to an empty parking lot, she's not sure where, and proceeded to rape her multiple times."

Alex shot a glance at Carrie. Her face had completely drained of color. "What about the girls?" she said.

"When the men brought Mrs. Johnson home, the girls were huddled together on their bed upstairs. They weren't hurt, but they were understandably terrified. The men gave Mrs. Johnson a message: 'Tell your husband to keep his mouth shut, or the kids are next.'"

The room was so silent Alex could hear his own heart thudding against his chest. "Mark, tell us what you know."

Johnson shook his head. "Promise me—"

Alex slammed his hand onto the table. "We can't promise you anything! Tell us what you know, and if we can protect your family, we will."

"I'm not sure!" Johnson wailed. "I never saw his face. I only overheard Roman on the phone with him a couple of times. There are rumors on all the dark net websites, but I'm not sure which are true or just legend. He's practically a ghost!"

"So you're telling me you can't even identify him?" Alex struggled to keep his voice even. Johnson shook his head. Alex pushed himself up from his chair and leaned across the table onto his fists. "You have nothing. We can't offer you or your family protection when you have nothing to offer in return. So congratulations—you've not only endangered the lives of countless children because of your sick behavior, now you've put your own kids in danger as well. Tell me, Mark, do you not see the irony in your situation?"

Johnson bore his gaze into Alex's, but he didn't say a word. Probably because the bastard knew he was right.

"You think it's somehow different when it's your own daughter sitting on some pervert's lap?" Alex continued. "Drugged so she doesn't squirm too much, but still lucid enough to cry and beg the man to stop hurting her?"

"Alex." Carrie's soft voice broke through his anger. He sat back down.

"Mr. Johnson is prepared to give as much information as he possibly can," Mr. Whitfield said. "We understand you'll do your very best to protect the family." Then he turned toward Johnson. "Mark, just tell them what you know. That's all you can do."

Johnson leaned back against his chair and wiped his hands across his face. "I know he's not from the US. He's not Russian, but something similar."

"I thought that was Jonkovic," Alex said.

"They came from the same country. They were close friends. Grew up together or something. Anyway, I never saw his face. I don't think many people have, at least not those of us who know him as El Maestro. He's wealthy; I know that. Travels quite a bit. I've heard that he dreams of being a famous author someday. He's already published a couple of books using a pen name."

"Do you know the pen name?" Carrie asked.

"No."

Alex pinched his nose. "So once again, you basically know nothing. Just some possible rumors."

"The pen name is something weird. Like a musical name or something. I want to say the first part is Treble, or something like that."

"Any idea what the books are about?" Carrie asked.

"Novels, for kids I think. But the word on the web was that he was aiming to start a whole new genre for kids, and adults like...like us."

Alex's stomach turned. "You mean like a pedophile genre? And someone published these books?"

"I don't think they're explicit. You have to read between the lines. There are a lot of books out there already that blur the lines. You just have to know what to look for."

"And I'm sure you do," Alex muttered. He realized he'd been feeling gentle pressure on his knee. When he looked down, he saw Carrie's hand. He covered it with his own.

"Mr. Johnson," she said. "Do you have anything else we can work with?"

He shook his head.

"Then I'm afraid it's not enough. I'll honor the agreement we offered before. That's the best I can do. Believe me, I wish I could do more. Your girls deserve better. Honestly, they deserve better than you."

Alex felt a surge of pride. He wanted to high-five her right there. She released his hand and gathered her things as she stood. "Mr. Johnson, does your wife have anywhere safe she can go with the girls?"

"She's already gone. Took them to her parents' house in Virginia. Says she don't ever want to see my face again."

Alex stood beside Carrie and crossed his arms over his chest. "I think that's probably best for all of them, don't you agree?"

Johnson dropped his head again, this time unable to hold back his sobs. Alex took small comfort in his pain. With any luck, his kids would be grown women before they ever saw him again, capable of understanding all that had happened around them.

But where did that leave his case? He was no closer to tracking down El Maestro than he'd been after interviewing Chuck. The pen name was barely a lead, and the chances of it panning out were about as good as winning the lottery. Something was going to have to break soon.

51.

"CARRIE, WAIT!"

She kept her feet moving, pretending not to hear Alex calling her name. Moving quickly along the row of cars in the parking deck, she hoped she'd reach hers before he caught up. It had been hard enough to be so close to him in the conference room, but being alone with him would be too much.

She hit the unlock button on her key fob as she neared the vehicle, but the footsteps were coming up close behind her. She was too slow. Or he was too fast. Either way, she was going to have to face him. So she turned to him just as she reached her car, her heart skipping a beat at the sight of him closing the distance between them.

"Did you not hear me calling you?" Alex's eyes blazed with frustration.

"I'm sorry. I heard you. I just...I didn't know what to say."

"So you decided to run away?"

The rise and fall of his chest just beneath his shirt drew her gaze. She had to make this stop somehow. "Look, we have to work together. I have to be able to do my job without any distractions." Her eyes traveled over his chest. "And all this tension between us is definitely a distraction."

"Look, let's just go somewhere and talk. If we just slow down and talk this out—"

"Alex, there's no more talking to do right now."

"Come on, we at least need to talk about what happened in there. We need to come up with a plan to move forward on this case."

"No." Carrie shook her head, forcing herself to stay strong. "It's your job to go out and gather the evidence. You make the case. I try it. That's it. Yes, there's some overlap, but if you do your job, and I do mine, we can minimize the overlap."

He moved closer, resting his hand on her hip. "Is that what you really want?"

She felt a blush creep over her cheeks. What did she want? Her job, or Alex? Could she have both?

"It doesn't matter what I want!" She managed to look up into his eyes, but that just made her ache for his kiss. She looked back down and gripped her hands together, rubbing her thumb over her palm, soothing the tension building in her body.

"Just turn the case over to Frank. He can finish this."

She stepped away from him and willed herself to stay calm. "And just how would that look to my boss? Like I can't handle a tough trial? In case you haven't noticed, I've worked my butt off to make sure this case is airtight and these sick, twisted men are brought to justice. I am not about to just hand it over to Frank!"

Alex put his hands up, and his mouth tipped into a grin. She couldn't believe he thought this was funny. When he reached for her again, she took another step back. "I'm serious, Alex."

He dropped his hands. "Okay, I get it. And you're right. You've worked your ass off, and you deserve to see it all the way through. So is this it then? You kicking me to the curb?"

Good Lord, did he have to make this so hard? "I thought you agreed with me last night that we weren't going to risk our jobs? Come on. One of us has got to be sensible here."

He nodded, looking around the garage. Other people were beginning to make their way to their cars. It was time to cut this short before someone in her office walked by. "All right then. I won't say anything else about it. Nothing but professional from me from now on. I promise."

He met her gaze, and it felt like his eyes would turn her inside out. The finality in his words stung more than she'd expected. And before she could say anything else, he turned and walked away.

Carrie thought her chest might explode, like it was desperately pulling her to follow him. But this was what she wanted, right? *Right?*

52.

ALEX TOSSED TWO BOOKS ONTO TONY'S DESK and dropped into a chair beside him, leaning it back on two legs and resting his hands behind his head. "I don't think I've ever seen a suspect so untraceable," he said.

Tony picked up the books and turned them over in his hands. "I was sure finding the books was going to be a huge break."

"Me too. I can't tell you how many musical books I had to skim through before I realized it was author's name I should be searching. I tell you, Amazon's search engine is amazing, but the info they sent me was a dead end. Fake name. Fake social security number."

"What about a bank account? I always say follow the money."

Alex shook his head. "The royalties go to a bank in the Caymans, and they don't want to play nice."

"Email?"

"Google sent me the same phony name. And every time the email is accessed, it's from an IP address masked by an onion router."

Tony's eyebrows shot up. "Damn."

"Yeah." Alex dropped his chair back level to the floor. "This guy's good. Like I said. Never seen a suspect able to hide himself with absolutely no missteps."

Tony surveyed the books in his hands. "You read either of these yet?"

"I read the children's book. Skimmed the novel. I can see what Johnson meant by reading between the lines. Given the right lens to look through, that kid's book is an outright grooming tool."

"What's it about?"

"A baby lion that's lost and alone, and some grown lion takes him in and teaches him it's okay to be different from all the other lions. Blah, blah, blah."

Despite his grim mood, Tony grinned. "So unrealistic. Everyone knows male lions kill cubs that aren't their own. Should've picked a seahorse or something. Don't they carry their babies around in a little pouch? Much more believable."

Alex laughed. "You should leave a review."

"What about this other one?" Tony held the young adult novel in his hand. "I guess the picture of the author on the back isn't real either?"

"That one's a little more clear in its intent. Seems to be about a teenage boy who's experimenting with his sexual preferences. Surprise, surprise, there's an older gentleman who points him in the *right* direction."

Suppressing a shudder, Tony handed the books back to Alex. "So what now?"

"Well, that's where you come in. Forensics is still sifting through all the phone data we got from each of the group members, including Meeks. But finding any matches that lead to our guy could take weeks, maybe months. So I emailed the author of the books from my undercover account."

"I thought the email address was a dead end?"

"Getting his true identity was, but I emailed him as a fan of the books. Told him I have a nephew who loved them, how much they meant to me as well. Stroked the ego like crazy."

"Please, do *not* use the word stroked." Tony chuckled, and Alex couldn't help but laugh too.

"Anyway, I told him how *amazing* it was that we live in the same city and asked the guy to meet me and my nephew for lunch so we could talk and he could sign my books. Doubt it'll go anywhere, but just in case it does, I'd like you to take over as the case agent of record so I can work the undercover angle."

Tony didn't respond immediately. In fact, he looked skeptical. He rubbed his brow for a moment before responding. "Alex, this means you're putting me in charge of the decisions for this case. I won't take over as case agent unless I'm really in charge."

"Right. So?"

"So, you're not exactly a follower. You really want me calling the shots? Especially a case you've put so much time and energy into already?"

"I trust you, man. No worries."

Tony still didn't look convinced, and Alex had to admit he wasn't sure about turning over the reins of his case. But he was out of options, and he couldn't ask anyone else to put himself in harm's way if he wasn't willing to do it himself. Going undercover was the only way, and rules dictated he couldn't be the case agent and the undercover agent at the same time. He had to make a choice.

"All right," Tony said. "I'll do it."

Alex blew out a deep breath and looked down at the books in his hands. For all he knew, this author might not even be El Maestro. He'd been so convinced he'd wrapped the whole case up. Had that only been a little over a week ago? Now he wasn't sure of anything.

"You all right?" Tony asked.

"Yeah, sure. Just need to catch a break. Every time I think I'm close to getting this guy, I hit another dead end."

"Is that all?" Tony's brow furrowed in concern.

"What do you mean?"

"What's going on with you and Carrie?"

"Nothing." The truth of that statement hurt more than he'd have liked it to. Every day for the past week had been a battle to keep from reaching out to her.

"Look, I know I messed with you before about it, but seriously, be careful. I don't need to tell you what can happen."

"Like I said, nothing's going on." Tony lifted an eyebrow, but he didn't press any further. Alex took the opportunity to end the conversation before he said more than he should. He stood and clapped Tony on the shoulder. "Thanks for your help. I'll let you know if I hear back from our guy."

"Sure thing. You want to grab a drink after work?"

Alex paused, not really feeling up to going out. But it had been a while since they'd hung out, and maybe that was just what he needed to forget about all the failures of the week. And especially to forget about Carrie. "Sure," he said. "I'll catch you later."

53.

THE TEACHER READ OVER THE EMAIL MES-
SAGE for the fourth time in two days. He'd
received a few fan emails before, and the sen-
timents expressed in the email weren't that unusual—many young men had reached out to him for
guidance—but the timing bothered him. If somehow the cops had tracked down his books, if Brian
or Mark had talked, this could be a trap.

The chair beneath him squeaked as he leaned
back and pondered his response, if any, to the request to meet with the fan and his young nephew.
He glanced around the quiet office, feeling the
boy's absence so deeply he ached. And of course he
missed Roman. The only person who'd ever truly
known him and loved him for exactly who he was,
was gone. It would be nice to talk to someone
again. It would be nice to feel adored.

But he had to keep his emotions in check. He couldn't afford any mistakes, especially right now. He sat forward and clicked on the reply button.

Dear Alex,
Thank you so much for the kind letter and request. I'm humbled by your praise. Although I would love to meet you and your nephew, I'm afraid I must decline for now. I'm simply too busy. Please give my regards to your nephew, and let him know I appreciate his enthusiasm for the story. I would be happy to mail you both signed copies of my books if you'll provide me with an address.
Kindest Regards,
Trebal Aknev

The Teacher stood from his chair and left the room to stretch his legs for a bit. He refilled his wine glass, pressed play on the remote for his audio system, and stepped out into the crisp night air. Bach drifted out of the house and onto the breeze. The deck just off the kitchen had a spectacular view of his secluded corner of Lake Allatoona. Though it was an enormous lake, with more tiny alcoves and branches than he could ever count, his house was situated in a cozy curve, almost like a cul-de-sac of a neighborhood.

He lowered himself onto the plush cushion of his lounge chair and sipped his wine. On nights like this, when the air was clear, the stars shone on the top of the water like tiny twinkling diamonds. The crickets had quieted with the onset of colder weather, but it was still peaceful to sit on the deck and enjoy the nightly sounds.

Of course, it had been so much better with the boy snuggled close beneath a blanket with him. He closed his eyes and reimagined those nights, glossing over the awkward early days when the boy was uncomfortable. He'd been so malleable. The memories warmed him, but they also made him wonder if he shouldn't have given the earlier email more thought. Brian was silenced. No doubt Mark had received his message. If the cops knew who he was, or anything about him, they'd have shown up at his door already.

A shiver ran through him, and he decided to return to the warmth of his home. Crossing the living room, he stopped in front of the fireplace to warm his hands. The music soothed his ache for his companion, but he couldn't shake it completely. He headed back into his office and sat down at his desk, pulling up the email once again.

There was a reply. His breath caught as he opened it.

Dear Mr. Aknev,

I completely understand that you're busy. I imagine you have fans writing you every day, gushing over your work. Of course I would love signed copies of the books. They've meant so much to me. Sometimes I feel so alone, and to know that others out there understand what I'm going through is enough to keep me going. If you ever find that you have the time to get together and share your wisdom, please let me know. It would be the greatest pleasure to meet you and thank you in person.

Sincerely,

Alex Bishop

Letting out his breath in a slow whistle, the Teacher read the message again. His words had reached someone. They'd touched this young man. He closed his eyes and imagined what he might look like, feeling an unexpected warmth spreading throughout his body. A simple lunch in a public place couldn't do any harm. He'd take precautions. He'd check out the situation before showing himself.

A quick check of the email address Alex had used sent off no alarms. Though he didn't have Roman's expertise in manipulating digital information, he knew enough to keep himself out of trouble and well-hidden. This Alex Bishop sounded interesting.

Yes. A quick lunch would tell him everything he needed to know. No cop would bring a minor into an investigation. If the guy made an excuse for his nephew not coming, or if he showed up alone...He'd have a plan in place.

54.

"I DON'T LIKE THIS, ALEX. WE CAN'T CONTROL this setting the way I'd prefer."

Alex met Tony's gaze and remembered his many promises to follow Tony's lead during the undercover operation. He straightened his shirt, making sure the camera button was situated correctly. "Look, he chose the location, and I didn't want to run the risk of him backing out."

Tony glanced over at Richards in the front seat of the van. "Everything look good? Audio? Video?"

Richards gave him a thumbs up. "He's good."

Then Tony turned to the agent seated beside Alex. "You ready to go?"

Chris Duncan nodded. "Absolutely." He'd only flown into town that morning, and his briefing had been short and sweet. He seemed to catch on quickly as to what was needed, but Alex was still skeptical. He'd sent a request to the National Undercover Coordinator for a male as young-looking as possible, and Chris did indeed look young. Hell, he might be able to pass for fourteen. But would it be enough? He had no idea what El Maestro's age of attraction was. Too late for second-guessing, though. They'd just have to make it work.

Tony bent down into Alex's line of sight. "I want to make sure we're clear. You do not try to go anywhere alone with this guy."

"Don't talk to me like a kid," Alex said. "I know what I'm doing." He pointed at Chris. "He's the one who's supposed to be a kid. Talk to him like that."

"You put me in charge, so I'm going to take every chance I get to boss you around. In fact, I'm making an executive decision to do the traffic stop on this guy once he leaves the restaurant."

"Good call," Alex said. They'd gone back and forth all day on whether a traffic stop would raise Aknev's suspicions.

"We have eyes on the target entering the restaurant," Richards called from the front of the van.

"Let's go," Alex said. He stepped out of the back of the van and waited for Chris to join him. Then he gave Tony a fist bump. "If I'm not back in five minutes, just wait longer."

Tony shook his head and laughed. "Seriously, new material. Get some."

Alex drove across the street and found a spot in the crowded parking lot of the strip mall near the café Aknev had suggested. He noted the unmarked car just a few rows away from the entrance where Craig and Carl sat ready to back them up if needed.

He glanced over at Chris beside him. "Ready?"

Chris put his baseball cap on. "Let's do it."

They exited the vehicle and headed into the café. Alex took a quick look around. Agent Tripp and another female agent from the drug group had volunteered to pose as diners, and Alex made eye contact with them seated in a booth to his right.

Then he looked to his left and saw an older gentleman approaching him with his hand extended. "You must be Mr. Bishop. I'm Trebal Aknev."

Alex shook his hand and took a long first look at the man who'd eluded him for so long. He was a couple of inches shorter than Alex, and like Jonkovic, appeared to be in good shape. His expensive suit fit him perfectly, accentuating his broad shoulders. And his handshake was firm, something Alex hadn't expected. This man, with his graying dark hair and open smile, looked nothing like the pedophiles Alex had ever arrested. He looked sophisticated, refined. Could he have the wrong guy?

"It's great to finally meet you," Alex said. He put his hand on Chris's back. "This is my nephew, Chris. He's a huge fan."

Aknev shook Chris's hand as well. "Nice to meet you also. Shall we take a seat?"

"Of course," Alex said. He followed Aknev over to a booth opposite the front windows. Aknev gestured for Alex and Chris to take the seat with its back to the front door, setting Alex's nerves on edge. He always faced the door. Always.

"Will this do?" Aknev asked.

Alex slid into the booth, followed by Chris. "It's perfect." He looked around the cafe as Aknev took his seat. The limited view made him uncomfortable, but he plastered on a smile. "I know you're a very busy man, so I wanted to thank you for taking the time to meet with us."

Aknev studied Chris for a moment. "How old are you, son?"

"Fourteen," Chris said in a slightly higher voice than he'd been using in the van. He tugged on his baseball cap and grinned shyly.

Nice, Alex thought. *He might pull this off after all.*

"And what did you like about the book?" Aknev continued.

Chris shrugged. "I don't know. I just felt like I could identify with Jamie. He seemed a lot like me."

Aknev glanced over at Alex, his eyebrows arched with curiosity. "And how about you? Anything in particular you enjoyed?"

Alex put on the most gushing smile he could. "Oh, I loved Jamie's story. I think we've all felt a little lost in a world that doesn't quite understand us. When he leaves home, the scene where he turns and looks back, that really got to me. I left home when I was a young teen too. The conflict inside of Jamie really resonated with me."

Aknev smiled, his eyes bright and friendly. "Well, I'm so pleased to know my words touched you." He paused over the word *touched*, just enough to emphasize it. Then he reached into the briefcase that had been tucked into his side of the booth the whole time. Alex mentally berated himself for not noticing it right away.

Aknev pulled out a copy of each of his books, crisp new copies, and passed them across the table. "Here you go. Both signed and dedicated to my loyal fans."

Alex and Chris took the books, and Chris turned his over in his hands. "Wow! I've never had a signed copy of a book before. Thank you so much, Mr. Aknev."

Alex beamed at Chris, barely having to pretend to be proud of him. The guy was good. Alex could almost forget he was a grown man. "I told you Mr. Aknev would be amazing, didn't I?"

Chris's smile lit up his whole face. "Can I go call my friend, James, and tell him about this?"

"Now, don't be rude," Alex scolded. "We came to see Mr. Aknev, not talk on the phone with your friends."

"Oh, let the boy make his call," Aknev said, chuckling.

"All right," Alex relented. "But tell me what to order for you."

Chris asked for a cheeseburger and fries before darting out the front door with his phone to his ear. Alex watched the door close behind him. He couldn't have been more pleased. Perfect execution. He turned back to Aknev with a huge smile. "Such a great kid."

"I can see that. You seem very close."

"Oh yes. Ever since he was little." Alex paused for effect. "It's a shame he has to grow up. He was such a beautiful little boy."

Alex watched for Aknev's reaction. His expression didn't change, remaining pleasant and friendly. "Well, I don't have any children of my own, but they are precious. I have some beautiful nephews...and nieces, of my own."

A waitress came to take their order, and Chris returned to the table shortly afterward. The conversation drifted from one meaningless topic to the next, with Aknev skillfully answering every one of Alex's questions with vague, unverifiable information. He'd come to America as a child from the Czech Republic, had grown up in the northeast with parents who had more money than anyone would ever need, and run away from home as a teenager because his father wanted him to be someone he couldn't be.

By the time they'd finished their meal, Alex felt he'd accomplished very little. Sure, they would have images of him from his button camera, but he'd learned nothing new about this mysterious man. If it weren't for the certainty in his gut that the man across the table from him was El Maestro, he'd probably just chalk him up as a friendly guy who'd written a coming-of-age story based on his own life. Nothing about him seemed dangerous.

"Well," Aknev said, gathering his things. "I must be going now. It was a pleasure to have met you both."

Chris slid out of the booth, followed by Alex. They all looked at each other for an awkward moment, and Alex racked his brain for a way to arrange another meeting. "Chris, why don't you go on out to the car, and I'll be right behind you."

Chris shrugged. "Okay. See ya!"

As Alex held the front door open for Aknev, he decided to just go for it. "Listen, Mr. Aknev, I really appreciate this. I can't tell you how much it meant to me and Chris." The door closed behind them. "I know this may seem forward, but I would love to get together again sometime. I've never found anyone else who actually understands me...you know?"

Aknev put his sunglasses on and smiled. "Alex, you seem very nice. I understand what you're going through. But I'm a very private person, and I don't spend much time socializing. I prefer to keep to myself. I hope you'll forgive me if it seems rude, but I'll have to pass this time."

Damn. This was not working out as he'd hoped. "I'm sorry to have imposed on you. I hope you write more books."

Aknev reached for Alex's hand and shook it, this time holding it for a moment. "You take care."

Then he turned and headed down the sidewalk. Alex watched him for a bit, but not too long. The other agents would have him in sight now. Maybe he didn't get a second date, but he'd finally made contact. And while they'd been enjoying a nice lunch, agents had already run his tags and found every bit of dirt on this guy possible. Before long, he'd have this guy locked away for life.

Alex headed across the parking lot to his car and climbed inside. Chris was waiting on him.

"That was a great job," Alex said. "I appreciate you flying out, reading that book, and catching on so quick."

"No problem," Chris said. "Creepy subject. So what's next?"

Alex backed out of the parking spot. "Traffic stop to get his information. Another email in a few days to see if he'll change his mind about getting together. I still don't have the evidence for a search warrant. But hopefully the traffic stop will be a huge step in the right direction."

Alex's phone buzzed. It was Craig. "What's up?" Alex asked.

"Someone's following you. Maybe."

"Maybe?"

"Could just be a random person who left right after you. But it was a black Mazda. I got the plates. Keep your eyes peeled."

"Will do. What about Aknev? Who's tailing him?"

"Garza. Looks like he's heading north. Cobb County's going to set up a checkpoint. We should have his license info within the next half hour."

"Okay. I'm going to drive around for a bit to see if I'm being followed. Meet you back at the office."

He hung up and glanced in his rearview mirror. Traffic on Cobb Parkway was heavy. There were no less than twenty cars behind, close enough to be following him. He made a left at the next intersection. Glancing back, he saw a black car make the turn as well.

"Well, we might have picked up a tail at lunch," Alex said.

"Guess we didn't convince Aknev," Chris said.

"No telling for sure without blowing my cover. We'll just drive around for a while and keep an eye on our backside."

55.

"GIVE IT ANOTHER THIRTY MINUTES," THE Teacher said into the phone as he headed north on Highway 5. "If he doesn't go anywhere interesting, then you can call it quits."

The insufferable idiot on the other end hung up. Garrett would never have needed such hand-holding. But he'd been needed to take care of other loose ends, and so Mush-For-Brains had been his only other option. The Teacher hadn't even bothered learning his name. Garrett would mind all the trivial matters in that area. He found that the less he knew of the men who worked under Garrett, the better off he was.

He removed his earpiece, preferring to think about the pleasant lunch he'd just had. And if Mush was correct, maybe this Alex Bishop person would be interesting to spend some time with. He'd barely taken note of the nephew once he'd realized that little detail had not been a ruse.

Something stirred within him, a memory. He'd once been a young man figuring out how all the pieces of himself could fit into the person in the mirror. He hadn't wanted to be just *one* thing, just *one* person, defined simply by whom he loved, and how he loved. He'd worked his whole life to become so much more—teacher, author, companion, mentor, and even friend. He thought of Roman, of all they'd shared growing up together, and he ached for that connection again. Could Alex be just what he needed?

Red and blue lights ahead of him snapped his thoughts back to the present. Three cars had stopped already, and the one in front of him slowed as well. The hairs on the back of his neck stood to attention, and he checked the middle console for his pistol. What could this be about?

He eased his car forward as the officers walked to each window and spoke with the drivers. Licenses were passed out the windows, and the officers passed them back after inspection. Were they looking for someone? For him? Had they linked him to Brian? To that worthless homeless man? His heart thundered. Maybe it was nothing. Just routine.

The car in front of him reached the two officers. Could he take them out? He looked around to see how many total were present. Looked like the two checking cars, and a third with a dog standing on the shoulder of the road. Then just past them, in the other lane, an officer was directing the opposite traffic to continue slowly. So four in total. Not good.

The car in front of him drove ahead. It was time. The Teacher rolled down his window as he inched forward to a stop. The taller officer with a beer gut leaned down into his window. "Afternoon, sir. I need to see your license and proof of insurance."

The Teacher reached for the wallet in his jacket pocket. "What's going on?"

"Just a routine checkpoint. Nothing to worry about."

The Teacher relaxed. Nothing to worry about. The officer took his license and proof of insurance and handed it to the other officer, who walked over to the police cruiser on the opposite shoulder. He sat in the driver's seat with the door open and appeared to begin typing on a computer.

"What's he doing with my information?" The Teacher asked.

"We're just running it through the system to make sure there are no outstanding tickets, warrants, etcetera."

"You didn't do that with the cars ahead of me."

"Now that would back things up to Kingdom come out here. We just do one every once in a while. You don't mind, do you?"

He did mind. And he wanted to say so. But he pressed his mouth closed and waited patiently. In another minute, the officer brought his papers back and handed them through the window. "All good. You're free to go. Have a nice evening."

With a curt nod, the Teacher took his cards and placed them inside his wallet. It hadn't exactly been pleasant, but it could have been worse. Much worse indeed.

56.

IT WAS WELL AFTER QUITTING TIME, AND ALEX'S stomach rumbled like crazy, but he wasn't going anywhere soon. Tony had assembled a meeting of the surveillance team with their supervisor, Nicole. As the information on El Maestro came trickling in, Tony added one paper after another to the spread on the conference room table.

"So our target's real name is Albert Cervenka," Tony said. "He came to the US as a child with his parents, who were very well off. We're still getting details on his schooling, but it appears he attended Columbia University and majored in business. He went on to start, own, and then sell several companies. You can read the report for the details. The important part is that we have known addresses for Mr. Cervenka. He has property in Miami, Virginia, and Massachusetts. He's got an apartment in down-

town Atlanta, and a secluded cabin on Lake Allatoona. The guy's loaded, and he has several places
to run to if he decides to bolt."

Alex paced behind Nicole and the others at the
table, unable to sit still. This was the guy. This was
El Maestro. And he could barely wait to slap handcuffs on the bastard. "What do you want to do
next?"

Tony didn't miss a beat. "We get trackers for
each of his registered vehicles. So far we have
three. The silver Mercedes he was driving yesterday, a red Porsche, and a black Audi. I've got a
small team at his lakeside cabin for now, keeping
tabs on him. I'd like to beef that up to a larger team
and get the trackers on tonight, and establish 24/7
surveillance." He swiveled his chair toward Nicole.
"How many guys can we borrow from the other
groups over the next week?"

"You've got top priority right now," she said.
"Hank's passed the word down to every group supervisor to get together teams we can rotate
through. You're good on the numbers."

Tony shook his head and caught Alex's gaze.
"Yeah, what we're missing is some hard evidence.
Anything yet from the detective over in Smyrna?"

"He's tracking down our homeless guy to see if
we can get a positive ID. He'll call me when he
finds him."

"Okay," Tony said. "So in the meantime we don't let this guy out of our sight."

As everyone gathered their things, Nicole told Alex he'd done a great job on the lunch that day. He thanked her, but couldn't shake the nagging feeling that he should've done more to get Cervenka to meet with him again. She thanked Tony on her way out, leaving the two of them alone.

"That was weird," Alex said.

"What?" Tony was still stacking his papers.

"Nicole's been way too nice to me ever since we were at the hospital for the Gomez kid. It's unnerving. I don't think I've been lectured once."

Tony laughed and threw his briefcase over his shoulder. "I'm sure once this case gets put to rest, everyone around here will go back to being themselves. Even you."

"What is that supposed to mean?"

"Just seems like this place has lost a bit of its humor, you included. I'm sure it's just the case."

Alex got the feeling he knew it wasn't just the case. As they headed for their cubicles, he said, "You want to grab a bite before we head out to the lake?"

"Sure. Why don't you ride with me? I'm meeting Carrie at Judge Mac's house to get the vehicle warrant signed. We can take care of that, grab a bite, and then—"

"I think I'll just meet you back here before we go to the lake."

Tony stopped short. "I knew it. I knew you'd slept with her. Now you're avoiding her."

Alex thought he might belt Tony in the mouth right there. "Would you shut your mouth? Are you trying to get me in trouble?"

Tony's face froze. "Sorry, man."

Alex walked ahead of him and turned into Tony's cubicle. He waited for Tony to catch up, then put his finger into Tony's chest. "Look, I never slept with her. All right? So get that out of your head."

Tony narrowed his eyes and pushed Alex's hand away. "You need to calm down. I don't care if you slept with her or not. I just don't want you jeopardizing the biggest case of your career—"

"Don't you mean *your* case?" Alex stepped back and leveled his gaze at Tony. "Funny how now that you're in charge, you're suddenly concerned about rules and jeopardizing cases. Because just a few weeks ago you were telling me to go for it."

"That was all in fun, and you knew it. I never meant for you to...what? Are you dating? What is it you're doing, anyway?"

Alex rolled his eyes. "I swear, there's nothing going on between me and Carrie." He dropped into Tony's chair and sighed. "We had a few...I don't know...not dates, really. We spent some time together outside of work, and we thought about getting involved, but we both agreed it was a bad idea.

So now there's nothing. And the case is fine. I swear."

Tony stood silently for a minute, unsure if he could buy Alex's story. But then he reached over and patted Alex on the back. "All right then. Just come with me to get the warrant signed. You have to work with her, so you're going to have to set aside whatever feelings you have."

Alex sighed again and pushed himself up from the chair. "All right. Let's go."

Tony was right. He'd have to find a way to work with her. But it wasn't going to be easy.

57.

ALEX FOLLOWED TONY AND CARRIE OUT OF Judge Mac's house and down to the circular driveway in front of his historic home. He'd signed the warrants with enthusiasm and wished them luck in "bringing the sick bastard to justice." Then he'd winked and gone back to his dinner. It was a light moment in what had been a tension-filled conversation.

The three of them paused in the driveway, and Tony thanked Carrie for the speed in obtaining the warrants. Alex shoved his hands into his pockets and wished he could shove away the ache in his chest just as easily.

Carrie smiled at Tony. "It was no problem. I want this guy as badly as the rest of you. Just wish we had the evidence for more."

Heat flooded Alex's face. "I've been doing everything I can. At least we know who he is now."

Carrie blushed, her eyes fluttering to his and then away. "I know you're working hard. It wasn't a criticism."

Tony's eyes widened slightly, and he glanced at Alex. "We're moving in the right direction now. The trackers will help us keep an eye on him, and I'm sure he'll slip up soon. We'll get him."

Alex wasn't so sure. "Detective Crouse still hasn't found our homeless guy. A positive ID would have been a big help."

Tony winced. "He may have met the same end as your boy Meeks."

Alex glanced at Carrie, her face losing color. She pinched her eyebrows together. "I should get going. You guys have work to do."

She turned away and headed for her car at the end of the driveway. Tony's car was parked on the opposite side of the circle. Alex turned to Tony, hoping he wasn't too transparent. "Hey, give me just a minute, and I'll catch up to you." His friend nodded.

Alex took a few hurried steps and fell in beside Carrie. "You all right?"

"Of course." She kept moving.

"You sure? You seem upset."

Reaching her car, she stopped and faced him, her expression barely hiding her anxiety. "Just be careful, okay? Cervenka's dangerous."

"So, you're worried about me? Is that it?"

"Don't act so surprised. Of course I'm worried about you."

His body warmed all over, and he fought the urge to pull her close. She rubbed her hands together, her thumb caressing her palm. She was fighting her feelings too.

"Don't worry," he said. "I know what I'm doing."

"I know. But still...Just be careful tonight."

Damn it all to hell. He took her hands in his. "Why don't you come over later? After we're done."

She shook her head, but she didn't pull her hands away. "You know that's a bad idea."

"Come anyway, bad idea or not. I just need to be around you, to talk to you."

She lifted her head, and though it was dark, he thought he saw moisture around her eyes. "I can't, Alex." Then she did pull away, opening her car door and sliding inside.

Alex took hold of the door and bent down. He could kick himself for being so needy, but he couldn't seem to stop. "If you change your mind, just come over. Okay?"

She reached for the door handle and tugged the door out of his grip. "I'm sorry. Really. Just call me when you're done. I want to know you're okay. I just can't come over."

She pulled the door closed and in a few seconds had backed out of the driveway. He watched her go, wishing he could take his frustration out on something. A punching bag maybe. He walked over to Tony's car and climbed inside.

"Y'all get things worked out?" Tony asked.

Alex pulled his seatbelt across his chest. "Sure. It's all worked out. I have once again fallen for someone I can't be with. I guess I'm just determined to put myself through hell."

"I didn't know it was that bad. I thought it was just, you know, fun." Tony shook his head. "You really care about her."

Alex slammed his head back against the seat and closed his eyes. "So stupid," he muttered. "You'd think I would learn eventually."

"Listen, I'm not an expert on women, and I don't really know anything about your relationships in the past. But you're a good man, Alex. I bet if you just cut yourself some slack and be patient, it will all work out eventually."

Alex let out a long breath. Things weren't going to work out, but he appreciated the pep talk. He opened his eyes and turned to Tony. "That's the nicest thing you've ever said to me. And I appreciate it. But if you don't knock it off, I'm going to turn you in for sexual harassment."

Tony laughed and started the car. "That's the Alex I know and love."

"Seriously. You're making me uncomfortable."

The laughter was just what Alex needed. It was time to put all thoughts of Carrie behind him, and concentrate on what lay ahead. From the reports Tony had received already, it sounded like the Lake Allatoona house would be a challenge. Cervenka was obviously paranoid, and the place was well-secured. Just the kind of challenge Alex needed to focus his mind on what mattered.

Nailing Cervenka.

58.

THE NEXT MORNING, ALEX DRUMMED HIS FINGERS on his desk, barely able to focus on the tasks that needed his attention. His paperwork was falling behind. Seemed like for every hour he actually went out and did real law enforcement, he had to spend five documenting everything. Such a waste of time.

His phone vibrated on his belt, and he took a quick look at the screen. A text from Carrie.

I thought you were going to call me when you got home last night? I was worried.

Alex rested his head in his hands. Maybe he shouldn't even respond. It seemed like nothing he did would get her out of his head. And nothing he did would bring her back to him. He typed a quick response, keeping it brief.

Got home late and went to bed.

He wouldn't mention how long he'd lain awake, hoping to hear a knock on his door. Another vibration.

Glad you made it home safe.

That seemed like a perfect place to cut off the conversation. He turned off the phone and stared at the computer screen before him, not seeing a damn thing. The phone buzzed again.

I'm sorry about last night. I didn't mean to blow you off.

Alex's fingers moved instinctively. *No problem. I understand.*

Silence. He stared at the frozen screen on his phone. Was that the end? Should he say something else? The dots at the bottom started blinking. There was more.

I miss you.

The words shot through him, leaving an ache as real as a bullet. What was she trying to do to him? He had no idea what he should say in return. The truth? Something to blow her off like she'd done to him? Maybe nothing at all. But in the end, he knew he'd tell her the truth.

Me too.

He turned the phone off again and put it back in its holster. He couldn't shut her out, couldn't have her, couldn't concentrate on meaningless paperwork. What next? He flipped open his laptop and logged into his undercover email account. Maybe he could reach out for Cervenka. Keeping an open line of communication couldn't hurt.

There were a couple of new messages: one that was junk, and one from Trebal Aknev. Alex clicked on it, not wanting to get his hopes up.

Dear Alex,

I wanted to apologize if I came across as rude yesterday. I've thought it over, and you must think I'm a real horse's ass. But I want you to know that having lunch with you and Chris was a delight. You remind me so much of myself when I was young and confused about the world. I shouldn't have dismissed your request so quickly. If you would still like to get together for dinner, I know a quaint little place just north of Woodstock that would be excellent for getting to know each other better. I'm available any evening for the next few days, or Monday or Tuesday of next week. Thank you again for such a pleasant time yesterday. I hope to see you again soon.

Kind Regards,
Trebal Aknev

Alex sat back in his chair and read over the message again. He couldn't believe it. What had changed his mind? He printed out a copy of the message and made a beeline for Tony's cubicle. Dropping the paper on Tony's desk, he grabbed the chair nearby to sit on.

"He wants another date," Alex said.

Tony picked up the letter and turned to face Alex with a huge smile. "Oh, honey! Congratulations—he's a real catch." He leaned forward. "So...what are you going to wear?"

Alex touched his finger to his chin and looked up at the ceiling. "Hmm, I was thinking about that navy blue button down shirt. It goes perfectly with my secret camera."

"Ah, you are a devil." Tony read through the message before dropping it onto the desk. Then he leaned back in his chair with his hands behind his head. "So, a small restaurant? Sounds a bit more intimate."

"Yeah, maybe I can actually get something this time that we can use."

"Any ideas on how to get him to slip up?"

"I was thinking about bringing up the arrests of the other guys. Say I saw it on the news and how tragic it was. Something along those lines."

"Hmm, that could backfire. Make him more suspicious. What else you got?"

"I'm not sure. I don't usually script these things out." Alex tried not to let Tony's second-guessing get under his skin. He was just doing his job.

"Well, you work on nailing down a date, and I'll line up the surveillance team. Let me know when you come up with a plan for your conversation. We can put something together hopefully that won't raise Cervenka's suspicions."

"Sure," Alex said. He stood and took a couple of steps before turning back to Tony. "Hey, thanks for working so hard on this. I can't say I particularly like handing over the reins, but I'm glad it's you."

Tony sighed and shook his head. "I thought we agreed, no more flirting at the office. Now run along."

Alex laughed and headed back to his cubicle. He pulled up the email again and worked on his response to Cervenka. He wanted to strike just the right chord, without seeming too desperate.

Dear Mr. Aknev,

I was so glad to receive your message this morning. I completely understood your desire for privacy, so I never thought you were rude. I would love to meet for dinner, and the restaurant sounds wonderful. I'm free on Thursday evening. Just let me know the time and address. I look forward to getting to know you better.

Sincerely,
Alex

That should do it. And now maybe he'd be able to get something to put this guy away for good.

59.

THE TEACHER SURVEYED THE SMALL RESTAU-
RANT that had become a safe haven over the
past few years. It was tucked into the woods
along a road that few seemed to travel. It was quiet,
intimate, and the food was good enough. He hoped
Alex would be able to find it with little trouble.

He'd been looking forward to the evening all
day. With Garrett returning to work earlier that
day, he'd been assured all loose ends had been ti-
died up, and nothing could lead back to himself. It
was finally time to put the whole nasty business of
Roman's mess behind him. Now he could focus on
being Trebal Aknev, accomplished author, and
mentor to a young man in need of guidance.

The bell over the door clinked, and Alex walked
through. Trebal's blood stirred at the sight of the
tall, muscular man. So much potential there. He

stood and waved Alex over to his table, extending his hand. Alex's hand was warm, and his handshake firm. Trebal noticed the calluses, from lifting weights no doubt. Intriguing.

"Good evening, Mr. Aknev," Alex said.

"Please, call me Trebal." They took their seats, and a waitress came over to take their drink orders. "I'll have some unsweetened tea, please. And be sure to put this on one check."

Alex put his hand up in protest. "That's extremely generous, but you really don't—"

"Please, it's the least I can do after my rude behavior on Monday."

Alex thanked him and smiled up at the waitress. He ordered tea as well, and after she left, turned his smile in Trebal's direction. "So, what do you recommend?"

"I like the fish here. The salmon is good. So's the snapper. But anything should be fine. I prefer this place more for the atmosphere than the food."

Alex leaned onto the table. "I can see why. It's very quiet. Not too many nosy customers staring."

Trebal's thoughts exactly. "Tell me a little more about yourself, Alex. Where are you from? What do you do?"

"Well, I grew up in North Carolina, near Raleigh. It was a fairly small town, and seemed like everyone knew your business. My stepdad and I didn't exactly get along. So I left home when I was fifteen. I've gone from one job to the next trying to find something I could love, but I just can't seem to make it happen. I'm between jobs right now."

"So how do you manage to meet your expenses when you're not working?"

Alex shrugged. "I get by. Friends help me out sometimes. My family will take me in if things get bad enough."

"I'm assuming you have siblings, since I met your nephew."

Alex smiled again. "Yes, my sister Chloe. We're not as close as I'd like, but Chris is amazing."

"What happened between you and your sister?" Trebal realized he'd been leaning closer to Alex, drawn in by the young man's warmth.

"She always seemed unhappy with my close relationship to Chris. I mean, I think I loved him more than she did. And she saw how much Chris loved me. I don't know. I guess she was jealous."

Trebal sat back in his chair as the waitress approached again. He ordered the grilled salmon while Alex went with the snapper. The interruption seemed to break the connection between them, and he found himself eager to reestablish it. He noticed Alex's eyes travelling over the dining room, pausing briefly in certain places. Was he memorizing the restaurant?

Alex brought his gaze back to Trebal. "How about you? Tell me more about the mysterious Trebal Aknev."

"Mysterious? Maybe a little. Only because I appreciate my privacy. I suppose it's an old habit that's difficult to break. I was mistreated pretty often as a child, picked on by more aggressive kids. Unfortunately, adults can be the same. I've just found very few people in life who truly understand me."

"I can relate to that."

Trebal studied him. That was probably true. A man with Alex's good looks probably felt obliged to meet certain expectations. Society could be so cruel when faced with enlightened men such as themselves. Perhaps he had the means for helping Alex find his inner peace.

"What kind of work are you interested in?" Trebal asked.

"I'd love to work with kids. I've had some jobs in the past where I got to do that, but it never seems to work out the way I hope."

"What do you mean?"

"Like this last job. I was tutoring some kids at the local Y, and this little boy really warmed up to me. He would bring a book over and want to sit in my lap and read. Such a sweet kid. Sometimes he would work on his homework with me, and he would never be content to just sit beside me. Always wanted to be between my knees at the table, or sitting in my lap on a beanbag. I guess his mother didn't like it, and she complained to my boss.

The whole thing just got uncomfortable, so I left. Broke my heart to say goodbye."

Trebal could understand. The love of a boy was like nothing else in the world. And the sadness in Alex's eyes moved him. "So now what will you do?"

"I don't know. You know what seems to be my main problem? I can't ever get close enough, not the way I'd like. It's very frustrating. I mean, I see others able to do it..." His voiced trailed off, and his gaze dropped. "I've said too much. You must think I'm a freak."

Trebal reached across the table and covered Alex's hand with his own. "Oh no, son. I don't think you're a freak. In fact, I think I could help you."

Alex lifted his gaze back to Trebal's. "Really? How?"

"Let me ask you, what did you mean when you said you see others do it?"

His smile returned, this time a tinge bashful. "I've seen videos and pictures online. It just looks so...I don't know. I mean, not the really bad stuff. Just, the sweetness of it." He dropped his forehead into his hand and groaned. "I know I sound like an idiot. But do you know what I mean? Have you ever seen...what I'm talking about?"

Trebal's nerves tightened. He still barely knew Alex, and this was heading into murky waters. He'd enjoyed the videos and images when he was younger, and when he and Roman had first begun figuring out how to make a profit from them. But he'd found over the years that their appeal dwindled. Videos were for amateurs.

He leaned onto the table and lowered his voice. "Son, what you're talking about, at least what I believe you're talking about, is illegal. You need to be careful. You never know who's tracking what you do online. I don't mess around with that stuff myself. Too risky."

"Wait, so then, was I wrong? I thought you and I were...you know...alike."

Trebal couldn't help but smile. Poor kid. He had no idea what opportunities were out there. "Listen, I believe you and I have some things in common. Things best left for a more private setting. You seem like a good kid. I'll help you out. Let's just enjoy our meal for now. We'll talk more private matters soon."

Disappointment flickered over Alex's expression. But then he smiled again. "So does this mean I'll get to see you again?"

Trebal's insides warmed at the thought of taking Alex back to the lake house. He could use a new project, and Alex was turning out to be even more enticing than he'd imagined. "Of course. Next time, I'll have you up to my lake house. You'll love it. Very secluded. We can talk openly there. No danger of being overheard or misunderstood."

60.

"**N**O, NO, NO! ABSOLUTELY NOT." NICOLE shook her head vehemently as she paced behind her desk.

Alex and Tony sat in their usual places, only this time it was no laughing matter. Alex had managed to convince Tony to move forward with the dinner at Cervenka's lake house, but Nicole was a whole different animal.

"This is a bad idea, guys," she continued. "We've only had surveillance on that house for a few days, and already it's a logistical nightmare. We can't seal it off because it's so close to the water. And we've nearly tripped off alarms three times! The guy has some serious security going on out there. And he's probably already killed at least two people we know of, and arranged the gang rape of a man's wife."

"All the more reason for someone to go in there who knows the risks and has been trained to handle them," Alex said, keeping his voice level.

"But if we can get someone inside, an informant that he already knows and trusts, we can get what we need without putting your life in danger. "Tony, come on. You know I'm right."

Tony glanced over at Alex, still looking pretty uncertain, then back at Nicole. "I understand where you're coming from. I have some reservations myself. But Alex has put everything on the line, and he's worked his ass off to bring this guy down. I think we should listen to him."

Nicole still didn't seem convinced. "Do you even have time to put together a proper op plan for this house?"

"Absolutely," Tony said.

"I'll help," Alex added. "I know this isn't ideal, but what else do we have? We've gotten nothing from vehicle trackers, nothing from computer forensics—"

"That will take more time—"

"Time we don't have. Who's to say he won't go after Johnson's kids? What about the next kid he's going to kidnap and keep as his own special toy? I looked in that man's eyes, and there isn't an ounce of light there. He is evil. And we have to do everything we can to get him while we have this golden opportunity in front of us."

"I don't know, guys," she said. "You're both damn good agents, but I don't like putting Alex in such a vulnerable position with someone as dangerous as Cervenka."

"Aw, thanks, Nicole." Alex grinned, trying to lighten the mood. "I didn't know you cared so much."

She pointed a finger at him. "This isn't funny."

"Of course not."

The finger turned to Tony. "I want to see the op plan by this afternoon. I want to go over it with Hank, someone from the Justice Department, everybody. Understand?"

Alex and Tony stood, thanking Nicole as they left before she could change her mind. Alex followed Tony to his cubicle and took a seat in his usual chair.

Tony fell into his chair and threw his hands up. "Well, looks like Operation Third Date is a go."

Alex had no desire to continue to argue the merits of his decision. But he knew Tony was sticking by him, despite his better judgment. "Thanks for supporting me in there."

"Of course. I mean, I think this is nuts. But if I was in your place, I'd want to do the same thing. And I know you'd stick by me."

"Absolutely."

"Then let's map out the lake house and get a plan in place to keep you safe."

Alex and Tony worked on the layout of the house for the next hour, taking into account the dock and boat behind the house, the shed in the backyard, the security cameras surrounding the house, and a myriad of other obstacles. Cervenka was no amateur. When it seemed like they had all the bases covered, they reviewed the assignments again.

"Okay," Tony said, pointing his pencil to the drawing. "Team Alpha will be in the woods north of the house and Bravo will be in the woods south of the house. There are several motion-activated wildlife cameras set up in those woods, so we'll have to be careful where we position each team member, but it looks like we can get good coverage of the sides of the house. That's not what worries me."

Tony pointed his pencil to the paper where he'd sketched the backyard, dock, and water's edge to the west. "Here's our problem area. At the end of the dock, we have a pole with a camera set up to see the dock, boat, and a good portion of the water's edge. It also rotates out to the open water every minute, so getting a team to cover this side of the house is tricky. I want Team Charlie in a boat just around the bend, ready to haul ass at a moment's notice. I'll be with Team Bravo and take a position here." He pointed behind the shed.

Alex sighed and leaned back in his chair. "I still say that's too vulnerable a position. Your backside is wide open."

Tony rubbed his forehead for a minute before turning his gaze on Alex. "Look, in all seriousness, this is the trickiest and most dangerous op I've ever been involved in, not to mention being the case agent. I'm going to do everything I can to cover to your back."

For once, Alex didn't feel the need to crack a joke. He clapped a hand on Tony's shoulder. "I wouldn't want anyone else, brother. Just make sure your back is covered as well."

61.

ALEX DRIED HIMSELF OFF AND PULLED ON some jeans before heading to his backdoor to let in Mutt for the night. Adrenaline was already pumping through his body from the anticipation of tomorrow's operation, so sleep was unlikely. He grabbed a beer out of the refrigerator and turned the lights off in the kitchen. Then he dropped onto the sofa to try to relax. Maybe he could zone out to *Forensic Files* or something.

He was searching through the onscreen guide when there was a knock at his door. Mutt leapt up and trotted over to the door, barking a warning at whoever was there. Placing his beer on the side table, Alex crossed the living room to the front door. Who could it be this late at night?

He couldn't help that idiotic part of him that hoped for one second it was Carrie. But she'd been clear about keeping her distance, so he willed that hope to the back of his mind. He leaned down and looked through the peephole, shocked when he saw that it actually was Carrie standing outside. His pulse raced to life. Had she changed her mind?

As he pulled open the door, she glared at him like she was ready to punch him, then blew past him and immediately began pacing his living room. "What do you think you're going to accomplish with this ridiculous plan? Are you trying to get yourself killed? Do you want me to suffer? Is that it?"

Alex stood watching her pace and shout, without a clue of what to say in response. Not that he could've gotten one in. She was hysterical. Her ponytail swung from side to side as she waved her arms in the air, and it was clear from the dark streaks on her cheeks that she'd been crying. Slowly he walked across the living room and stood what seemed to be a safe distance away until she finished.

At last Carrie let out a groan, threw up her hands, and turned to him with accusing eyes. "Well? Aren't you going to say anything?"

"Are you all right?" It was a dumb question. She was obviously not all right. But his mind had drawn a blank.

Her eyes widened, and she threw her hands out to the side. "No! I'm not all right with you doing something stupid that's going to get you killed!"

"Okay, listen, we can talk about this if you want. I'll explain exactly what's going on. But you really need to calm down."

She groaned again and went back to pacing. Apparently, calming down wasn't an option. "I already know what's going on. Tony told me everything when I went down to the office today."

"Did they call you in for legal counsel?"

"I thought it was for an operation with an informant, until Tony said it was you going into that house."

"I really don't understand what has you so upset. I specifically remember you telling me to do my part of the case, getting the evidence, and you would do your part. Sounded to me like you wanted nothing more to do with me than was absolutely necessary. So that's what I'm doing. This is my job, and I'm damn good at it. I don't need you to come in here, acting hysterical."

Abruptly, Carrie stopped pacing. She slammed her mouth into a tight line. "I know you're good at your job. I just think it's reckless to put yourself and everyone else that has to cover you in harm's way."

Alex nearly laughed. "What do you think we do? Only arrest the bad guys that don't seem too dangerous? This is exactly what we're trained for. You should know that. Besides, would you be this upset if it was Tony or another agent going in there? Is this your idea of keeping our relationship professional?"

"Stop throwing that in my face! I can't help how I feel."

"And how exactly do you feel, Carrie?" Alex threw up his hands, unable to contain the anger building inside of him. "It can't be anything too serious because you can surely toss me aside whenever things get too hard."

"Toss you aside?" Her voice struck a new octave. "*Toss you aside?*"

"Yes!"

"That's ridiculous! You were the one who said you had to see this case through. I was trying to do the right thing and support you."

Alex shook his head and moved closer. All the frustration of the past few weeks was about to explode out of him. "I was willing to risk everything to be with you. I would've taken the chance. You're worth the risk. But you couldn't do it. And the only reason I can think of that makes sense is that I'm not worth it."

She shoved her finger into his chest, tears streaming over her cheeks. "You don't know me at all! I've been dying inside. All I think about is you, every day, and every night."

Alex's anger began to lose its hold. Hadn't he felt the same way? So then why was she doing this?

"I just can't stand the thought of you going into that house with no protection." She covered her face with her hands. " No one else in there with you. If he decides to point a gun at your head and pull the trigger, what's to stop him?"

"You're just going to have to trust me," Alex said, caressing her damp cheek with his thumb. She gazed up at him with such turmoil in her expression. "Come on, take a deep breath. Just relax for a minute. Shut everything else out. It's just you and me. Nothing else matters." He touched his forehead to hers, and she slid her hands up his bare chest, wrapping them around his neck. Warmth spread from her hands all the way down to his toes.

"Just for the record," she said. "You are worth the risk. I...I just...I wanted to protect you, to protect us."

He touched his lips to hers, aching for the slightest response. When she kissed him back, it was like a fire spreading over his whole body. He wrapped his arms around her waist, lifting her off the floor as their kiss deepened. No more waiting. No more second-guessing.

They tumbled onto the sofa, and he moved his lips to her throat. She moaned, sending ripples of lust through him. Her hands gripped his hair, pulling his head up so she could look him in the eyes.

"I can't lose you," she said.

"You won't. I promise." He kissed her again and smiled. "Just no more of this professional crap, okay? Screw being professional. Deal?"

She smiled. "Deal." He pushed her mouth open with his, sinking into the desires he'd been holding at bay for too long.

"Alex, tomorrow—"

"No tomorrow." His hand slipped beneath her shirt, caressing her warm skin. "Just right now. That's all that exists. Just you and me. Okay?"

She bit her lip and nodded. "Just...can we...take things slow?"

He made a concerted effort to slow his thumping heart. The last thing he wanted was to scare her off. "Carrie, I don't want to pressure you. I just want to make sure we want the same thing. I want to be with you, only you. Is that what you want?"

"Yes," she said, lifting her lips back to his. "I only want to be with you."

Alex reached around her waist and pulled her tight against his body. He could do slow. It might kill him. But she was worth it.

62.

ALEX STOOD PATIENTLY OUTSIDE THE SUR-
VEILLANCE van as Tony did one more check
of all the equipment. Tension had been high
all day, as they'd prepped each team on its respon-
sibilities. As the last few moments crept closer, Tony appeared increasingly nervous. There had been
no jokes all day.

Richards came around the side of the van and
handed Alex a thumb drive. "We put some photos
on there of kids. Nothing illegal; just some border-
line stuff. Should make it seem a little more valid."

Alex thanked him and shoved the thumb drive in
the pocket of his coat. Tony approached and looked
over his camera button again. "Everything looks
good. Audio's coming through. What's the code
word for trouble?"

Alex grinned. "Help?"

"Very cute. Seriously. What is it?"

"How about Tony the Tiger?"

"Too long."

"Dude, lighten up. This is going to work out. We've got this bastard tonight."

Tony studied him. "Why are you so calm? You look...almost happy. What's going on?"

Alex did his best not to laugh. "I'll tell you later, okay?"

"Hmm...well just remember, I'll be behind the shed ready to cover you as soon as you give the word. Which is...?"

"Flintstone."

Tony shook his head, finally letting out a chuckle. "Okay, Flintstone it is." He put his fist out. "Let's do this."

Alex bumped fists and pulled open the car door. As Tony headed past him toward the van, he called out, "Hey! If I'm not back in five minutes..."

"I'll just wait longer." Tony gave a half-hearted salute before climbing into the passenger side of the van.

Alex slid into his undercover car and drove toward the main road. Taking a left onto the dirt road that led to Cervenka's lake house, he glanced in the rear-view mirror to see the surveillance van turn off into the woods. Adrenaline pumped through him as he parked his car in front of the house and stepped out. He took a quick look around, noting the cameras on each corner. The house was situated in a clearing stretching all the way down to the water's edge, with about fifty yards between the house and the woods on each side.

As he walked up the front steps and onto the porch, he was keenly aware of being surrounded by both the enemy and his own team. And yet, he was very much on his own. He rang the doorbell and stepped back, taking in the layout of the front porch. Nothing of any consequence; just some wooden rocking chairs and flowerpots.

The door opened to Cervenka and a large Rottweiler at his side. Alex didn't remember anyone mentioning a dog. How had they missed the dog? That was Surveillance 101. Hopefully they were seeing it now, and making the necessary adjustments.

"Welcome, my friend!" Cervenka gave Alex a huge smile. "Come on in. This is Beau. He's pretty harmless. Just keeps an eye on things for me, but I don't think he'd hurt a flea."

Alex stepped into the foyer and shook Cervenka's hand. Beau sniffed him. "Hey there, Beau. You smell my puppy?"

"You have a dog as well?" Cervenka asked.

Alex straightened as Beau pushed his muzzle into his hand. He rubbed the dog's head. "Sure do. A mutt that showed up at my door about a year ago. I think he adopted me more than I adopted him."

Cervenka laughed and showed Alex into the living room. "Well, make yourself at home. I have a little more work to do on dinner, but it should be ready shortly. Would you like a drink? Some wine maybe?"

"Sure." He'd rather have a beer, but knew that fitting into Cervenka's world was key to gaining his trust.

Cervenka returned to the living room moments later and handed Alex a glass of red wine. "Can I take your coat? I'll just go put it in the bedroom, then make the finishing touches to dinner."

Alex sipped at the wine as he took a look around. The open floor plan had the living room, dining room, and kitchen all in one large space, with only the island in the kitchen area offering some separation. Cervenka closed a door to Alex's left and crossed over to the kitchen. He grabbed a remote off the island and hit a button, soft music filling the room.

"This is a nice place," Alex said.

Cervenka went over to the oven and pulled it open. "Thank you. I love it out here. Very private." He straightened, holding a small dish of potatoes and carrots.

Alex walked over to the bay windows that opened to the backyard and the view of the lake. He noticed the shed and the dock, along with the boat that could pass for a yacht. Was Tony in position already? "That's a great boat. You use it often?"

Cervenka leaned onto the island and smiled. "Oh yes. It's loaded. I can go out on the lake for days at a time."

"You ever do any fishing?"

"Sometimes. Not often. I find fishing a bit frustrating. I much prefer catching."

Alex laughed and shook his finger at Cervenka. "You just have to go with someone who knows what they're doing. Maybe I could take you out sometime and show you some tricks."

Cervenka carried two full plates over to the dining table. "That would be very nice." He set them down and motioned for Alex to take a seat. "I'll just grab the bread, and we'll be ready." Alex took the seat he'd pointed to, once again uneasy with his back to his surroundings. But at least he had the front door in view. Cervenka returned with a basket of bread and set it before him. "Let's dig in."

Alex sliced into his steak. He took a bite, savoring the juice and spices. He had to hand it to the guy. He could cook a damn good steak. "This is amazing. Very tender."

Cervenka grinned. "The trick is to use very young meat."

Alex suddenly lost his appetite. The quicker he got to the evidence, the better. "So, the other day at lunch," he began, "you said we'd be able to speak more openly here. So, may I ask you something?"

Cervenka swallowed. "Of course."

"You and I, we have many things in common. I mentioned that I was having trouble finding the same joy in my own life that I'd seen with others in the videos and images online. You seemed...willing to help me."

Cervenka leaned back in his chair and rested his fork against his plate. "Alex, what is it you really want?"

Alex's throat tightened. Had he said too much already? "Ah, I'm not sure what you mean."

"Do you want to find real happiness? A special connection that fulfills you? Or do you just want to get off on watching the poor idiots online, while also risking getting yourself thrown in prison?"

Alex set his fork down and leaned closer. "Mr. Aknev, of course I want someone special."

"Then I can help you, son." He resumed eating, and Alex choked down another bite of steak. Then Cervenka wiped his mouth with his napkin. "Listen, I understand the appeal of the videos and images you see. I've been there. But they aren't the end goal. They can be nice...a sort of snack, if you will. But they aren't the main course. And you have to treat them as such."

Alex's stomach churned. He'd seen too many of those *snacks*, and took a moment to indulge a mental image of the special kind of punishment Cervenka would get in prison. But then he pushed that aside. It wouldn't help him convince Cervenka to hand over any evidence.

"So then, what advice can you give me?" Alex asked.

The pleasure on Cervenka's face was sickening. "Ah, much. Let's start with your current activities. You must stay away from online videos. Big Brother is always watching, and it's only a matter of time before you trip one of their invisible booby traps."

"They can track what I'm doing online?"

"Yes. There are measures you can take to better protect yourself, but in the end, there's only one way to avoid Big Brother."

Alex plastered on an amazed expression. "What do I have to do?"

"It's simple, really." Cervenka shrugged. "You gather your own collection of the best, and only the best, videos. You keep them on a separate drive that's easy to carry around, easy to destroy. And you do not share. You do not send them to anyone. You do not get them from anyone else. In fact, if you are extremely wise and careful, you learn how to make your own."

Cervenka rested his fork again and pointed at Alex's wine. "You know, I appreciate your kindness, but I'm happy to get you something else if the wine isn't to your liking."

"Oh, no. The wine is good."

"Would you prefer a beer?"

"Maybe after dinner," Alex said. He took a sip of the wine to further his point. "So, I was wondering. If I don't download any videos from the web or share with anyone, how am I ever going to build up my own collection?"

Cervenka smiled like a kind grandfather sharing his secrets to a favorite family recipe. It was unnerving to discuss such heinous acts so carelessly. Alex pushed down the bile stirring in his stomach.

"Listen," Cervenka said. "I will help you out. But I need you to understand some rules first. Can you do that?"

Alex nodded. *Finally.*

63.

THE TEACHER WATCHED ALEX'S FACE FOR ANY hesitation, seeing none. He was pleased Alex hung on his every word. He'd be as pliable as silk. "All right, now you must agree to never, under any circumstances, share what I give you. Understand?"

Alex nodded, his eagerness titillating every nerve in the Teacher's body. He pushed himself up from the table. "Why don't I start the process of copying just a few things over for you? Then we can sit out on the back deck and continue our conversation around the fire pit."

"That sounds wonderful," Alex said. "I even have a thumb drive with me. Didn't you say I should keep it on something I can carry and easily dispose of? That seems perfect?"

The Teacher sensed something, just for a moment. Was he too eager? The poor kid's view of the world was so narrow. No wonder he was obsessed with videos. The Teacher would enjoy broadening his horizons. But still, he'd come with a thumb drive. Was that odd?

"That will do just fine," he replied. "Where is it?"

"It's in my coat pocket."

"Well, then I'll just run back to my room, get the thumb drive, and start the file transfer. You relax and make yourself at home. It shouldn't take long."

The Teacher headed for his bedroom and took the coat off his bed. He reached into the pocket and sure enough, there was a thumb drive. He pulled it out and looked it over as he walked to his desk. Once seated, he placed it in the USB port and opened the drive.

Several pictures were already on there: Six measly pictures of kids playing at the park. One of a little boy splashing in a fountain with his shirt off. Pitiful. Alex really did need his help. Out of habit, he clicked on the metadata of the image of the boy. It was wiped completely clean. For someone who seemed so ignorant of security measures, this seemed odd.

One red flag he could ignore, but two were a different matter. Frowning, he put on his headset that had a direct, secure connection to the boat and pressed the call button. Within a few seconds, Garrett answered. "Yeah?"

"Can you do something for me?"

"Of course. What do you need?"

"I might be a tad paranoid, but could you run a check on all the cameras and see if anything seems strange? Also, check to see if we have any video or audio signals in the immediate area."

"I'm on it."

"One more thing," the Teacher said. "I have a thumb drive in my main computer with some images on it. Can you run that little trick Roman taught you and see where exactly these pictures have come from and who has accessed them?"

"Sure thing. By the way, all cameras are functioning properly. I don't see anything unusual at this point."

The Teacher's nerves settled slightly. He looked out the back window toward the dock where the boat sat. He was just being paranoid, but it was what had kept him one step ahead of the police all these years.

"Hang on," Garrett said. "I am picking up some audio. Sounds like there might be police in the area."

The Teacher's gut tightened. Was that a shadow he saw move near the shed? He'd have to find a way to get Alex out of the house. Maybe the below-ground passage out to the dock? Garrett's voice broke through again. "There's another signal. It sounds like classical music."

The Teacher's heart dropped into his stomach. "Is it Beethoven's *Adieux*?"

"Ah, I don't know about that, but there's also a video signal and it's your dining room on camera."

"The pictures," the Teacher said, his voice shaking. He typed in a web address for the article on Roman's death. "Where are those pictures from?"

"Give me just one moment."

The Teacher bit his fist to keep from slamming it into the desk. The picture from the article loaded and he searched the background. If he was right...

"Okay," Garrett said. "We have a problem. The images were accessed by a computer registered to the Department of Homeland Security."

The Teacher ripped off the headset and paced his bedroom. How could he have been such a fool? He'd let them right into his home! And Alex was one of them. How could he have been so careless?

This wasn't the time to panic. He had to figure out what to do right now. He slipped the headset back on. "Garrett, are you still there?"

"Yes, sir."

"We'll need to get out of here quickly. Get the boat ready."

"Yes, sir."

"I'll need about ten minutes. Can you isolate the audio and video coming from my house?"

"I believe so."

"Can you create a loop and set it to run for ten minutes?"

"Yes, sir."

The Teacher glanced out the back window, certain that he'd seen a shadow behind the shed that didn't belong. "Good. I don't want anyone seeing what's about to happen in here."

Killing a federal agent while backup was most likely nearby wasn't the wisest course of action. He'd have to be smart. But Alex would have to pay for this.

64.

ALEX GREW INCREASINGLY UNEASY THE LONGER Cervenka stayed in the bedroom. He stood and paced near the windows, keen to get the thumb drive and exit the house with the evidence to put Cervenka away for life. But this was taking too long. He should've been back already. Something wasn't right.

"You doing all right out here?" Cervenka asked from behind him.

Alex started and turned around. "Oh yes. Just admiring the view." Something was different. Cervenka had a tenseness to his posture that hadn't been there earlier. He smiled at Alex, but it seemed forced.

"Let me get you that beer," Cervenka said, as he headed into the kitchen.

Alex stood in the dining room, debating whether Cervenka's behavior was odd enough to signal his team. But he didn't have the thumb drive in hand, and without it, he really had nothing. If they stormed in now, and somehow still missed the evidence, they'd blow the one shot they had at him. No, whatever had spooked Cervenka, it couldn't be too bad. He just needed to turn on the charm.

Cervenka returned with the beer and handed it over. "Come," he said. "Let's relax while the computer does its thing."

He directed Alex over to the sofa and sat him down facing the television. Then Cervenka went around behind the recliner. He leaned onto the back of it and sipped his wine. He was definitely on edge, and Alex's own body began to react to it. His stomach tightened, and his heart pounded away in his ears.

Cervenka smiled at him and motioned with his hand. "Drink up, my friend. We must relax! You will have a wonderful time here. I have so much to show you. But drink up, so we can have some fun."

Alex tipped the beer back, studying Cervenka the whole time. How was he going to get this back on track? "So, you said before that you would help me. What other ways can you help?"

Cervenka placed his glass on the side table between the recliner and the sofa, and narrowed his eyes at Alex, like he was waiting for something.

Alex's stomach took a serious dip. Cervenka moved beside the recliner.

"Alex, I would love to help you. I really would. But I'm starting to get the feeling you don't want my help. Not really."

"Oh but I do," Alex said. His head swam, and the room wavered just a bit. Had he downed his beer too quickly? He'd only had the glass of wine and a few gulps of beer. No way should he be this affected. The floor swayed, and for a moment he felt like he might fall off the sofa. This definitely wasn't right. He glanced over at Cervenka, who had moved closer to the kitchen.

Alex reached down into his boot and yanked out his pistol, pointing it at Cervenka. "Stop right there! I'm a federal agent with Home...Homeland..." The room swayed again and he took a side step to steady himself. "Flint...Flintstone." When Cervenka came back into focus, Alex saw he had a gun pointed right back at him.

"You must be the scum that took my Roman from me," Cervenka said. "I looked up the articles online, and bam, there you were. Standing in the background at the hospital."

Alex stumbled sideways again and tried to center his aim on Cervenka's head, but it wouldn't stay still. His body wanted to crumple into a deep sleep, but he forced himself to concentrate. Cervenka had moved again.

Alex stumbled toward the kitchen, grabbing onto the back of the recliner for support. He aimed at Cervenka's back. "I said freeze!"

Cervenka turned around with a snarky smile. "Alex, or whoever you are, I doubt you could hit a train at this point."

"There are agents surrounding the house," Alex said. "You won't get out of here."

"Watch me." Then he let out a short whistle, and the dog ran to his side.

Instead of heading out the back door, Cervenka made an abrupt turn that seemed to take him through the wall. Alex couldn't tell if he'd imagined it, his head was so fuzzy. He stumbled into the kitchen, still trying to train his gun. A door in the wall stood slightly ajar. He reached for the crack, nearly falling over.

He had to clear his head. What had Cervenka put in his drink? He shook his head and fixed on the stairs. When his legs buckled, he slid the rest of the way down, coming to a painful stop as he crashed into a wall at the bottom. His face throbbed.

Pushing himself up, Alex turned in every direction, finally catching a glimpse of another door. He shook his head again. Now it was throbbing all over. Where was the back up? Why weren't agents storming into the house by now?

Then he smelled it. Smoke. Where was it coming from? He didn't have time to figure it out. He stumbled over to the door and practically fell through it to a tunnel on the other side. Out of nowhere, pain shot through his face again, and he fell to his side. He opened his eyes to see Cervenka standing over him, his gun pointed at his chest.

"Come on, Alex," he said. "I actually liked you. Don't make me kill you."

Alex rolled onto all fours and tried to push himself up. A bolt of intense pain shot through his stomach. He dropped to the floor again.

"Stop trying to get up!"

Alex's head was ringing; his stomach roiled. Where was his gun? He rolled onto his side again, and this time saw Cervenka's feet moving away from him down the tunnel. He felt along the damp floor until he found his gun. Then he lifted himself again and began to crawl.

65.

THE TEACHER RAN DOWN THE TUNNEL, HIS thoughts racing. He should have killed Alex. Should he go back? There was no time. Agents would be swarming as soon as they smelled the smoke in his bedroom, or as soon as they caught the looping video.

He rushed up the slope as the tunnel neared its opening beneath the dock. Water dripped from the ceiling, and Beau sat waiting on him. He took a quick glance back. The moron was still trying to come for him, crashing into the walls as he tried to run.

The Teacher strapped Beau into the pulley system he'd installed for emergencies. Then he climbed the ladder and pushed open the hatch at the top. Stepping into the mud, he peered out into the backyard of his precious house. He'd never see it again, thanks to *Alex*. He'd make him pay for this. He heard shouts from the woods. There was no more time.

He pulled Beau up before making his way out from under the dock and headed up the bank. His chest heaved as he stood up straight and looked around once more. Now he could hear yelling from both sides of the house. Men were moving around inside. Too bad he hadn't rigged a bomb for such an occasion.

Beau took off running down the dock, always eager for a boat ride. The Teacher turned for the dock when a voice too close to ignore came out of the darkness. "Freeze right there!"

The Teacher turned slightly to his left. He'd forgotten about the shadow near the shed. He put his hands up and backed away from the dock.

"I said for you to freeze!"

The Teacher stopped. It should be far enough anyway. The agent, dressed completely in black and pointing a pistol at his chest, moved out of the shadows.

"Where's Alex?" he yelled.

The Teacher shrugged. "Who?"

The agent appeared to be talking into thin air. "I have the suspect in the backyard near the dock. Possible agent down inside the house. Get the ambulance here now!"

The Teacher couldn't help but smile. "Yes, there's definitely an agent down. And it's you." He heard the zip of a bullet, and the agent slumped to the ground.

66.

LEX TRIED THREE TIMES TO CLIMB THE LAD-
DER, slipping off each time. His head hit it at
least twice, and his ribs hurt so much he
could barely breathe. He reached up once more for
the rung closest to him, sucked in a breath, and
lifted his body to the next rung. He repeated the
painful process again, his ribcage exploding. Sparks
surrounded his vision.

He took another rung, then another, and finally
he reached the opening at the top. Resting on his
elbows for a moment, before inching out of the
tunnel, Alex lay on his back in the mud trying to
breathe, his vision still uncertain. From the distance he could hear yelling and a siren, but the
sounds barely registered.

Forcing himself to roll over, Alex pushed himself
up to standing. His stomach swam. Plunging one

step ahead of the other, he dragged himself up the bank. At the end of the dock, he could see Cervenka frozen in place, his hands raised. Relief flooded him as he realized the sick bastard hadn't gotten away.

He pulled his aching body the rest of the way up the bank, and lifted himself up to his knees. But then a bullet zipped through the air. A body crumpled to the ground, and another took off onto the dock. It was Cervenka.

Alex rolled onto his side and pointed his gun at the back of the man running down the dock. He fired several shots before a searing heat streaked through his chest, followed by another in his leg. He rolled away from more bullets hitting the ground around him. A motor roared to life and then began to die as it sped it away.

Alex clutched his chest just below the collarbone. His whole body throbbed. But then what he'd seen before Cervenka took off down the dock hit him.

"Tony!"

Somehow he rolled onto his side and crawled toward the end of the dock. Agents swarmed around him, rushing to Tony's side. Alex couldn't breathe. He had to see if it was Tony. He pushed away the hands trying to help him. "Is it Tony? Is he okay?"

Through the crowd he could just make out Craig kneeling beside the lifeless body. He lifted his gaze to Alex's and shook his head.

67.

ALEX STARED AT HIS TELEVISION, UNABLE TO hear it, unable to comprehend the images on the screen. He couldn't get the television to replace the screen in his own mind that kept replaying the shot that had killed Tony. He'd slowed it down, watched it frame by frame. *Tony standing with his pistol pointed at Cervenka. Tony falling to the ground. Cervenka running. Tony standing. Tony falling. Cervenka running.*

He couldn't make his legs move fast enough.

He heard the doorbell in some distant corner of his mind. Then barking. He ignored it. He replayed the scene again. *Tony standing. Tony falling. Cervenka running.* He could've gotten there sooner if he hadn't been drugged.

A door behind him slammed and the barking stopped. He shut his eyes and tried to make the images go away. When he opened them again, Carrie was kneeling in front of him. Her eyes were kind, concerned. His chest tightened at the sight of her.

"Hey there," she said. "You going to the funeral?"

He was still in his boxers. "No."

She sighed, but said nothing more. She moved onto the sofa beside him. The shift in his position, even though it was slight, sent a ripple of pain from the gunshot wound just below his collarbone out through his shoulder, along with a sharp stab to his ribcage. Three cracked ribs, a busted shoulder, and a laceration on his left thigh from the second bullet grazing him—that was what he'd gotten for all his brilliant investigative skills. And Tony was dead.

The playback rolled again. *Tony standing...Alex taking a deep breath, a moment of relief...Tony falling to the ground.* It was that fraction of a moment when he'd paused, when he'd believed everything was okay. That was all it took for hell to bust wide open.

Carrie shifted beside him and laid her head against his good shoulder. A wave of sorrow flooded through him. He'd crumble if he let it take hold of him. So he stiffened and pushed himself forward to the edge of the sofa. He had to get up. Had to move. The pain didn't matter. He leaned forward just a bit to stand, enduring the stab to his ribs. He pushed himself up and sucked in a shallow breath.

"Why are you shutting me out?" Carrie said from behind him.

"I'm not." He hobbled around the end of the sofa in the direction of the kitchen.

"Yes, you are." Her voice trailed behind him. He assumed the rest of her was following him as well. "You haven't answered your phone. You haven't answered your door. You haven't spoken to anyone, including me, in three days! And now you're not going to Tony's funeral?"

He opened the refrigerator and grabbed a beer, setting it on the counter and popping the tab with his one available hand. He didn't need a lecture. But he was certain he was about to receive one anyway, and it would go down better with a beer.

"Alex, are you even listening to me?"

He took a long swig before making eye contact. "Do I have a choice?"

She pressed her lips into the thin pink line he knew so well. "You should come to the funeral. It would mean a lot to—"

"I'll pay my respects to Tony in my own way."

"And how's that? By getting drunk and sulking in front of the television?"

He slammed the can onto the counter. "Look, I know you love to tell me how to do my job, but don't come in here and tell me how to grieve!"

"Because you have that down so well, right?"

"Exactly!"

She shook her head, frustration seeping out of her. He didn't care. Maybe if he pissed her off enough, she'd leave him alone. He needed to figure out a way to make things right. To make sure Cervenka got exactly what he deserved.

"Alex," she said. "You don't have to go through this alone. I'm here for you." She took a step toward him and reached for his good arm.

Some part of him ached to let her touch him. He could let go of the dam holding back his emotions, and let the flood of grief overwhelm him. But what would that accomplish? Nothing. So he pulled away. He had to stay strong. She only weakened him.

"You should go. I'll be fine."

"What are you going to do?"

"I'm going to make things right. I've already failed enough people trying to catch that sick bastard. I'm not going to fail again."

"You haven't failed anyone. What are you talking about?"

"Samuel, Meeks, Tony, even Chuck!"

"Who's Chuck?"

Alex sighed and pinched his nose. "The homeless guy. Detective Crouse never found him. He's probably dead and buried, and not a single person on the face of the earth even missed him."

"Oh Alex, none of those awful circumstances were your fault." There were tears in Carrie's eyes. "You're not to blame."

"It's always the same story with me. The people I love...the people I'm supposed to protect...I can't. I'm useless."

"That's your problem, right there!"

"What?"

"You think that somehow you're supposed to save everyone. That you're supposed to be God—"

"Do not bring God into this!" Heat flooded his whole body. "This has nothing to do with him. And I certainly do not want to *be* God."

She sighed and looked down at her watch. "I'm going to be late. Please think about coming to the funeral. You should say goodbye."

She walked over and stood on her tiptoes, kissing him gently on the lips. Then she left him standing there in the kitchen. Just like he'd wanted all along. But it didn't feel the way he'd hoped.

Gingerly, Alex hobbled back to his bedroom and lowered himself onto the bed. He couldn't take any more loss. No more goodbyes. He'd failed. He couldn't save anyone.

You aren't supposed to.

He lay back against the mattress and yelled at the ceiling. "Then what am I doing here?"

The room was silent.

"If I'm not supposed to save anyone, why am I even trying? Why even hunt down the monsters out there hurting these kids? I can't save anyone!"

You're not supposed to.

"But you are!" Rage came rushing out of him, sending every curse he could think of flying out of his mouth. "You *are* supposed to save them! You were supposed to save them. You were supposed to save Evan! You were supposed to save Tony! Even Meeks...At least he was trying. You were supposed to save them!"

His voice gave out, and he covered his face with his elbow. He hadn't even realized he'd started sobbing. "You were supposed to save them."

I did.

His sobs stilled. His heart slowed. How was that possible? The thought made no sense. But there was something in it...certainty. He pushed himself back up to sitting, wondering what had just happened. Had he finally lost his mind? Or was God actually speaking to him?

And if so, what the hell was he talking about?

68.

ALEX TRIED TO PASS UNNOTICED AS HE approached the group gathered around the grave. Three large tents sheltered the casket and family. Spread around them had to be close to two hundred mourners. He could hardly believe it. There were agents from every group in the Atlanta office as far as he could tell, along with many other agencies. He spotted Carrie in a group of lawyers from the US Attorney's office. Cops in uniform from various precincts lined the small road leading up the hill to Tony's burial lot. But even more surprising was the number of faces he didn't recognize at all. At least half of the people there were complete strangers.

He crossed the cemetery with his head down, unable to meet the eyes he felt on him as he approached. The cold wind sliced through him as his

jacket flapped loosely over his right arm, held tightly to his chest by a sling. He moved into a spot
about thirty feet away from the casket and beside
Nicole. He felt her turn toward him, but he kept his
eyes on the minister standing at the head of the
casket. He was determined to stay strong, even if
that meant he couldn't look at anyone.

The minister held a Bible open in his hands, and
he looked around the crowd as he spoke, his voice
full of emotion. "My dear friends, we are all suffering deep sorrow at the loss of our brother, our colleague, our friend, our son. But we must remember
not to mourn as the rest of the world mourns, as if
we have no hope. Tony wouldn't want that. He
wouldn't want us to weep for him. He'd want us to
remember his laughter, his joy in serving others,
his love for his family, and most of all his love for
his Lord."

Alex's nerves shot to attention. *His Lord?* The
minister talked as if he knew Tony, as he continued
to tell the crowd how Tony had served in their
church, had mentored troubled youth, and even
traveled to other countries to serve. It dawned on
Alex that he had never really known Tony outside
of work. Had he ever mentioned church? Maybe.
Alex had probably shut that out. Just like he'd done
to everyone else.

Alex glanced at the minister, and he could've
sworn the guy was looking and speaking only to

him. "Tony Blake was a man of great integrity, but he would be the first to tell you he wasn't perfect. He never tried to be. But he trusted in God. And he'd want you to trust in God as well."

Alex dropped his head, unable to listen to any more. He took a step back and to the side so he couldn't see the minister or the casket any longer. His chest throbbed. How could he have not known?

He kept his eyes on the ground for the rest of the service, only looking up when the color guard gave the twenty-one gun solute. An American flag was tightly folded and placed in the arms of a woman whom Alex had never met, but assumed was Tony's mother. Beside her, three young women wept. His sisters? He'd mentioned a sister once. Hadn't he?

Shame clouded around him, and his eyes stung. What had he missed out on by keeping his walls so tall and so strong? A closer friendship? Maybe. But wouldn't that have made his loss hurt even more?

As the crowd began to wander away, Alex made his way toward the casket. Others stood close by, hugging the family and passing on condolences. He heard a young man talking of Tony's help in getting him straightened out. A teenaged girl behind him asked her friend if she remembered the paintball fight at the youth group trip to the mountains when Tony had taught their team SWAT maneuvers to help them win.

Finally he reached the casket and laid his hand on the top. Who was this man inside? Why was he the one to die? "It should've been me," Alex whispered as he stepped back. "I'm so sorry."

His left hand tingled as fingers, light as feathers, brushed against the skin. "You okay?" Carrie said. He could barely swallow, let alone speak. He took her hand and gave it a squeeze. She didn't let go. "I'm glad you decided to come," she said. "He really cared for you."

He cleared his throat. "Did you know?"

"Know what?"

He glanced sideways at her. "That he was a Christian? That he did all those things for his church?"

She nodded. "We only talked about it once or twice, when he asked me why I didn't drink. I told him a little about my history, and I don't know...we just talked about how God had reached down and saved us from bad situations."

God had saved him. Long before Alex had failed. That's what the voice, or his thoughts, or whatever that had been, was trying to tell him. "It doesn't make any sense."

"What doesn't?"

He dropped her hand and turned to her. "Why would God let Tony die, when he was doing so many good things? His life mattered. It just doesn't make sense."

"Alex, do you think that your life *doesn't* matter?"

He dropped his gaze, his chest aching so hard he could barely breathe. He looked down at the casket, then at the people still lingering with Tony's family. Who would come to his funeral? He hadn't spoken to his sister in three years, or his mother, or his friends back home. Would anyone miss him? No, his life didn't matter. Because he hadn't wanted it to.

Maybe it was time to change that. Maybe it was time to let go of the past. Let go of his anger. Let go of his walls. Maybe it was time to trust in something, in someone, bigger than himself.

He looked back down at Carrie, admiring her strength, her peace. He remembered the way she'd lit up when playing football with Reggie. Her life mattered too.

"I need to go," he said. He needed to think. Needed to make some decisions.

"Alex, wait."

He shrugged off her hand on his arm and headed down the hill toward his car. As he passed by the line of government cars, he caught sight of Nicole talking with Special Agent in Charge Hank Carpenter and several other agents. The intensity in Nicole's expression made him wonder if there was news about Cervenka. He changed course for the group.

"We should head back to the office for this," said James Carroll, the Assistant Special Agent in

Charge who oversaw both Alex's group and the drug group.

Nicole spotted Alex and put her hand up to pause the conversation. "Alex, you should go home and get some rest."

He had no intention of resting until he'd seen this case through to the end. "Have you gotten anything on Cervenka?"

Hank lowered his chin. "Looks like we have a location."

Alex's heart pounded. "Where?"

"His private plane turned up in Miami. He's got a house down there. We have agents ready to move in. Headquarters is monitoring. We were just about to go to the office and keep up with it ourselves."

"I'm there." Alex ignored the concern from Nicole.

Hank nodded. "All right then, let's get moving."

69.

ALEX COULDN'T SIT STILL, SO HE PACED THE hallway outside the conference room while everyone waited for nightfall. The Miami team was ready to go. If he'd had any shot of making it happen, Alex would've flown there to bust Cervenka himself. It was killing him to sit on the sidelines.

Nicole closed the door behind her as she joined him. "You okay?"

He stopped pacing. "Just wish I was there to finish the job."

"I know this has been a tough week. You don't have to be here."

"Yes I do."

She sighed. "Okay. Well, I'm going to the break room for some soda. You want anything?"

He shook his head and went back to pacing. A moment later, his phone buzzed.

Where are you? It was Carrie. He typed a quick response.

At the office. Miami agents are about to arrest Cervenka. Where are you?

Your house.

Hank stuck his head out the door. "We're getting started."

Alex punched in a quick message on his phone. *Arrest going down now. Will call when over.*

He stepped into the conference room and heard the radio communication of the Miami agents as they busted down the door of Cervenka's house. They cleared one room after another, all of them empty. As the seconds dragged into minutes, Alex knew they'd missed him again.

He listened long enough to hear the agents decide to end the search, and then left without a word, slamming the doors behind him. Once in his car he sat for a moment, unblinking, then pounded his fist on the steering wheel, and laid his head back against the seat, closing his eyes. No one could just disappear. He'd have to show up somewhere sooner or later.

His phone buzzed again. Carrie.

How did it go?

No one home.

Alex cranked the car and headed for home. At the red light, he glanced down at the phone again.

Aw. That's too bad. Come home and let's talk about it.

On my way.

The light changed and he sped along Camp Creek Parkway, racking his brain for anything that might be a clue to Cervenka's whereabouts. But by the time he'd pulled into his driveway, nothing had come to mind. He was exhausted, and all he wanted was to lie in his bed with Carrie in his arms.

He climbed out of his car and walked over to hers, expecting to find her waiting on him. But her car was empty. Maybe she'd decided to go for a walk. He pulled out his phone and sent her a text.

I'm here. Where are you?

He waited, but nothing came. He tried calling her, but it rang through to voicemail.

Alex's stomach knotted. Something wasn't right. He took his flashlight from his car and gripped it the best he could with his right hand against his chest. Then he stuffed his pistol in his back pocket. He walked over to the front door and tried the knob. Locked.

Swearing, he fumbled with his key and unlocked the door, wondering if he wasn't overreacting. But better safe than sorry. He dropped the keys and grabbed his gun from his pocket, holding it close as he slowly pushed the door open with his good shoulder.

The flashlight illuminated the foyer and living room, casting long shadows. He eased to his left to check the guest bathroom, again tucking the gun close to his shoulder. He took a deep breath and flung himself around the doorframe, pointing the pistol into the bathroom. Nothing.

Alex's skin tingled, the hairs standing on end. It was too quiet. Mutt should be scratching the back door to get in by now. Easing back into the living room, he circled around the edge of it to the kitchen and back door. He pulled aside the curtain that hung over the glass window on the door. No Mutt.

He should call for backup, but that would mean putting down his gun. No way that was happening. He'd clear the house first. Then call.

He continued through the kitchen into the hallway that led back to his bedroom, sliding along the wall. Then he froze. He'd heard something. A moan? His door was slightly ajar. He pushed it open and slipped inside, his arm and pistol aimed straight toward the sound.

Something hard flew down onto his arm, crushing Alex's elbow. He spun toward the man behind his door and slammed his whole left side into him, sending them both into the wall. Something fell from the man's hands and thudded against the carpet. Alex brought his knee up into his groin. He moaned and crumbled.

Then everything went dark.

70.

FOR A MOMENT, ALL ALEX KNEW WAS THE AGONY radiating through his head. Where was he? It didn't take long for everything to come rushing back. He'd been attacked coming into his bedroom.

He coughed. His chest felt like it had been split wide open, and stabs of pain shot out from his wounded shoulder down into his elbow. A foot dug into his ribs, sending sparks of light through his vision.

"Get up."

He knew that voice.

The foot dug harder, this time pushing him until he had to roll away. His gun was gone. Had Cervenka found the small one on his ankle too? He pressed the outside of his left leg against the floor. Nothing. *Damn.*

A light flashed in his eyes, blinding him as hands grabbed his left arm and wrenched it behind his back. The pressure drove him to his knees. "I said to get up!"

The voice wasn't coming from the man holding him. Slowly his eyes focused, and he struggled to his feet. The lamp on his nightstand flipped on, and he could finally take in his situation. He couldn't see him, but he could tell the guy behind him was slightly taller, possibly stronger than Alex, considering the state of his injuries. Cervenka sat next to the door in a chair taken from the dining table, one leg crossed over the other and a sickening smile on his face. He was clutching something in his lap—Carrie's phone.

To his right, a shorter guy, stocky and looking ready to fight, stood beside the lamp. He was smaller than Alex. Manageable. But then he heard the moans from the bed and saw Carrie. She sat with her back against the headboard, her hands tied above her to the top rail. Her mouth was taped, and tears streamed out of her eyes.

Rage flew through Alex, and he shoved against the weight of the man behind him. But his arm was wrenched again, nearly shredding the tendons in his left shoulder. He bent over to relieve the pain. "Cervenka, you bastard!" he yelled. "You touch her, and I swear to God you are dead!"

Cervenka dropped his foot to the floor and leaned onto his elbows. "Alex, please. Why are you so angry? I've only come to help you."

Enraged, Alex shoved against the man behind him again, who responded by driving Alex's head into the wall, sending a shock of throbbing pain through his skull. A knee flew into his abdomen. His stomach swam, and he dropped to the floor.

"Garrett, don't kill him yet. You'll ruin our fun. Put him on his knees," Cervenka said.

Alex was gathering for another attempt to fight, but a huge hand wrapped around his throat and squeezed. His legs responded, almost involuntarily pushing away from the grasp. Garrett's brute strength lifted him up, and once again his left arm was wrenched back until he was forced to bend over. His knees buckled beneath him. Something, a rope of some kind, tightened around his throat, but he could still suck in short, painful breaths.

Cervenka bent over into his line of sight. "Oh come on, *Agent Walker*. Stop fighting so much. I'm going to give you exactly what you want. Remember those videos you were so interested in? I'm going to help you start your own personal collection, just like we discussed." He straightened and pointed to the shorter guy. "Andrew here has agreed to be the main character in our presentation. Your friend—Carrie, is it?—has not so much agreed to play the other role, but we'll work with her as best we can, eh?"

He turned back to Garrett. "Keep him conscious. He'll want to see this. Action!"

Alex tried to stand, but the rope squeezed so tight around his throat, that for a moment everything went black. But Carrie's scream jolted him back to consciousness. Andrew had ripped the tape from her mouth and pulled her hands down from the rail. He grabbed her by the waist and yanked her toward the side of the bed.

"Alex! Alex!" Her hands flailed against the zip tie around her wrists.

Alex tried to yell, to tell her to fight, but all he could do was cough. He had to get a grip. He had to assess what he could do. There was a way out of this if he could only think for a second.

"Mr. Cervenka," said Garrett from behind Alex. "This is taking too long already. Let me kill him. We can take the girl elsewhere for this."

Cervenka shook his head. "I want him to see it."

Alex's heart thundered, fear coursing through his body.

Cervenka turned back to Andrew. "Get on with it!"

Breaking free momentarily, Carrie managed to kick Andrew into the wall behind him, but he lunged for her again. She screamed as Andrew struck her across the face and yanked her to her feet. Then he shoved her back onto the bed, face down.

Alex bucked against Garrett's hold, but he barely budged. His mind raced through his training, but he couldn't focus. Couldn't breathe. The rope around his throat tightened again. Carrie's screams were like knives piercing his chest.

I can't save her. I can't save her. Please, God! Please save her!

There was a moment, just as Alex felt every ounce of rage in his body begin to explode, when the room went absolutely still. His anger evaporated. And a small, quiet voice spoke to him.

You're not alone. Trust Me. And fight.

Alex sucked in every ounce of strength he had left, twisted to his right and flung his right elbow, sling and all, into Garrett's knee. It was enough to loosen Garrett's hold on the rope around his throat for a fraction of a second. Alex's arm went numb, but he was able to keep his momentum moving into Garrett's knee, knocking him back. Alex climbed on top of him, throwing his numb fists into Garrett's head. As Garrett threw his hips up and rolled Alex off, a bullet zipped into the carpet beside them. Garrett brought his elbow right into Alex's collarbone.

Another bullet.

Garrett leapt off Alex and screamed at Cervenka. "What the hell are you doing?"

Cervenka fired again. Alex's chest exploded into white-hot pain.

Cervenka turned toward the bed. In what remained of his peripheral vision, Alex thought Andrew bounced off the wall again. He couldn't tell. Could barely see.

"I've had enough of this," Cervenka said. He lifted the gun toward Carrie.

Fight.

Garrett's back was still turned. Cervenka poised to shoot. Alex shoved himself up, pushing Garrett into the path of the gun just as it fired. Garrett hit the floor with a dead thump. Cervenka stumbled backward. Alex lunged again, knocking Cervenka into the wall. He seized the hand holding the gun, twisting until he felt the finger snap. Cervenka screamed, but wouldn't let go. Alex squeezed, and the gun fired into Cervenka's chest. His eyes went wide, and he sucked in a sharp breath. Then Cervenka went limp.

As Cervenka fell to the floor, Alex turned to the bed. Andrew had abandoned his attack, but now he stood against the wall, clutching Carrie by the throat.

Alex sucked in a wet, raspy breath and aimed the gun at Andrew's head. "Let. Her. Go."

Wildly, Andrew's eyes scanned the room. Alex heard a distant siren. "Look, it's over. Let her go. I will shoot you. And I promise you, I don't miss."

Andrew thought about it for only a moment before releasing his grip on Carrie's throat. She sobbed and threw her elbow right into his gut. *Good girl,* Alex thought. Andrew dropped to his knees, and Carrie rushed to Alex's side.

"Oh God! Are you okay?" She cupped his face in her palms, ignoring the blood dripping from the lacerations made from the zip tie still binding her wrists.

"Are you? Did he hurt you?"

She shook her head. "I'm okay. But you need an ambulance, now."

He nodded and handed her the gun. "Point this at him until the police get here. If he moves, shoot his ass." She took the gun from him, and he slid down onto the floor, completely spent.

"Alex?"

He laid his head back against the bed. "I'll be okay. Just keep your eyes on the scum over there..."

Alex stared at the ceiling, listening to Carrie's ragged breathing and the approaching siren until he couldn't hold his eyes open any longer.

71.

ALEX'S EYES DRIFTED OPEN TO THE MOVE-
MENT around him. Counting. "One, two,
three." Excruciating pain shot through his
chest. Then he was floating through the air, and the
darkness returned.

Jostling woke him again. He sucked in air from
the mask on his face. A man in a white shirt leaned
over him. "Mr. Walker?" The man blurred. He
spoke over Alex to someone else. "He's drifting in
and out. Watch his BP." It faded to black again.

Then there were lights, flashing above him, one
after another. A trail of fluorescence, so fast they
blended into a stream. He was flying. He could feel
the wind rushing over him. His body ached. It was
so cold. He wanted to ask for a warm blanket, but
the mask absorbed his words. He was so tired. He
closed his eyes again.

Something woke him. Air being sucked into a vent. Or maybe pushed out. The sound was behind him. He couldn't quite lift his eyelids. He couldn't move either. But everything ached so badly, he didn't want to. He managed to open his eyes enough to see a nurse seated beside him. She was making notes, and she dropped her chin to eye him over the rim of her glasses.

"Well, well. Look who's decided to live after all." She smiled. "Nice to meet you, Agent Walker." She stood and slid the mask up to his forehead. "Better?"

He nodded the best he could, but the movement sent a burst of pain down his neck and out through his collarbone. She made another note. "Can you tell me your name?"

"A—Alex," he managed.

She smiled again. "Well, Alex. You have caused no small amount of drama around here this evening. Now, you just hang in here with me for a few minutes, and we'll get you settled into a room so you can rest."

He checked her nametag. Janine. She set her clipboard down and moved behind his head. He wiggled his fingers and toes. Still working, but every part of him, from head to foot, felt like it had been crushed beneath a truck.

The sucking sound stopped. Janine came around to the other side with a syringe. She pushed a clear liquid into the IV in his arm. "This should help with the pain."

She moved away, and he closed his eyes again.

The next time he awakened, light streamed into his hospital room as if it were the middle of the day. There were flowers everywhere. Nicole, Craig, and Carrie sat in chairs near the window. Alex sucked in a shallow breath, the ache radiating all through him. Another nurse moved around his bed, checking the machines and pushing more clear fluid into his IV. This one was Rachel. She was younger, maybe in her thirties. She too smiled when she asked how he was feeling.

"Terrible," he said.

"Would you like me to sit you up a little?"

"Yes, please."

She adjusted the bed and showed him the remote near his hand. "Press the call button if you need anything. The doctor will come by to see you soon."

As she left, the others circled around his bed. Nicole stood to his right, dark circles under her eyes. Craig hung toward his feet, and Carrie came over to his left. She lifted his hand from the bed and kissed the back of it.

"Are you okay?" Carrie said. "I mean, of course you're not okay, but...are you—"

"I'm okay," he said.

He glanced over at Nicole, whose face barely registered her surprise. She looked from Alex to Carrie and back at Alex again. "Well, you managed to get yourself in quite a situation, Walker."

"Is Cervenka—?"

"Oh, he's dead. So's the big guy, Garrett Thomas. We were able to make him as Tony's shooter."

Alex let out a shallow sigh of relief. *Justice.* "What about the other one? I think his name was Andrew."

"In custody," Craig said.

Alex squeezed Carrie's hand. Her face was still swollen around her cheek, her neck was bruised, and her wrists were bandaged. "Are you okay? Did that piece of...did he hurt you?"

"I'm all right," she said, her thumb stroking the back of his hand. "Once you started fighting with the other two, he just pushed me around until he got me up to shield himself."

"I should have killed him too," Alex muttered.

Nicole touched his arm. "I'm going to step out for a bit and let everyone know how you're doing. The waiting room is packed."

She lifted an eyebrow at Carrie before walking around the end of his bed. Craig cleared his throat and excused himself as well.

"So I guess our big secret isn't so secret anymore," he said once the door had closed.

"Ah, no. I think it's pretty much headline news at this point."

"I'm sorry."

She rubbed her hand along his arm, soothing some of the pain still shooting out of his shoulder. "I'm not. You're worth it. Besides, I don't think it'll matter too much in the end. I won't be trying any of the cases that have to do with Cervenka now that I'm a witness to his crimes."

"I imagine we'll still face some questions, maybe a reprimand."

"Probably, but from what I hear you're used to those." She grinned at him, and leaned in closer. "Is it okay to kiss you now?"

"Absolutely."

Her lips brushed over his. "Thank you."

"For what? Nearly getting you killed?"

She sighed and scooted a chair to his side, then resumed rubbing his arm. "Please, Alex, no more of this crap where you blame yourself for everything. Bad things happen. That's part of life. But good things happen too. You saved me. That was a good thing."

He had to admit she was right. "Are you really okay? That had to be scary."

She bit her lip and dropped her gaze. "I don't know. But I'll be okay again..." After a moment's pause, her eyes returned to his. "I'll be okay. As soon as we get you out of here and put all of this behind us."

"Amen to that."

"I was thinking that maybe you could come stay with me for a little while. You'll need some help until you can get around better. Plus, I think your house is still a crime scene."

His stomach warmed at the thought of being with her every day. He couldn't help but smile. "Only on one condition."

"Name it."

"Take me to church with you."

Her eyes widened, and then she grinned like it was the most wonderful request she'd ever heard. "Well, you have to promise not to swing from the rafters. We're not that kind of church."

He tried to hold in his chuckle, but it came out more like a cough. "Ah, don't make me laugh. It hurts."

She rested her chin on her hands, her elbows propped on the side of his bed. Her eyes danced. Watching her, Alex realized that despite everything, he felt happy. "I figure it's time to let go of the anger that's been eating away at me. I don't have everything figured out. I guess I never will. I mean, if God exists, and I suspect he does, I'd like to ask him a few questions."

"I'm still doing that myself, so maybe we can do it together."

"Sounds perfect." His eyelids grew heavy again, as the medicine began to work its magic. But a thought sent his eyes open wide. "What about Mutt? I couldn't find him—"

"I found him. He's okay. He's staying with me. He was outside the fence. He must have gone crazy when all the fighting broke out. That's how the police got there. Your neighbor called them about the dog barking."

Alex nearly laughed again. So crabby old Mrs. Anderson's hatred for Mutt had been their saving grace. How ironic. "But wait, can you keep a dog at your apartment?"

She squeezed her shoulders up, giving him a mischievous look. "Well, I figured we were so good at keeping our other secret, what was one more?"

He struggled to keep his eyes open for another moment. "God, you're adorable. I love you."

She tilted her head to the side, flashing the smile that had undone him. "I love you too."

As the hospital room faded once more to black, Alex could close his eyes with peace in his heart. His body would heal, and soon, the rest of him would too.

The End

Acknowledgements

This book was born from many emails I've received over the past couple of years from readers of my first book *Love's Providence* asking, "What about Alex?" He's always been a character that was close to my heart, so I want to thank those readers who loved him and inspired me to continue his story.

I'm equally grateful to my husband, whose stories over the years have always been more entertaining than mine. His adventures in law enforcement have been a wonderful treasure to pull ideas from, and he's always happy to answer my what-if questions.

Thank you to my kids, who put up with a mom who's often distracted, and sometimes very sleepy from late-night writing sessions. But most of all thank you for being the source of so much laughter and fun.

Thank you to Brynoy Sutherland, an editor who manages to be ruthless and encouraging all at the same time. You take my stumbles and make them into a beautiful, graceful dance.

Thank you to Amy Hobbs, who manages to still answer every request with enthusiasm. You cover designs and website design always amaze me.

And lastly, thank you to the readers who email me encouraging words and share your experiences with these characters. You keep this dream of mine going, and make it worth all the sacrifice.

About the Author

J.L. Hays first played with the idea of writing crime fiction as she listened to her husband tell of his adventures over the years, first as a local cop, then a detective, and finally as a federal agent. He has inspired her to create characters that are genuine and flawed, people who protect us from monsters we don't even know are out there. She is the author of *The Kill Code*, as well as two short stories, *A Heart's Tale* and *Fallout.*.

During the day, she homeschools her two precious boys, and by night she writes until she can no longer hold her eyes open. You can find out more about J.L. Hays at her website: www.jenniferhwestall.com/jl-hays/

www.ingramcontent.com/pod-product-compliance
Lightning Source LLC
Chambersburg PA
CBHW060139260626
47160CB00001B/43

* 9 7 8 0 9 9 0 8 7 5 9 6 3 *